STELLA OF AKROTIRI: ORIGINS

LINDA RAE SANDE

Twisted Teacup
PUBLISHING

Stella of Akrotiri: Origins

This is a work of fiction. The events and characters described herein are imaginary and are not intended to refer to specific places or living persons. The opinions expressed in this manuscript are solely the opinions of the author and do not represent the opinions or thoughts of the publisher. The author has represented and warranted full ownership and/or legal right to publish all the materials in this book.

Stella of Akrotiri: Origins

PROLOGUE

1631 BC, at the Palace of Knossos on Creta, the capital of the Minoan civilization

Squinting as they emerged from the shadow of the palace and into afternoon sunshine that was both bright and hot, Darius of Agremon listened intently as the King of the Minoans both praised and scolded him.

"As *lochagos* of the coastguardsmen, you have no equal on your island," Cydon said as they made their way down the steps of the palace. "No one with whom to commiserate."

Darius allowed a grunt, a bit surprised by the king's words. The man had never seemed interested in Darius' personal life, nor had he mentioned much of his own. "I have no complaints, and therefore no need to commiserate," Darius replied. After the cool confines of the palace in which they had been discussing matters of new trading routes, valuable cargo, and protection from pirates, the heat was a harsh reminder it was summer in the Aegean.

"You have *ypolochagoi*, though," the king stated, referring to the lieutenants who oversaw the watchtowers and the coastguardsmen who manned them.

"Seven of them," Darius acknowledged. "One for each watchtower. I meet with each one at least once a sennight. Unless there is trouble, of course, in which case I see them more often."

He wasn't about to admit he liked to join the coastguardsmen on raids against the few pirates who managed to make it onto the island of Strongili. He had learned his fighting skills over decades of practice, in many different lands, and with a variety of weapons, and he wanted to stay sharp.

Cydon frowned. "Which means you are not taking your day of rest," he scolded.

"I have no need of rest when much of what I do is to ride a horse," Darius argued. Then he dipped his head. This was the King of the Minoans to whom he was speaking—at the man's invitation. He had no right to counter the ruler's words. "Apologies, my king."

King Cydon paused when they were once again in the shade, this respite courtesy of the olive trees that lined the main thoroughfare of Knossos. "You need not apologize, Darius. I may be your king, but I am not your ruler."

Despite having lived in many countries in his lifetime —he had lived six-hundred years, as near as he could figure—Darius had never encountered one in which the king wasn't so much a monarch but rather a trade negotiator. That, and a keeper of the trade agreements made with allies of the Minoans. But it also meant Cydon had to defend the trade routes that came under his jurisdiction. Ensure shipments made it to their destination. Keep trading partners satisfied.

Minoa's reach extended throughout the Aegean, so every island with valuable goods had to be protected from pirates or invasion by enemies. The coastguardsmen of Strongili were essentially the king's army on that island, and Darius was their leader.

"And I am not about to order you to do something that is not in your nature," Cydon added.

"I appreciate that," Darius replied with a smirk.

"However, may I suggest you take a wife?"

His brows cocked in surprise, Darius stared at the king for several heartbeats. Before he could put voice to a word of protest, Cydon added, "A wife is a woman with whom you can spend your evenings. Your days of rest. A place to put your cock at night and in the mornings," he went on, as if he were explaining the concept of a female partner to a young boy.

"I have had wives in the past," Darius replied, almost embarrassed at hearing the king's tutorial. At Cydon's raised eyebrow, he added, "Two of them."

He had actually had three wives, but to mention that number would have the king suspicious. Darius wasn't about to admit he was six-hundred years old when he looked no older than forty summers.

Cydon frowned. "Death in the childbed?"

Darius dipped his head, deciding it was easiest to have the king believe that particular scenario for one of his wives. "And disease," he said. Admitting one had died of old age was out of the question. His second wife had lived to be over eighty.

"Sympathies," Cydon replied in a quiet voice. "Still, you are a..." He paused, realizing he couldn't say that Darius was still a young man. There were slight crinkles

3

at the edges of his eyes, and his chiseled features had long since lost the softness of youth. His close-cropped hair looked as if it would display flecks of gray in the next year or so. "You are a man in need of a reason to go home at night," Cydon stated. "Which is why I am giving you one."

For a moment, Darius thought the king was bestowing a wife on him before he realized they were discussing homes. "I have an oikos," Darius argued.

"Ah, but not one you are anxious to go to very often," Cydon countered.

The hairs on the back of Darius' neck lifted, and he regarded the king with a face that could have been carved from stone. Had someone been watching him and reporting back to the king? One of his trusted lieutenants, perhaps? "It is not a bastion of luxury, if that is what you are implying," Darius replied carefully.

"Then I have guessed right," the king said with triumph.

Darius relaxed a bit, realizing he wasn't the subject of some royal spy's efforts to learn more about him.

"There is a villa on the north shore of Strongili. Near the settlement you know as Tholos. That villa is now yours," Cydon said with a nod. "A housekeeper—one you already know from your time here on Creta—is seeing to it everything is in place for your arrival in two days' time. She will see to your meals when you are in residence. I have seen to a stable for your horse, and amenities to match those you seem to appreciate most while you are here in my palace," he went on, his joy at describing Darius' new home evident in his enthusiasm and huge grin.

"Gratitude, my king," Darius murmured, realizing at once he couldn't turn down the offer—even if he didn't make it to the north end of the island more than one or two days every sennight. "But... why?"

Cydon gave a shake of his head. "I cannot have my very best lochagos living in a *tent*," he replied, pausing for a moment. "There is a cost, of course." When Darius didn't say anything but merely allowed a shrug, Cydon added, "You will train the new recruits."

Contrary to the king's assumption that training recruits would be abhorrent, this was welcome news to Darius. He had expressed concern only the year before that some watchmen were lax in their duties. That some coastguardsmen lacked training with certain weapons. That most were unfamiliar with tactics invaders might employ to gain access to an island. "I am honored. I accept, of course," Darius said with a nod.

"You will need to choose two of your ypolochagoi to train as potential lochagos. So there will be someone to take your place while you are training new watchmen here on Creta," Cydon warned. "Your best and most trusted men."

Darius nodded. "I have two such men," he replied. Glaukos was of an age and level of experience he could trust in his stead. Klumenos was another, but would require more seasoning before Darius could leave the island in his hands.

Cydon nodded. "And you will need to find a wife."

Darius blinked, stunned by the king's decree. "And if I cannot find one who would abide my frequent absences from the villa?" He hardly thought it fair to marry and then leave a woman to live alone for days at a time.

Although there were no doubt women who would prefer such an arrangement, he had never met one.

"At least *look* for a wife," Cydon replied. "Or arrange a betrothal in the very least, if you find one who is not yet old enough to wed."

Thinking of every woman on Strongili who had not yet taken a husband—and he knew most of them—Darius felt a lead weight drop into his stomach. None of them would marry him but one, and she was a prostitute. He hadn't even spent a night in her bed!

But perhaps there was a young woman somewhere on Strongili. Someone who might one day be old enough to agree to marry him.

As an Immortal, he had all the time in the world. As a lochagos, it seemed he was on a deadline.

"I will do as you say," Darius agreed. "It may take some time to find one, but I shall be on the hunt for a bride."

King Cydon smiled before they were interrupted by one of his advisors. "Let us hope it happens before my successor ascends the throne," he said. "I should like to meet the woman you choose. Safe travels, Lochagos," he added, before heading back to the palace with the advisor.

Darius watched them go, grimacing at the thought of what he was expected to do.

1

A NIGHT ON THE BEACH

A beach near Akrotiri on the island of Strongili, in the center of the Minoan civilization

The flames of a small fire danced about in the late evening breeze as Darius of Agremon sat on the red sands of a beach. Tired, but not weary enough to give in to sleep, he contemplated his latest trip to Creta.

His only reason for making the seventy *milion* crossing was to meet with the king. He did so on a regular basis, always during every other new moon, always at the palace at Knossos, and never for very long. There wasn't much to tell King Cydon. They rarely spoke of anything other than the security of the islands under the king's control. The need to prevent pirates and marauders from either landing on the islands or disrupting important shipments from reaching the center of the Minoan trading juggernaut.

As Strongili's lochagos, Darius would apprise Cydon of any current threats to the island and to Creta. Request more watchtowers and the coastguardsmen to man them.

Then Darius would find passage on a northbound ship, ready to spend the return trip sleeping so he could resume his command of Strongili's coastguard when the ship docked in the morning.

Today's crossing was made on a ship heavy with cargo. Possessed of a huge crew featuring muscled oarsmen, the ship set a new record for speed when it made it into the port near Akrotiri by sundown.

So much for having arranged a cabin in which to spend the night.

Had they arrived at dawn the following day as expected, Darius would have made his way on horseback to the tent he kept on one of the mountains in the southern half of the island. Spent the rest of the day there, and then made the trip to a small *oikos* he owned on the north end of the island the following day. But with the sun having set and no desire to travel in the dark, he decided to spend the night in Akrotiri.

Not wanting to impose on either of the coast-guardsmen he knew who lived there—both had wives and families—Darius instead arranged for a bed and an early supper at an inn near the port. Unable to sleep, he had ventured onto the red beach and discovered the still-hot embers of an abandoned fire. A bit of kindling and dried driftwood brought the fire back to life.

His thoughts strayed to his meeting with Cydon. At first, he wasn't sure why his earlier conversation with the reigning King of Minoa had him so bothered.

Although King Cydon had praised Darius time and again for his skills as lochagos, his other comments as to his personal life had stung in a way Darius couldn't seem to shake.

You are a man in need of a reason to go home at night.

Didn't the security of the island take precedence over the condition of his living quarters?

You will need to find a wife.

The thought of taking another mortal to wife bothered Darius. Was it fair to wed a woman who could never bear his child? After three wives, he knew he could not father a babe.

The dying fire briefly flared back to life just then, pulling Darius from his reverie. At the same moment, a slight tingle at the edge of his consciousness should have had him on alert. Had him reaching for a weapon and preparing a fight to the death. But something about the sensation seemed more friend than foe. More relaxed than dangerous. More welcome than not.

Angling his head to glance up at the high ground over-looking the red beach, he couldn't make out anything—or anyone—watching from above. But the musical sound of a young girl's giggle, barely heard over the wind, had him grinning.

Leave it to the young to find humor in my quandary.

A few minutes later, Darius of Agremon made his way back to the inn and slept harder than he had in years.

2

A VIEW FROM ABOVE

Meanwhile, on the cliff above the beach

Curiosity had the baby goat hopping to where Stella sat cross-legged at the edge of the cliff overlooking the red beach. A plaintive bleat preceded the animal's drop to the ground next to Stella, and a moment later, his head was resting on the young girl's knee.

"I miss her, too," Stella whispered, referring to the female goat that had died the week before. The one who had given birth to this particular kid. She had been too young to give birth, and so it was no surprise to Stella that she would die when she did.

Helena, Stella's mother, expected the newborn to die before the sun rose. But Stella had seen to feeding the goat from a small bottle with a makeshift nipple. She even stayed awake the entire first night just to be sure the babe survived, and now it seemed she had a constant companion and a friend for life.

Stella absently rested a hand on the baby goat's head,

her attention on the beach below. Specifically on the remains of a bonfire that had just been abandoned.

Earlier that evening, she had been drawn to the cliff's edge by the raucous sounds of several young men. Engaged in loud conversation and rough play, they had finally gathered around the bonfire one of them had built with driftwood. Unable to hear their words, Stella had been about to go inside for the night. The goat had fallen asleep, though, and she didn't wish to wake him just yet.

The fire seemed to die all at once, the flames guttering as its fuel supply dwindled. Soon the boys drifted toward Akrotiri, calls of farewell signaling an end to their evening gathering. Darkness replaced the purple and peach twilight, and the soothing sounds of occasional waves washing ashore interrupted the quiet.

Her eyelids drooping, Stella was about to drift off to sleep when a slight tickle had her eyes snapping open.

The tickle was familiar. She experienced such a sensation when she climbed the oldest of her father's olive trees. Only one person on the island caused the same tickle.

A large man—an important man—who visited her father every summer to order olives and *olio* from the next harvest.

She turned her attention to the red beach below.

That very man was making his way to the remains of the fire. The tickle in her head increased until she was grinning with happiness.

What was it about him that had her feeling such delight in her head?

Seen up close, she thought him almost frightening. He had strange markings on his skin, and his manner was always so serious, as if he wanted everyone to fear him. She knew he was an important person on the island, but he was not so important that he lived in a palace.

He wasn't the king.

Her mother, Helena, had taught her the king, Cydon, lived in a beautiful palace on Creta, a large island to the south. She had never been to Creta, nor had she seen King Cydon, but she had seen the man on the beach. Sometimes Stella saw him with other men, all on horses, rushing off to the east or to the west, their bows loaded with arrows or their swords raised as if they sought to do battle.

She never saw whatever—or whomever—they pursued with their weapons. But she heard her father speak of pirates. Heard him talk of invaders from other lands intent on stealing the valuable goods of Strongili.

The man on the beach was the lochagos of the coast-guardsmen, Helena had once explained. *Our protector.*

Stella closed her eyes and concentrated on the man who now sat at the edge of a fire he had relit using driftwood. After he settled onto the red sands, his muscled forearms wrapped around his bent legs and his chin dropped to rest atop his knees. Although she couldn't see his eyes from this far away, she was sure his gaze fell on the flames.

Fire was always mesmerizing. Hypnotic. Comforting. Even on a hot night such as this. Stella had half a mind to negotiate the goat path that led down toward Akrotiri so she could join him.

The moon hadn't come up yet, though. The path wasn't visible in the dark. What if he didn't want her company? Her questions? Her comfort?

Contact with another who was like him? For she was sure he was as aware of her as she was aware of him.

He just didn't know it yet. He wasn't paying attention to the tickle in his head.

Stella gently moved the baby goat's head from her knee and stood up. For several minutes, she simply stared at the lochagos. Concentrated on him and his mood, stunned to discover he felt lost. Confused.

Old.

Her brows furrowing in shared confusion, Stella watched as he lifted his head and seemed to finally acknowledge he wasn't alone.

Studying him as he was now, Stella thought he no longer seemed so large and imposing in such a position. No longer the frightening leader of the coastguardsmen who were said to vanquish any pirates and behead all the marauders who dared land on the island.

For a moment, Stella was sure he spotted her atop the cliff. Finally!

She thought of the very funniest memory she had—of the baby goat and how he hopped instead of walked everywhere he went—and she giggled in delight.

The man's alert state abated, and his serious manner slowly changed to one of amusement. Another moment, and he stood up and made the short trek back to Akrotiri.

Instead of taking satisfaction in what she had managed to accomplish, Stella frowned. At no point had the lochagos acknowledged *her*. At no point had he waved in her direction. He hadn't even sent a thankful thought in response to her efforts to ease his mind.

Perhaps he wasn't like her at all.

Just old, like the ancient olive trees.

Allowing a long sigh, Stella led the baby goat to the stables behind the oikos and settled onto a straw pallet for the night. A few more days, and the baby goat would no longer be so lonely.

Stella, on the other hand, might remain lonely for a long time.

AN ANCIENT OLIVE TREE

A sennight later

Given the importance of the tree that stood before him, Darius of Agremon couldn't help but feel a bit underwhelmed. It was not particularly tall, nor was it wide. The leaves weren't fragrant or colorful, although they stayed on the tree year-round. The green fruit was quite small, and the trunk was reminiscent of a gnarled old man he had once come across in his travels. If he hadn't been told it was over a thousand years old, he would have guessed the tree was far younger.

Perhaps it was the age of it that had him staring at it for so long. For the first time in his life, Darius had discovered a living thing that was older than him.

"There are two-hundred more just like it in my orchards," Andros said as he watched the commander of the Strongili coastguardsmen regard his favorite olive tree. "Not as old, of course, but they produce the best olives in all of the Aegean Islands. The best olive olio in all the world, when we combine the black and the green fruit together in the press."

Darius gave a nod as his gaze traveled down the crooked rows of olive trees that populated the south end of the largest land mass of Strongili. Although it would have been easy to accuse the olive grower of boasting, he could tell by the man's passion he spoke the truth. Having tasted the products of the old but not-so-exotic trees, Darius had to agree.

Which made bargaining with the man that much more difficult.

"So, what will it cost me to keep my men in olives and olio this next year?" he asked as he placed one of his palms against the tree's trunk. Just as he did so, a slight tingle made itself apparent at the edge of his consciousness at the same moment his horse nickered softly. He gave a start and glanced around, his hand breaking contact with the tree as he did so. The tingle disappeared, and he held his breath as he contemplated what had just happened.

"The same as last year," Andros replied with a shrug, unaware of what the commander had just experienced. "Your service to our island is necessary," he added, when he noted Darius' look of surprise. "We all know the Egyptians or Hittites could lay waste to our lands should they wish to."

Darius nodded, although inside he bristled at the implication the Hittites could overtake the island. *Not on my watch*, he almost said. Those two potential enemies as well as Mycenaeans and pirates were the reason he and his men were charged with defending Strongili, Creta, and the other nearby islands that made up the center of the Minoan civilization.

Since most of the cities on the islands were built atop hills that allowed for fortification, his men were stationed at watchtowers and ports next to the shore that surrounded the mostly round island. Should a ship filled with marauders be spotted, it was possible for his men to stop an invasion before it started.

"Gratitude for your words," Darius said then, just as the familiar tingle returned in his head. Once again, the Sorraia lifted his head and nickered. Darius frowned when he realized he wasn't even touching the tree trunk. His gaze swept across the orchard in an attempt to determine what—or who—might have caused the odd sensation, one he had learned over hundreds of years ago foretold the presence of another like him.

An Immortal.

When he didn't immediately spot anyone else in the orchard, he was about to turn his attention back to Andros when movement in one of the trees had him reaching for his sword.

"Oh, do not mind her, sir," Andros said with a shake of his head, one hand held out as if he could prevent Darius from raising his weapon. "She is just curious."

Furrowing a brow, Darius stared at the tree, finally spotting a flash of color among the leaves. "Who is she?" he asked in a whisper, remembering just then the young girl's giggle he had heard when he was on the beach the sennight before. The sound chasing away his dark thoughts and replacing them with amusement. The reminder of them later that night sending him into a deep sleep that left him more refreshed than he had felt in a very long time.

Andros dipped his head. "My daughter, Stella. She is young, but quite good at climbing the trees, especially at harvest." When the commander gave him a sideways glance, he added, "She has hands that are perfect for removing olives from the branches. My Helena says it is like watching her slide the pearls off of a necklace."

Finally allowing a grin, Darius regarded the farmer a moment. "And when it is not time to harvest?"

Andros motioned towards a pair of boulders and took a seat on the lower one. "She uses a knife to cut out the tiny branches that do not bear fruit," he replied as Darius leaned on the larger boulder. Andros held out a gnarled hand, aged with liver spots and years of labor. "Something I can no longer do well."

A quick glance at Andros' arthritic fingers confirmed the man was too old to be climbing in olive trees, but it also had Darius wondering if Andros' wife was far younger than him. The girl in the olive tree couldn't be older than nine or ten summers. "Does your wife work in the orchards then?" he asked.

Andros shook his head. "Only at harvest. She helps to pick up the olives from the burlap we spread beneath the trees. Like me, she is no longer young enough to do what Stella does."

Darius dared another glance in the direction of the tree in which he had spotted Stella, but he couldn't see any evidence of her through the sage green leaves.

He couldn't help but notice the pleasant tingle in his head was no longer present, though.

"Your older children must help, I suppose," he hinted, wanting to know if Stella was the youngest.

"We have no other children," Andros said with a shake of his head. "Stella was a gift from the gods." When he noted how the commander stared at him, his dour expression suggesting he didn't believe in deities, Andros added with a shrug, "We were blessed."

Giving a non-committal grunt, Darius half-asked, "If you do not have other children to help you..." He paused and waved at the orchard behind him. "You must employ others for the harvest, no?"

This time, Andros nodded. "I hire the men from Akrotiri who also gather the saffron. The two crops come in at different times, so those men are available when I need them. In the autumn, before the nights are too cold," he explained. "They help cart the olives to the mill where they are pressed for the olio."

Darius nodded his understanding. Saffron was the most lucrative of all the crops on Strongili, its yellow used in the manufacture of dyes for fabrics. "Perhaps I shall have to come watch while your daughter slides the pearls from the necklaces," he said with a grin.

Andros smiled, his white teeth gleaming in the harsh sun. "You are welcome to do so, but be warned. She may put you to work picking them up."

His smile matching that of Andros', Darius said, "Perhaps she will." He straightened and pushed his red cape from his shoulders. "I would not be adverse to a day of labor." With that, he mounted his Sorraia, the horse once again lifting his head as if to listen. Darius gave another glance in the direction of the olive trees before he took his leave of the orchard.

4

PIRATES

A sennight later

Darius watched as two of his men dispatched the last of the five pirates that had attempted a raid on an outbound ship from Perisa. Their boat, half sunk but stuck in the sands of the black beach, would make a suitable fishing boat should some enterprising young man dig it out.

How such a small craft had made it to the island on the rough waters of the Mediterranean, Darius was wont to know. None of the pirates spoke a language he understood, though, and his men and those of the targeted ship were ruthless in dispatching the first three pirates.

Their bodies were somewhere beneath the surface of the water.

"I spotted your warning shot from above," Darius said as he indicated the steep hill behind him. "I see I am too late to have any fun, though," he added as he indicated the bodies at his feet. "How did you know they were pirates?"

Glaukos, one of Darius' most trusted lieutenants, glanced over Darius' shoulder. "We saw them come 'round from the north," he explained. He motioned toward the sea with the helm he carried in one hand, its boar's tusks threatening to impale anyone who came too close. "At the very same time Orestes set sail for Creta. Four of my men were in a packet seeing to the launch of the *Eritha* when they sent up the fire."

The warning signal, a flaming arrow shot straight up into the sky, was one of the means by which the coast-guardsmen knew a threat existed. For boats still out at sea, smoke signals from bonfires provided the notice necessary to gather troops to the threatened beach.

Orestes captained *Eritha*, a vessel that transported saffron, olive oil, and textiles the seventy milion to Creta. His frequent and successful sailings were a source of pride for the seaman. He had yet to lose a shipment, let alone a ship, to the waters of the Aegean.

Or to marauders.

"And your men?" Darius asked, his gaze taking a quick survey of the contingent stationed on the southeast side of the island.

"All accounted for, sir," Glaukos replied. "Orestes lost two oarsmen, though. Arrows got both of them."

Darius hissed. "I will give him my apologies—"

"I have already given mine," Glaukos interrupted, and then ducked his head when he noted Darius' frown. "I have... I have failed in my duties," he added.

Darius took a deep breath. Glaukos was his very best ypolochagoi. He didn't want the man feeling guilty over something he couldn't have prevented. "Could you have taken either arrow in place of the oarsmen who did?"

Glaukos furrowed a brow. "No, sir."

"Then you can hardly count this a failure," Darius said in a voice kept low so that only his lieutenant could hear. "I will not hear your resignation, nor will you be allowed to fall on a sword. Do I make myself clear?"

Startled at hearing the commander's orders, Glaukos nodded. "Yes, Lochagos."

"Take what can be salvaged from the bodies and see to it they are buried."

"Buried?" Glaukos repeated. "Not... burned?"

His attention going to the two pirates that had just had their throats slit, Darius gave his head a shake. "Pirates do not deserve to be burned," he replied. "Let the creatures of the earth have them."

"Yes, Lochagos."

Darius made his way to where the *Eritha* was docked, heartened to find the ship's captain giving orders.

"Orestes," Darius called out as he approached, his dun-colored horse following close behind.

The captain paused in his conference with a crewman and gave the commander a nod. "Darius of Agremon," he said by way of a greeting. "I could hardly think this is a matter worthy of your attention," he added as he held out his hand.

Darius took Orestes' hand and gave it a firm shake. "Any incident that threatens Strongili is a worthy matter," he replied. "Apologies for the loss of your men."

An expression of appreciation passed over Orestes' face. "They were good men. Old, though, and not long for this earth. Much like us, no?" he teased.

Wondering if his face appeared more worn than usual —he hadn't heard this many comments about this age since his assignment on the island had begun—Darius scrubbed a hand over a cheek. "Still, two men are two men too many," he countered. "Will you still launch today?"

"Indeed," Orestes replied. "I was just about to give the order."

"Take some of my men," Darius insisted. "Just in case—"

"I have no room for them," Orestes interrupted, one hand waving in front of him, as if to punctuate his words. "And even if I did, I would rather they stay guarding the shore. For my return. In two sennights, I should think. Perhaps less if my wife does not welcome my return to Creta." This remark was followed with a roll of his eyes.

"I hear gifts of gold are always welcome by those who have been left alone for too long," Darius hinted. "Maybe a gemstone or two." He had learned the hard way with his second wife, although he could barely remember her.

Orestes grinned. "I have acquired a most stunning piece for my Karantha. A necklace made of gold with pearls," he added, his eyebrows lifting.

"Sounds expensive," Darius remarked.

"It was. But my cock shall have a willing home for several nights. Maybe for my entire stay on Creta," Orestes said in a lowered voice.

Darius nodded his understanding. "Then safe travels, old man," he said before dipping his head.

When he was sure his orders were being carried out by Glaukos' men, Darius mounted his horse and was about to make his way up the steep incline to the middle of the island when several men on horseback approached on the beach from the south. He paused when he recognized one of his lieutenants. "Klumenos!" he called out.

The coastguardman's eyes scanned the scene before him before he turned his attention to Darius. "Lochagos. We saw the signal and came as soon as we could," he said as he pulled his horse alongside Darius' Sorraia.

"Five pirates in a boat far too small to have made a crossing," Darius said, one eyebrow arching up.

"Which means they came from somewhere near?" Klumenos guessed. Two of his men joined them, also on horseback, listening in on their conference.

"That is my guess," Darius agreed. "How would you like to dispatch a nest of snakes?" he asked, knowing the man was probably hungry for action. Klumenos' men had the responsibility for guarding the entire southern shore of the island, but they saw little in the way of action. Most ships that arrived at that port came by way of Creta.

Klumenos glanced at his men, who nodded their agreement. "I should like my odds better with two, perhaps three more men," he said.

Darius glanced over towards Glaukos and his men. "Take four of them. Glaukos, too, if you do not mind another ypolochago. He is anxious to take revenge. Two oarsmen were killed by pirates before they were intercepted."

Nodding, Klumenos glanced in the direction of his fellow coastguardman. "And you, Darius? Do you wish to join us on our hunt for snakes?"

The commander gave a shake of his head. "Snake hunting is for the young," he replied with a laugh. "Just do not get yourself bit by a viper."

Klumenos grinned and saluted, and he and his men were off at a gallop to the other end of the black beach.

Darius watched as they hurried off, a sense of melancholy settling over him. Talk of age had him anxious to spend time in the company of someone far younger.

And he knew exactly where he could find her.

5

A MEETING IN AN ORCHARD

An hour later

The pounding of the sea against the black shore faded as the horse made quick work of the gradual climb from Perisa to the pass between two mountains and the road heading west. Darius had his mount pause as he turned to survey the horizon from the highest point of his journey. Although he no longer had a view of the beach, he did spot the *Eritha* well on its journey south to Creta. A few fishing boats dotted the sea near the pristine beaches, but he could see no other ships from this vantage.

He knew another place from which he could scan the southern horizon. Andros' oikos sat near a slight cliff, the city of Akrotiri spread out below. Getting there would require Darius make his way along the southern beaches or inland over undulating hills and through Andros' olive orchard. On a warm day such as this, he was already planning to go through the orchard. The trees would provide some shade as he made his way.

At the edge of the grove, he half-expected to feel the

slight tingle he had come to realize was the signature of Stella's Essence. Had she been older, or if she had already died for the first time, he knew her Essence would be more pronounced, the tingling sensation it caused more noticeable. Having learned of her existence only the week before, Darius had spent the past few nights wondering if she was truly another Immortal.

Anticipation had him wanting to urge his horse to trot faster—run, perhaps—but he had no need to hurry, and he feared he might miss her if he allowed his horse the rein.

About halfway through the orchard, the tingle tickled at the edge of his awareness, and he slowed his horse to a walk. He glanced to his left and right, looking for the colorful fabric of a skirt amongst the leaves of the trees. When the tingle increased in intensity, he halted the Sorraia and studied the trees. He could detect no movement in their branches, nor any color outside of the sage green of the leaves. There was no sound of birds or insects. The quiet in the orchard was almost unnerving, which made him wonder why his mount suddenly nickered.

The *thump* of an olive hitting his head had him giving a start.

He might have expected such an occurrence should he be parked beneath one of the trees, but he had stopped his horse between a row of them.

Listening carefully for the sounds of tree branches cracking or leaves rustling, he allowed a chuckle when a second olive hit his shoulder.

"Another direct hit!" he called out, making sure to keep his expression from appearing dour. He didn't want to scare his assailant.

The sound of a giggle gave away the young girl's location. Seeing Stella's grinning face staring at him from between two branches, Darius realized the color of her skirt was nearly the same as those of the leaves of the black olive tree in which she was sitting. "Your aim is excellent, young lady," he called out.

"You are so close, I could not miss," Stella countered as she lowered herself onto a branch closer to the ground. She sat on it, her legs dangling below the lowest branches. "Are you searching for my father?"

Darius had his mount approach the tree, and he halted the beast when he was nearly under the young girl. "No. But I am gladdened to find you," he responded. "I had hoped to introduce myself when I last visited Andros."

Glancing around as if she thought he might be speaking to someone else, Stella finally asked, "To me?"

He gave a nod along with a look of amusement, deciding the young girl wasn't as precocious as he first thought. "I am Darius of Agremon."

Stella furrowed a brow. "I have not heard of Agremon. Is it on the other end of the island?"

Darius shook his head. "It is... it is far east of here. In a much larger land than this," he replied. His gaze went to her feet. She wore thin leather sandals, the ties wrapped around her calves to keep them in place. "And you? Where are you from?"

Stella regarded him with suspicion a moment before she said, "Akrotiri." She straightened on the branch and announced, "I am Stella of Akrotiri." And then she giggled, the musical sound bringing a smile to Darius' face. He was sure he recognized that giggle from his night on the beach. He almost asked what she had found so amusing, but decided he didn't want to embarrass the young girl.

His smile had her suddenly sobering. "You don't look as old as father says you are."

Darius blinked. He was about to reply with a comment about how old he really was, but thought better of it. No need to give away his age to one who probably hadn't seen ten winters. "What makes you say that?" he asked.

She dimpled and gave a shake of her head. "He said you have the soul of a very old man."

Dipping his head, Darius considered this bit of news. Perhaps having an old soul wasn't the same as being old. "And you? How old are you?"

Stella's attention was on his horse, though, her swinging legs having attracted the attention of the Sorraia. "How old is your horse?"

Darius ran his hand along his mount's neck. "Four springs, I think," replied.

Brightening at this, Stella said, "I am ten summers. What do you call him?"

Not having given his mount a name—he thought to decide on something once he had ridden him more than a month or two—Darius wasn't sure how to respond. "Perhaps you can help in that regard."

Her swinging legs came to a halt and her eyes widened. "Help?" she repeated.

"Give him a name. What would you call him?"

Stella seemed uncertain for a moment. "I think I would need to ride him before I could give him a name."

Darius allowed a smirk, recognizing her ploy for what it was. "Have you ever ridden a horse before?"

Shaking her head, Stella clambered down from the tree and moved to stand in front of the Sorraia.

Alarmed at what the horse might do—Stella had positioned herself directly in front of the beast—Darius was about to dismount. But the horse merely nickered and then lowered his head until Stella's hand could come to rest on the side of his nose.

"Take care," he warned. "I should not want you trampled—"

"Ssh!" she interrupted, holding a finger to her lips as she leaned to her right.

Blinking, Darius stared at her. How dare she *shush* him! And how dare she touch his horse! But he was mesmerized as he watched her return her attention to the beast. He knew she was saying something, but her whispers didn't quite make their way to his ears, and he leaned forward in an effort to hear.

In the meantime, his horse continued to nicker, as if he was conversing with the child. Darius rolled his eyes in dismay, wondering how much longer Stella intended to treat the horse as a plaything. Then she was suddenly standing next to where his leg gripped his mount, her arms raised as if she expected him to lift her onto the horse.

He paused a moment before he leaned down and captured her beneath her arms. Lifting her onto the leather saddle at the same time he repositioned himself to give her room behind the pommel, Darius nearly gave a start. The mere act of touching her had a pleasant sensation replacing the slight tingle in his head.

He wondered if she had the same sense of him.

When she was settled, both legs hanging over the left

side, she turned her gaze onto him. "You shall call him Augustine."

Darius blinked again. "Oh, I shall now?" he replied, nearly rolling his eyes with amusement.

"It means 'majestic'—"

"I know what it means," he countered, and then wondered how it was she knew the name's meaning. She was but ten summers old!

"He likes being your horse."

"Does he?" Darius couldn't help the hint of pride he felt at hearing her words.

"Yes. You are a man of great importance, and he knows it," she stated. "But sometimes you hit him too hard with the flat of your hand. It hurts him—"

"I do not hit him," Darius argued, straightening in the saddle. Any hint of humor he had felt the moment before dissipated.

"Not intentionally, of course," she agreed. "Just when you are trying to pat him on the shoulder—"

"Withers," he interrupted. "They are... they are called withers," he explained.

Stella blinked. "Then you are patting him too hard on his withers when he has done well."

Frowning, Darius stared at Stella for a moment before the edges of his lips quirked. "You got all that out of him, did you?"

She nodded, unaware he was teasing her. "And more. He is three springs old. He loves to run. Should you ever have cause to race another, he would like that very much. He is lonely, and he is very thirsty."

Darius stared at the red-headed girl for a long time before his brows furrowed. "It has been some time since he had water," he agreed, deciding it better he not address the comment about the horse being lonely.

Was he expected to acquire another horse to provide companionship? At least there were horses on the lands surrounding his new villa on the north end of the island. He had plans to return there in a few days.

"There is a trough at my father's oikos he can drink from," she suggested. "I do not think he will mind that the goats drink from it." She pointed to the south.

"Then I suppose we should see to it his thirst is slaked." Placing an arm around her in an effort to ensure she didn't bounce off the horse, Darius knocked his heels into the underside of the horse and had them off at a fast trot through the middle of the orchard.

He couldn't help but notice how Stella beamed in delight, one of her hands pressed against the Sorraia's mane as they made their way. He couldn't help but smile, too, her enthusiasm for the ride infectious.

"I will have to explain to your father why it is I have taken you from your work on this day," he said, wondering how much of her day she was expected to spend in the olive trees.

"He will not be at the oikos," she replied. "He took Helena to Akrotiri," she added when she saw how he frowned.

"He left you alone?" Darius asked, a hint of alarm sounding in his voice.

Stella grinned. "I am not alone. I am with you," she countered.

"It is not safe for you to be up in the trees without protection," he argued. "Why, I just came from where my men had seen to ridding this island of some pirates."

The grin disappeared from Stella's face as she regarded him a moment, their ride forgotten. "So they *are* pirates?" she half-asked, her reddish brown eyebrows furrowing with concern.

With the oikos in sight, Darius slowed the horse until it was just walking. "What do you mean, they are pirates?"

Stella pointed due south. "There is a ship in the tiny cove down there," she said. "I have never seen it before."

Alarmed, Darius quickly dismounted. Tossing his cape behind his shoulders, he reached up to capture her beneath her arms. "Show me," he ordered as he lifted her down from the horse.

"You can see it from over there," she said as she pointed to where the wooded land fell off in the form of a slight cliff. Before she headed in that direction, she helped herself to the horse's reins. She quickly led the beast to the trough, her small feet running while Augustine followed at a quick walk.

When she was sure the horse was drinking, she took one of Darius' hands and led him to the edge of the cliff. From this vantage, he could clearly see Akrotiri below and to the south as well as the cove to the left that she claimed held pirates.

Staring down at the unfamiliar ship—it's bottom was broad, and there were two masts for sails—Darius looked for signs of life but didn't see anyone on board. He turned to her and asked, "How long has it been there?"

Stella angled her head, as if in thought. "It was not there two nights ago, but it was there yesterday morning," she replied. "I told Helena when she was teaching me yesterday, but she said I was imagining things. That it was just a fishing boat." She glanced up at him. "I thought it too large to be a fishing boat."

Darius regarded the girl for a moment, rather charmed by her manner. He was also curious as to why she referred to her mother as 'Helena' rather than 'mother'. She referred to Andros as her father.

"From where do you think they have sailed?" Stella asked, turning her attention back to him.

He shook his head. "Until I get a look at one of them, I cannot say, and even then, I might not know."

Her shoulders sagged, as if she were disappointed by his response. "I think they are from the lands to the south. Not Creta, though. Maybe Egypt. Or Assyria," she said, her eyes widening as she watched for his reaction.

"Assyria is due east," Darius said with a shake of his head. "And how is it you even know of the lands to the south?" he asked, turning to regard her in surprise.

She allowed a shrug. "Helena teaches me many things. She is not of Strongili, and knows much about Creta and other islands. Like you, she is old."

Having heard entirely too much about age on this day, Darius regarded her with a combination of humor and offense. "Old?" he repeated. "Just how old do you think I am?"

Her head angling to one side, Stella regarded him for a long time before she reached up and touched his bare arm. A shiver passed through him just then, as if the essence of her immortality was attempting to merge with his.

"Six-hundred years?" she guessed, and then giggled when she noted his look of shock. "Five-and-thirty?" she quickly amended, her shoulders rising up so her head seemed to turtle between them. "I just guessed."

He relaxed a bit at hearing her amended number, and finally allowed a grin. "You have the right of it," he murmured.

In more ways than one.

Her first guess nearly matched his own. He didn't know exactly how many years had passed before he started to keep track of the passage of time. He knew he was different from most when his first wife showed signs of age and she complained that he looked the same as the day they were wed. Back then, there was only his reflection in the surface of water to show him what he looked like to others.

Darius was torn between wanting to stay with Stella—to learn more about how she had come to be—and discovering more about the visiting ship below.

He decided he needed to attend to his duty. Had there been a fire nearby, he might have shot up an arrow as a warning signal. But he didn't yet know enough about the ship, and he didn't want to alarm the coastguardsmen if it really was just a fishing boat usually moored somewhere else on the island.

Either way, Klumenos would not appreciate learning of a vessel that had landed under his watch, but stranger things had happened.

Darius was about to head for the trough—once his horse had had enough to drink, he feared he might wander off—but he turned to find it standing directly behind Stella.

She turned and reached up to capture the Sorraia's head between her small hands. Augustine immediately lowered his head, and she kissed his nose. "Farewell, my friend," she murmured.

A stab of jealousy caught Darius just then, and he chided himself for the reaction. He had never been jealous of his horse before. He knelt down, his head even with Stella's. "Do I get a kiss?"

All at once, Stella displayed a streak of shyness. "I can afford you a kiss for farewell and a kiss for welcome," she said in a quiet voice. "I am too young to bestow kisses of affection."

Darius struggled to keep from grinning just then. Her manner was so serious!

"Then a kiss of farewell," he agreed. He leaned down and bussed her small lips, managing to keep a straight face as she pursed hers into a rosebud. The light tingling sensation at the edge of his brain flared into an intense tingle, and for the first time in a very long time, he felt young again.

"Until your father returns, perhaps it would be best if you stayed inside. I should not want a pirate to make off with you," he half-teased.

Stella nodded her understanding. "I will go hide in a tree."

Darius mounted his newly-named horse, gave her a wave, and headed off the way he had come. Even before the tingle in his head subsided, he knew he would look forward to seeing her again.

Perhaps when next they met, she would bestow a kiss in greeting as well as in farewell.

6

A CHILD CONTEMPLATES A HORSE

Stella watched the leader of the coastguardsmen ride off to the north, disappointed he had taken his leave so soon. From the moment he had appeared in the olive orchard, she had known it was him from the tickle she had felt at the edge of her thoughts.

Did the man have any idea how thrilled she had been at riding his horse? Such a magnificent beast! And one that had been born in a land far from Strongili. Chosen for his sure-footed hooves and stamina, the Sorraia was perfect for the terrain of the mountainous island. Proud but lonely, the beast was well aware his master was a man of importance on the island. A man of great responsibility.

And a man of advanced age.

Darius of Agremon certainly didn't look as if he were six-hundred years old, but when she touched him, there had been that shiver of awareness that passed through her. Of knowledge that she was in the presence of a man who had seen much, suffered as a result, and continued to live only because he had no choice.

An old soul, indeed.

She could almost feel sorry for him.

Except she could not. He rode a magnificent horse. A horse she hoped she might one day ride by herself.

Daring one more glance in the direction of the ship anchored in the small cove below—there was no one about on the deck nor anywhere nearby—Stella made her way into her father's oikos.

Hurrying to the small room in which she slept every night, Stella pulled a sheet of papyrus from beneath her short bedstead. Her father had allowed her to purchase several sheets of the imported paper when they last visited the *agora* in Akrotiri. Although she could have used her allowance—her pay for her work in the olive grove— for toys or sweets, she always chose to buy the papyrus from Egypt or colored dyes she could mix with water or olive olio. With a small brush made of goat hair, she applied the colors onto the wet papyrus to make paintings.

While delivering olives to a multi-storied oikos in Akrotiri, she had seen the frescos on the walls and hoped to one day paint one on a wall in her own bedchamber. By the end of the next year, she might be able to acquire the lime necessary to make plaster.

A man in town had explained that an artisan needed to spread only as much of the wet plaster on the wall as could be colored during a session of painting. Once the plaster was too dry, it would no longer take the pigment.

Sure she could do such a thing, Stella practiced her craft on papyrus, making sure to apply only the amount of water she could color with her pigments in a single sitting. Once the papyrus was dry, she could move on to a different part of the painting, working her brush and the colors into a scene as vibrant as her imagination.

Sometime soon, she intended to create a painting to rival that of the fresco she had seen in the oikos in Akrotiri.

Stella placed the sheet of papyrus atop a thin, fired-clay tray. After crossing her legs, she pulled the tray onto her lap and regarded the blank canvas with a grin of excitement. Using a stick of charcoal her father had carved for her, she began to draw the outlines of the Sorraia.

Augustine.

Such a noble horse. Proud, and not just because of his master's status on the island.

He certainly wasn't born on the island—Darius had confirmed that with his words about the beast having come from a land far away—but Augustine had endured much in the trip over water that brought him to Strongili. For seven days, stormy seas, lightning, wind and rain were followed by blistering heat. Barely weaned, he would have died of fright if there hadn't been other horses of his kind on the same ship. At least he had been given enough to drink. Not like today, when Darius seemed oblivious to the midday heat and the toll it took on the horse to climb and descend the mountains.

Why didn't Darius know this about his mount?

Stella sensed that he was aware of their shared traits. Of how she knew he was near even before she looked for him from between the tree branches. He knew she was there—she was sure of it as she watched his body tense and his mind still as he searched for her.

And yet, he hadn't been aware of the gust of steam that escaped from the ground near Augustine's hoof. The horse certainly knew. She saw how his nostrils flared at the smell of the noxious odor that accompanied the steam. The same smell as the broken rotten eggs in Helena's hen house.

Stella wrinkled her nose before returning her attention to the drawing before her, somewhat dismayed when she couldn't remember if Augustine had any distinctive markings on his body.

Finally content to simply paint him as she remembered him, she mixed a series of ochres and browns from her ground dyes and set to work with her brushes.

An hour later, she regarded her still-wet painting with a grin. Once the papyrus dried, she would darken some of the browns where Augustine's coat was in shadow and add the details of his eyes, nostrils, and ears.

"Am I to surmise the Lochagos Darius has been here today?"

Stella gave a start, glad she no longer held a pigment-filled brush that might have obliterated some of what she had accomplished. She looked up to find her father leaning over her, his hands on his knees as he surveyed her work.

"He was, and it is not finished," she murmured.

"Was he after more olio?" Andros asked, hope in his voice.

"I do not think so," Stella replied, realizing just then she wasn't sure why Darius had come to the olive orchard. She had meant to ask. But she was easily distracted by Augustine and by the lochagos' determination to see what might be a pirate ship. "He was riding between the trees and saw me. I showed him the strange ship down below," she added.

Andros frowned. "What ship?"

Before Stella could even answer, her father turned on his heel and left her room. After a moment, she knew he had left the oikos. Setting aside the papyrus and placing her brushes into a clay pot of water, she got to her feet and quickly made her way to where her father stood staring down at the cove below the cliff's edge. Helena, busy seeing to her goats, seemed oblivious to her husband's concern.

"When did you first see this?" he asked, his frown nearly matching the one Darius had displayed earlier that afternoon.

Stella repeated what she had told Darius. "The lochagos said he was going to have his men see to them," she added, noting her father's consternation. "Why are you worried?"

Andros turned his attention on her for only a moment. "I am not. Especially if Darius has his men looking into it," he replied, attempting a manner of nonchalance.

Furrowing a reddish-brown brow, Stella regarded her father for a moment and then allowed a sigh. "You are a poor liar, Father," she whispered on a sigh.

Allowing a chuckle, Andros said, "As long as you are the only one who knows it, my daughter."

Stella dared a glance in Helena's direction, quickly averting her eyes when she realized her mother had been watching them with interest.

Helena knew her father was a poor liar, too. The older woman had known as much for longer than Stella had been in their household. But being a wife to a well-regarded farmer on Strongili required Helena simply do her duty and provide help where she could.

She did so with the goats and chickens and otherwise spent her time on the loom making beautiful fabrics Andros could trade for goods and gold.

"Now. How are my olive trees on this fine day?" Andros asked as he led them back toward the oikos.

"Except for the tree that is too close to the heated ground, the trees are all well," Stella replied. That single tree, north of the main grove and well away from the others, displayed signs of stress as its leaves withered and fell. Very little fruit grew on it, so Stella no longer pruned it.

Andros frowned. "Heated ground?" he repeated in alarm.

"Another steam vent appeared today—right in the middle of the orchard—although this one was far enough away from a tree that I do not expect it will hurt one," she explained. "It nearly hurt Augustine, though."

"Augustine?" Andros repeated.

Stella nodded. "The lochagos' horse. It nearly burned one of his hooves," she said in a hoarse whisper. "And it smelled ever so bad."

Andros regarded his daughter for a long time before nodding toward the oikos. "You will tell me of these steam vents over supper," he said as he led the way.

By the end of the evening meal, Andros finally understood why his olive orchard was no longer producing as many olives as it once did.

7

A MYSTERY BEGINS

Two hours after Darius left Stella

Klumenos, Glaukos, and their men weren't where Darius expected he might find the coastguardsmen. Given the direction from which the pirates had sailed in their attempt to board the *Eritha*, Darius thought he would spot them just north of Perisa. From his vantage above that location, he could see no evidence of pirates—or of anyone, for that matter.

The appearance of two horses, their heads showing between the leaves of trees, had him pausing in his descent down the slight incline.

Although he had been following a donkey path at first, it led off in the direction of Perisa. He wanted to end up north of the outcropping just beyond Perisa, perhaps as far as Kamari. When a foot trail through the foliage made itself apparent, he took it. He allowed Augustine a bit of rein, the Sorraia negotiating the path at his own speed while Darius studied the shoreline below.

Upon spotting more horses, he halted his mount and listened.

Expecting to hear voices, he was frustrated at hearing only the slight sound of waves crashing onto the black shore. He allowed Augustine a few more steps and then had him pause again. Another riderless horse came into view, which had the hairs on the back of Darius' neck coming to attention.

Where were his men?

Another few steps, and he allowed a sigh of relief when one of Glaukos' men came into view. He was holding onto the reins of his horse, although he wasn't mounted. Apparently, the others had dismounted and continued on foot while this man was left to mind the horses.

Pursing his lips, Darius made the sound of a bird's whistle and watched, hoping the man might look in his direction. He did it again after a moment, waving a hand when the sentry turned to survey the hill above him.

Darius knew he had been spotted when the sentry whistled back and then motioned that he should join him.

Augustine made the descent slowly, serpentining his way down the slope until they reached the flattened area upon which seven horses and the sentry were located.

"Greetings, Lochagos," the coastguardsman said in a hoarse whisper.

"Where is Klumenos?"

The sentry gave a nod to the north. "He has taken some men to the caves while Glaukos awaits on the other end of the shore."

From this location, Darius could make out Glaukos and three of his men seated around a fire at the beach.

From his vantage, they appeared to be men simply gathered about a small fire—not a contingent of warriors ready to do battle. "You think the pirates are hiding in the caves?" he asked in a whisper.

The sentry nodded. "Footprints in the sand have given them away," he said, his finger directed to a series of disturbances in the otherwise pristine black beach. "We have not yet found a ship, though."

Darius took a breath before saying, "It may be in a cove near Akrotiri. Arrived sometime the night before last."

Frowning, the sentry shook his head. "There are coastguardsmen there," he whispered. "Surely a boat would have been spotted, especially if it made it into the cove."

Nodding his agreement, Darius said, "Or it was mistaken for a fishing boat."

The sentry seemed to consider this possibility before he finally nodded. "A costly mistake," he murmured.

"Perhaps," Darius whispered, just before his brows furrowed. "What are you called?" he asked, sure he had seen the sentry before.

"Aries, son of Glaukos."

"Ah," Darius responded. "Learn well, and one day you might replace him," he said. In the growing gloom of dusk —he secretly wished he had been on the other side of the island to pay witness to a glorious sunset—the nearby islands to the south and east were barely visible on the horizon. "When will you raid the caves?"

Aries gave a shrug. "I thought Klumenos might have done so by now," he replied, his attention going to where the ypolochago and his men had disappeared earlier that evening.

Darius glanced in the direction of where Glaukos and his men were gathered around a bonfire. The hairs on his forearms stirred, but not because of a breeze. "Have you heard anything at all? A signal, perhaps?"

Shaking his head, the sentry's attention was still on the area where he had last seen Klumenos. "Nothing, Lochagos. But they may be delaying in an attempt to learn more about the invaders."

"Or they may already be dead," Darius whispered hoarsely. He untied a saddlebag from the back of the horse and slung it over his shoulder. "Take my horse," he added as he held out the reins.

Ignoring Aries' look of alarm, Darius made his way toward Glaukos and the fire, his gait slow and as relaxed as he could manage lest anyone was watching him. Surely the invaders would have a lookout posted, and he didn't want to appear as if he were ready for a fight.

Glaukos' men certainly were. Three tensed and half-stood once it was apparent he was headed in their direction. A murmured command had them taking their seats on small boulders that had been assembled around the fire.

"Lochagos," Glaukos said with a hint of question. "Has something happened?"

"You tell me," Darius countered, easing himself down to the coarse black sand and resting his elbows on his knees.

"I wait, but I do so only because Ypolochago Klumenos told me to give him until the moon appeared completely." Glaukos pointed to where just half of the mostly-full moon was rising in the east. With its reflection on the fairly still water, it looked as if it was already full above the horizon. "If we hear nothing, or see nothing, then we are to raid the caves."

At least the moon would provide some light. As would the torches each man had planted in the sand next to where they sat. "With your permission, I think I should like to join your raiding party on this night," Darius said, his eyes glimmering in the firelight.

Glaukos glanced around at his men. "We would be honored to have you and your weapon, Lochagos," he replied, his words supported by the nodding heads and grunts of approval coming from the men surrounding the fire.

"Have you eaten?" Darius asked.

Several heads bobbed, and one man indicated the fire-charred carcasses of two hares, their hides drying on the other side of the fire pit. Darius opened his saddlebag and pulled out a bunch of grapes. He divided it in two, passing the small bunches to the men on either side of him. Then he pulled out another bunch and did the same to those who sat across from him. He helped himself to the loose grapes at the bottom of the bag, wishing he had arrived in time to enjoy some of the meat.

"Gratitude, Lochagos," one of the men said before he seemed to swallow several grapes without chewing. His eyes widened when he looked first toward the moon and then toward the caves. "Arrow!" he said with urgency.

All eyes turned to follow the arc of a flaming arrow as it shot up into the twilight before coming to a halt and then diving down toward the water.

"That's our signal," Glaukos hissed as he got to his feet.

The men were already up from their seats, though, a

few leaving behind their torches as they hurried towards the caves. Not as quick to rise from the black sand, Darius helped himself to a torch, jogged to join the rest, and took up a position at the rear of the group.

Given Klumenos seemed to have shared a plan with Glaukos, Darius simply followed the orders the lieutenant called out. His sword in one hand and the lit torch in another, he was left to stand guard outside the cave opening. Knowing he would need both hands if a battle ensued, Darius planted the base of the torch in the black sand so it provided light for the cave's opening but didn't blind him should someone come out of the cave.

He stepped to the side and listened intently. Whoever had shot the arrow had apparently done so and then returned to the cave, for no other coastguardsmen could be seen on the beach. In the deepening twilight, he could barely make out the horses still grouped at the base of the mountain. Another few minutes, and they would be impossible to see.

The sound of a scuffle within the cave had Darius poised for a fight. He knew this particular cave was deep. Knew that its cavernous interior provided protection from wind and water, given how it angled to the north. The depth of it extended to the mountain's base. Any number of pirates could easily hide in the back, although there was only one way in and out.

The sound of a warning whistle made its way to Darius' ear, a clear indication that the first man out of the cave was a foe. He crouched to one side of the opening opposite where he had left the torch, his sword raised and the hilt clutched in both hands.

At the very moment the man emerged from the cave,

Darius brought down the weapon in a wide arc. The blade should have intersected a mid-section—should have sliced the man in half—but it missed the escapee entirely. Darius watched in dismay as the small man, down on all fours, scrambled away from the cave's opening towards the safety of darkness.

But Darius was quick to pull a dagger from his sandal tie. He threw the blade toward the nearly naked man, satisfied when he heard a howl of pain. The dagger's blade, buried deep in the man's thigh, hindered his forward momentum and had him reaching back with a flailing hand as he attempted to get a hold of it to remove it.

Darius stood over him with his sword raised and finally reached down and retrieved his dagger. The tang of fresh blood filled the air, as did a screech of pain. Using his foot, Darius pushed the man over until he was on his back.

"Where are you from?" Darius asked from between gritted teeth.

When the moaning man didn't respond, Darius asked the question again in three other languages. The last one had the prisoner's eyes widening in surprise.

"Gutium, yes," came a strangled response. "I am Gutian."

Darius frowned. He had thought the Gutians and Sumeria—the Akkadian Empire—long gone since the Babylonians had taken control of that part of the world nearly two centuries ago. "Why?" He ignored the chain of men who were emerging from the cave, each man's ankles tied with rope to an ankle of the man behind them. The line was flanked by all the coastguardsmen that had been on duty that afternoon. In the dim light from the torch, it was evident several of the intruders had been wounded by blows to their heads and upper bodies. "Why?" Darius repeated when his prisoner didn't respond.

"Gold. We... we seek gold. And silver."

Well aware the wounded man would not live much longer—he was bleeding out—Darius lowered his sword. "You have come to the wrong island," he said in the man's language. "There is no gold here. Who sent you?"

Klumenos joined him then and regarded the dying man as he struggled to catch his breath. The battle in the cave had obviously been heated. "You understand his words?" Klumenos asked in hushed tones.

"He speaks an ancient language," Darius whispered, not adding that he had at one time used the Gutian language because he had lived in the region from which this prisoner hailed. "But that doesn't mean he is from the east." He raised his voice to repeat his query. "Who sent you here?" Although he was glad for the light from the nearly full moon, it cast an eery glow over the beach.

"No one. We came of our own accord."

"You speak lies," Darius accused, his gaze going to the line of nine men Glaukos and his team had pinned against the outside of the cave. "Who sent you?" he called out, using the same language the dying man spoke.

"We were told of riches. Gold and pearls. Silver and gemstones," one of the younger men replied. "This is the center of Minoa, is it not?"

A series of angry words, spoken in a slightly different language from Gutian and directed at the one who had responded, had the younger man cowering in fear.

Darius walked up to the line of men and studied their

features. The one who had spoken first was so young, he could have still been a boy. The one who had rebuked the boy appeared older than the others and was probably their leader.

As to the language the leader had used, Darius recognized it as one he had also spoken, although not so long ago. Akkadian. The language of Babylonia and Assyria.

"From where do you come?" he asked in Akkadian. Despite remembering how to say the words, he couldn't recall exactly where he had said them. In the course of only a few minutes, some of his past had flashed through his mind in a series of disjointed images.

Several prisoners straightened and regarded Darius in wonder. "The mountains known as Zagros," one of them finally said. "But we have been gone from there for two summers."

"You are far from your home," Darius remarked, the image of the Zagros Mountains forming in his memory. Although he had lived in their shadow, he had done so as part of a nomadic life.

"As are you," another said.

Darius furrowed a brow. He hardly knew where his original home was located. It had been nearly six centuries since he had been near the mountain range. "What do you know of me?"

The prisoners exchanged nervous glances. "You spoke Gutian. How is this possible if you are not from Gutium?"

Rising to his full height had him towering over the line of prisoners, and he felt a hint of satisfaction when several suddenly cowered. "We trade with all peoples," he stated. "As you say, this is the center of Minoa." He turned his attention to Klumenos. "What do you wish to do with your prisoners?" he asked.

Klumenos gave him a look of surprise, obviously expecting the leader of the coastguardsmen to make that determination. "If it were truly up to me, I would put them to work in the saffron fields. As slaves, if it were allowed."

Darius gave a grunt. "I hardly think men from the hills would make good farmers," he whispered hoarsely.

"We are sailors," the oldest prisoner said, which had Glaukos threatening him with his sword. Darius noted how the man didn't flinch but stared at his captor with a steely gaze. From his comment, it was obvious the man understood the Minoan language.

"Pirates, you mean," Klumenos hissed.

"We came seeking trade," the leader countered. "We offer grain for gold and silver."

"Hiding in caves?" Glaukos countered in disbelief, just then realizing the man understood the Minoan language.

"We could not find accommodations," the boy said then.

"Do you all speak our language?" Glaukos asked, his brows furrowed.

"Some do," the leader replied on a sigh. "As I said, we came to trade. We are not..." He struggled for a moment, as if he didn't know the word for pirates. "Invaders."

"Where is your ship?" Darius asked, waving a hand to indicate the eastern horizon.

A few of the men gave quizzical glances in the direction of their leader. He seemed to hesitate before he asked, "If I tell you, what assurances do I have that you will not rob it of its cargo?"

Darius once again straightened. "I will not raid the hold of your ship, nor will my men," he stated.

The older man nodded. "I am Perakles. The captain of the *South Winds*, which I left anchored in a cove on the south end of the island."

"Near Akrotiri?" Darius half-asked.

Perakles gave a start. "I went there first. Alone. I was told grain was not traded there, though. I was directed to come to Perisa."

Darius frowned. "By whom?" Not having experience in trading grains—Darius only negotiated with Andros for olive oil, and he paid coin for it—he wasn't aware of who saw to the local grain trade. He did know it was occasionally available at the agora.

The captain shrugged. "My queries directed me to seek a man in Perisa, who it seems has made his way to Creta."

Rolling his eyes, Darius said, "Orestes," at the same time as Klumenos. Neither were surprised when the man recognized the name and nodded vigorously.

The two coastguardsmen regarded one another with lifted brows before they turned their attention back to the ship captain. "He will not return to this island for another sennight," Darius said. "After he has had enough of his wife."

"Or she has had enough of him," Klumenos whispered.

Perakles blinked and then his eyes widened in understanding. A look of disappointment crossed his face. "I fear for the grain in the meantime," he remarked.

"Is your hold not sound?" Klumenos asked.

Obviously offended, Perakles gave a huff. "The ship's hold is more solid than any ship its size. My fear is of thieves," he replied. "I left only one man to guard it, but he is weak of flesh and no doubt spending this night in the bed of a prostitute."

"And if there is no prostitute?" Klumenos countered, knowing there were only a few in Akrotiri and none who would entertain strangers in their beds.

"A widow?" Perakles guessed. "Lukios is handsome enough, and he speaks your language."

Darius nodded his understanding. "If we release you, where will you go on this night?"

Perakles pointed toward the cave entrance. "Back into the cave. We intended to sleep there on this night. And then we shall make our way back to our ship at first light to await Orestes' return," he said.

Sighing, Darius waved for Glaukos and Klumenos to join him several steps away from the strangers. "What are your thoughts?"

Klumenos sighed. "Am I mad to believe him?" he asked. "He seems sincere."

"I was prepared to kill every one of them," Glaukos said before allowing a sigh of his own. "But they are not men of war. They have but only a few weapons."

"What did you find among their possessions?"

Glaukos shrugged. "Idols, pallets for sleeping, a few items of clothing. Nothing much of note," he replied.

"And you?" Darius asked as he turned his attention on Klumenos. "What would you do with them?"

The lean man dared a glance back at the line of men and gave a shake of his head. "I would escort them back to their ship and see that they departed our shores," he answered.

"And the grain?"

Glaukos leaned in and said, "If they have a goodly

amount, perhaps *we* should put in a bid for it, Lochagos," he suggested. "My oikos is in need of stores for the winter."

"As is mine," Klumenos chimed in.

Darius furrowed a brow. "Which means all the coastguardsmen could benefit," he reasoned. He had some gold. Some silver, too. No pearls or gemstones, though. At least none that he would be willing to trade.

A thought of the young girl, Stella, had him wondering what she might like in the way of jewels. When she was old enough, what might he bestow on her in honor of their eventual joining? He hoped she would like the gold and pearl ring and the bracelet of colorful gemstones he had kept safe in his trunk. There were other jewels, as well.

He gave his head a shake, embarrassed by the thought he would be caught daydreaming. "Allow them the use of the cave for the night," Darius said, knowing he wouldn't be going to his own villa that night. Paradisos was too far away, especially this time of the night. "Then escort them to their ship once the sun is up."

Glaukos nodded. "And if the grain is good? What are we to use as payment?"

Darius had some gold coins stashed in a hole beneath his tent he could use to buy the grain, but he would have to retrieve it.

He glanced over at the path that led up and to the side of the mountain. His tent was beyond where the trail disappeared, located on a flat of ground that allowed for a view of both sides of the island. Set up against a stand of trees, the large tent provided privacy as well as safety from interlopers.

Given the light from the moon, he decided his horse could negotiate the path.

"I will see to acquiring some coin and meet you at their ship in the morning," Darius finally replied. He glanced back at the fire at the other end of the beach, noting how its flames were no longer visible.

"Understood," Klumenos said. "We will take shelter in the cave. At the front," he said, obviously disappointed he wouldn't be spending the night in his own bed.

"I will tell the boy guarding the horses of our plan," Darius offered, well aware the young man had been watching the proceedings from the back of the beach. The herd of horses were quiet now that the sun was down.

A snort erupted from Klumenos. "Aries is nearly eighteen summers."

"As I said, a boy," Darius replied, although he did so with a grin.

Knowing the sky would be black soon, Darius retrieved his saddlebag from near the fire, took his horse from the guard named Aries, and explained the plan to him. Without a backward glance, he mounted Augustine and made his way up to his tent.

He spent the night in a sound sleep.

Visions of a red-headed young woman were all he wanted to remember the following morning.

8

NEGOTIATING FOR GRAIN

The following morning

Darius loaded a saddlebag with several purses of gold coins, wincing when he realized how heavy the bags would be for his horse.

Augustine, he thought with a grin. Stella had been so serious with her edict. "Augustine, let us see if we cannot make this load a bit easier to carry," he said in a low voice.

The horse nickered softly, much like he had done with Stella.

"Do not expect me to talk to you all the time," the lochagos continued. "We have work to do on this day."

His nickering continuing, Augustine tossed his head.

Darius gently placed a hand on the horse's withers and nearly pulled it away just as quickly. The flare of awareness that erupted in his head had him understanding why Stella had done it the day before. It wasn't that the horse spoke to him exactly, but simply acknowledged him as his master. Smoothing his palm over the horse's hide, he nearly laughed as the horse continued to nicker. "Enough," Darius murmured.

Evenly distributing the purses into two bags, Darius finally decided to rebury a few of the purses in his tent. He didn't want to take the chance of losing the coins should he be robbed along the way, nor did he believe the traders had that much grain to trade. The ship he had spotted from Andros' overlook hadn't been that large, so he doubted there was much cargo in its hold.

Although he had no idea how much grain cost these days, he wasn't about to spend more than his annual wages to secure it for his men. The sellers would simply have to find others to buy the rest if what he took in gold wasn't enough to pay for all of it.

As for transporting the grain, he would have one of his men see to those details once the transaction was complete.

Securing his tent's opening, Darius mounted Augustine and headed south. He was tempted to go through Andros' olive orchard on the way—a glimpse of Stella would assure him she was safe—and then make his way down the goat path to Akrotiri. Reason prevailed, though. Allowing his horse to pick its way down the mountainside, he was gladdened to join several of his coastguardsmen on the beach south of where the traders had been discovered.

"It appeared there was trouble last night?" Argurios half-asked as Darius came to a halt next to their watchtower. The small village of Theros wasn't far. "I saw Glaukos leading men down the beach."

"Men from the east. He thought they were pirates, but they may be traders in grain. I will know in the next couple of hours," Darius replied, before telling Argurios and his two men what had happened.

The mention of grain had the three murmuring. "May we help?"

"Indeed. Follow me, but stay back and keep watch as I continue to their ship. It could be a trap, and I do not wish to lose any men over what could be a ruse," Darius explained.

"Understood," Argurios replied, turning to order his men to retrieve their horses. "I shall remain here and keep watch. I will send up an arrow and smoke should I spot any ships," he added.

"If all goes well, I should have your men back to you before the sun is high." With that, Darius continued south on the beach, eventually followed by the watchmen.

JUST BEFORE THE cove came into sight, Darius slowed his mount and gave final instructions to the men. From his vantage, he could see Klumenos' men down near the water's edge, although Glaukos and his crew were nowhere to be seen. Continuing along the beach, the cove and its ship came into view. Several of Perakles' men were on board, while Glaukos had a few lined up on the beach, still in their rope shackles.

Darius whistled and waited until Glaukos acknowledged the signal. When his lieutenant gave a wave, Darius made his way to the ship. Perakles, standing with those in ropes, straightened at the sight of the lochagos and gave him a nod.

"We did not discuss price last night," Perakles said before Darius could get out a greeting.

"We did not discuss how much grain you have for sale," Darius countered.

"Enough for all your men, certainly."

"Is that all?"

Perakles winced. "I still hope to make a deal for the remainder with Orestes, or perhaps someone on Creta."

Darius held out a gold coin, the profile of the Minoan king displayed in relief. "One of these for each sack of grain?" he guessed.

"Three," Perakles countered, barely glancing at the gold. At Darius' look of doubt, he added, "They are large sacks."

"Then let us see these sacks," Darius replied.

Up on board the ship, the crew was bringing up grain from the hold and stacking it near the ramp.

"My men believe you will simply take all of it and leave us with nothing," Perakles said as he watched one of his crewman walk down the ramp with a sack over one shoulder.

"My men believe this is a trap. That your grain is rotted."

When a second man descended with a sack of grain, Darius moved to the end of the ramp and ordered the man to open it.

Giving his captain a quick glance, as if to be sure he was allowed to do as the lochagos demanded, the crewman pulled away the rope tie and opened the fabric bag.

"Now dig in with your hand to the bottom and pull some up."

The man did as he was told, the golden grains separating as his hand delved into the sack nearly to his armpit. When he pulled up a handful of grain, it appeared unspoiled, nor was there evidence of insects.

"What are you called?"

The crewman replied, "Tyrus."

"Did you grow this grain, Tyrus?" Darius asked, recognizing emmer. Not exactly like the wheat they imported from the lands to the north, but it would do to feed many families.

The man shook his head. "My brothers are farmers. The yield was too great last year, though—"

"Too great?" Darius interrupted, his tone suggesting disbelief.

"Yes. There were few buyers in our lands—the weather was good to us—so Perakles said he would add it to his cargo for this trip if we could get it to the port where his ship was docked."

Struggling to remember the distance to the Zagros Mountains, Darius frowned. "From where did you come? How far did you travel?"

Tyrus dipped his head. "Akkad," he replied, which had Darius reeling for a moment. Although he was sure he had never lived in the center of the Akkadian Empire, it was close to Kunara, a village that he did occupy in his very early days.

At least, he did until the city burned.

"Three of us followed the trade route to Ugarit—"

"That is over five-hundred milion!" Darius claimed.

"Indeed," Tyrus affirmed with a nod. "But we did so with a caravan. Once in Ugarit, we joined Perakles' crew." At Darius' questioning glance, he added, "Farming does not suit us."

Still wondering if he could trust Perakles, Darius

pretended interest in what was in the sack. "Where does Perakles usually trade?" he asked in a quiet voice.

"The lands south of here. But he does not like the Hyskos—"

"Hyskos?" Darius repeated, his head jerking up to regard the crewman. Now there was a tribal name he hadn't heard in some time.

Tyrus leaned in. "It is said the Egyptians have fallen to their influence, but others say the Hyskos have prevailed over Egypt in battle and now rule the entire country," he explained. "Perakles refuses to trade with them. Instead, he wishes to trade with Minoans." He paused and lowered his voice. "He was not aware of how difficult it would be, though."

Perakles probably hadn't considered the number of coastguardsmen that could be found on all the islands near Creta. Probably hadn't thought he would be considered a pirate when his unfamiliar vessel arrived on Strongili.

"He should have sailed on to Creta, but I am glad he did not," Darius murmured. He took his leave of Tyrus and made his way back to stand before Perakles. "Do you have fifty sacks of grain?"

Perakles allowed a look of offense. "Is that all you want?" he asked in dismay.

"I can take one-hundred for two-hundred coins," Darius offered. A quick glance at the small ship had him wondering how much cargo it could carry.

"Two-hundred-and-fifty for one-hundred sacks," Perakles countered. He quickly added, "Not all will be emmer, though."

Darius frowned. "But something just as edible?" he guessed.

Perakles nodded. "Since you speak our language, and you look as if you do so because you once lived among our kind, you must know of the other crops. Crops better even than emmer," he said with an arched brow. "There are pistachios and almonds. Barley, too."

Pistachios. The word brought back pleasant memories of the green nut he had enjoyed as a boy. A food that had staved off his hunger in the winters.

"I will give you one-hundred sacks for two-hundred-and-fifty coins," Perakles stated.

"Done." Darius gave the gold coin to Perakles and shouted orders to his men. When he turned his attention back to the captain, he said, "You will sail on to Creta." He pointed due south. "I will give you a token and a pennon you can fly on your sail. The harbormaster will let you dock when he sees you have both. But be warned, Captain, that should you cheat us in any way, you will not leave Creta on your ship."

Perakles eyes widened, as if he was surprised by Darius' words. "Understood." Then he angled his head closer to Darius. "You are not going to rob me?" he asked.

Darius furrowed a brow. "As long as you do not cheat me."

"Gratitude, Lochagos." After a moment, he asked, "Why did you make this deal and not make us wait for Orestes?"

Shrugging, Darius wasn't about to tell the captain that Orestes would probably charge him double for the same number of sacks. "I did not wish to have my men guard you for another sennight while we waited for Orestes' return. They have more important duties," he explained.

Perakles held out a gnarled hand. "Gratitude."

Darius grasped the man's hand and gave him a nod. When he turned around, he discovered a chain of men were passing the sacks of grain from one to another until the last man set them on an already growing pile on the cove's red beach.

Returning to his horse, Darius pulled three purses from his saddlebag. He knew each one held a hundred coins, but he doubted the captain would take his word for it. Carrying them back to the captain, he handed two of them over.

"Two-hundred," he said before untying the cord securing the third. He opened the purse and dumped about twenty-five coins into the palm of his hand and gave the third purse to Perakles, who struggled to hold onto the first two given their weight. "Fifty, and some extra for your men," he murmured. "For the trouble we have put them through." Then he gave a nod and returned to his horse to deposit the extra coins and pull out a yellow pennon from his saddlebag. The cloth, woven from linen and dyed using saffron, would notify the harbormaster that this ship had come from Strongili but that he should use caution when dealing with the crew.

Augustine nickered as Darius climbed onto his back and then inexplicably turned around and faced the overlook.

About to chide his horse for the unexpected move, Darius glanced up and grinned when he spotted Stella waving. He wondered how long she had been watching them, especially now that he realized the telltale tingle at the edge of his consciousness was barely there and had been since his arrival in the cove. The young girl had probably paid witness to the entire exchange.

Darius gave a wave and was sure he heard the musical sound of her giggle before the wind took it away.

When he turned his horse around again, he noted Glaukos frowning. He urged Augustine forward until the horse stood before the lieutenant. Darius dismounted, noting how Glaukos regarded him with a look of worry. "What is it?" he asked.

Glaukos pointed to the pile of grain sacks on the small beach. "How are we to transport it?" he asked in dismay.

Darius gave a shrug. "A sack on every horse and the rest by donkey. See to it every coastguardsman on the island gets two sacks," he ordered.

Nodding, Glaukos allowed a huge grin. "Yes, Lochagos. But what about the rest?"

"I will take two on my horse right now. Split the rest between you and Klumenos for the horses."

"Gratitude," Glaukos replied, his eyes widening. His family would have enough grain for the rest of the year.

A half-hour later, sails hoisted and filling with wind the opposite of its namesake, Perakles' ship made its way out of the cove and headed south to Creta.

Seeing that Klumenos was not convinced of the trader's trustworthiness, Darius made his way to where the lieutenant was examining sack after sack of grain. He had opened each one, peering in or shoving his hand in and lifting up a sampling of the contents. "Did you find any filled with sand?" Darius asked, noting Klumenos was arranging the bags into neat piles—after he had retied them.

"Not a one, although this bag is different from most."

"How so?"

Klumenos shrugged. "It appears to be a grain, but it is rather unusual," he noted, holding out a handful for the lochagos to see.

"Barley," Darius remarked, a memory surfacing from his boyhood. "Boil it in water with vegetables, or, if you are of a mind to make your own beer, it will work for that, too."

Giving an appreciative nod, Klumenos opened another sack that he had set aside from the others. "Are these edible?" he asked, a small green pellet held between his thumb and forefinger.

Darius allowed a laugh. "It is a dried pea, you idiot," he replied. He had memories of eating those, as well, although he couldn't recall liking the soup his first wife made from them. "Your woman will know what to do with them."

"Soup?" Klumenos guessed.

Nodding, Darius regarded the other sacks. "If these are not distributed by nightfall, be sure they are covered with oil cloth," he ordered.

"Yes, Lochagos," Klumenos replied.

"I will see to mine right now." Darius reached down and hefted a sack into each of his fists, his biceps bulging with the effort.

Although his own household wouldn't have need of two sacks of emmer, he knew of one that would appreciate such a gift.

And Augustine would appreciate not having to carry two of the sacks all the way to Paradisos.

9

NEGOTIATING A SETTLEMENT

The following day

"She is not yours, is she?" Darius half-asked, his gaze darting to where Stella was gathering twigs and small branches she had cut from the insides of the trees onto a burlap sheet. She wore the same style of skirt most of the women on the island wore, but also a tunic of lightweight fabric, and she went about her work humming. A small animal had captured her attention just then, and she bent to watch it for a moment before returning to her work.

"She is my daughter," Andros argued, his chin rising with his claim. As soon as the lochagos' attention was back on him, the piercing blue eyes the only challenge to his words, he relented. "She has been since Helena found her, abandoned in a basket. She was left beneath the olive tree closest to our oikos," he admitted, his manner guarded. "The morning after Helena prayed for a child." He paused and turned his gaze back onto the young girl. "Her hair was not nearly as red back then. More...

orange," he murmured with a grin. The hair color alone had been cause for caution upon finding the baby. Most Minoan females had very dark, sometimes black hair.

"Still a babe?" Darius asked, his brows furrowing. Never before had he encountered another Immortal so young. The fact that she was still growing meant she hadn't yet died her first death. Once that happened—if it did happen—she would appear the same for the rest of eternity. Or until her Essence passed into another Immortal, should she ever have cause to give up the body she now inhabited.

Andros nodded. "Helena said she could not have been there long. She was nearly a newborn, wrapped in a linen cloth and sleeping quite soundly." He paused before he lowered his voice. "The gods have been good to us. We could not produce as much fruit as we do without her."

Darius considered the farmer's words. "She has a pleasant disposition," he remarked, almost as if he were regarding a horse for sale at the *agora*.

"Indeed. And Helena is teaching her to read and write her numbers," Andros said then. "She is... smart. Clever for one so young."

Darius couldn't argue with that. He followed the old man's gaze and watched as Stella pulled the fabric sheet closer to where they stood. She paused, though, one hand moving to the side of her head as if she were in pain. Her eyes darted to the left and right, and she turned in a circle, apparently in search of someone.

At the same moment, the tingle Darius associated with her presence tickled his own brain, and he allowed a sigh.

The thought of experiencing that pleasant tingle all the time had him deciding right then to offer for the girl.

When she was old enough, he would take her to wife. "I wish for her to be my betrothed," he announced, just before he stood up and lifted a sack of grain from the back of Augustine. He set it down before the farmer.

Andros regarded the gift and stared at him, his astonishment apparent. "She is but eight winters old," he stated.

"Ten summers," Darius countered, remembering her words. "But I would not take her to wife until she is... sixteen or seventeen," Darius replied, not sure when most of the girls on Strongili were old enough to wed. Despite having been on the island for over two decades, he hadn't given a thought to taking another wife. Now that Cydon had taken notice of his lack of a mate, though, it seemed imperative he at least look like he was betrothed.

Frowning, Andros regarded Darius a moment before he said, "Pardon, Lochagos, but you are not a young man. Another six or seven years, and you will be... you will be *too old* to take my daughter to wife."

Despite the comment, Darius grinned. "I will be no older than I am now. And I am young in spirit," he replied. Even younger when he was in Stella's presence, but he didn't think it necessary to mention it to the girl's adoptive father.

He reconsidered his last comment. Before what had happened two days earlier, when Stella had touched his arm in an effort to determine his age, he hadn't felt young in centuries. But the thought of continuing his life with a wife he wouldn't lose to death after only a couple of decades gave him hope just then. Gave him something to look forward to.

And he was tired of being alone.

"I cannot do without her," Andros replied in a quiet voice.

"You would keep her here, working in the trees, for the rest of her life?" Darius asked gently. "She will grow to resent you."

Andros' expression betrayed his sadness at the thought. "What would you have me do?"

"I will give you coin. Enough so that you can hire someone to take her place," Darius offered. "It is not for another six years, at least."

"It would take three men to do what she does," Andros argued.

"Then I will give you enough coin for three men. More, if need be." Despite his purchase of the grain the day before, he had coin aplenty. Gold, too, should the coins from Creta prove worthless in a decade. He had been collecting gold for centuries once he learned it was the universal currency among most peoples.

Glancing out to find his daughter had resumed her work, Andros finally nodded. "Seven years," he murmured. "Should the gods take me before then, you will give the coin to Helena."

Darius frowned. "Agreed, but with the proviso it might be six years."

Andros finally dipped his head. "It is your gold."

Seven years was not so long to wait, Darius thought as he mounted his horse. Not when he'd been alive for six hundred years.

He thought of how he had something to look forward to now. A reason to continue living on the island. A reason to continue in his position as lochagos.

When Stella paused in her work to wave at him, her smile wide, he grinned and waved back.

He would look forward to seeing her wave and smile, too.

10

A HARVEST IN JEOPARDY

Three years later

Her hands on her hips, Stella regarded the second oldest olive tree in her father's orchard and sighed. Despite having taken special care with the pruning the past few years, she realized the tree had barely enough fruit to warrant including it in the upcoming harvest.

She would have felt annoyed—angry, even, given she thought she had done what was necessary to revive the ancient tree—but for a pleasant tingle that foretold the arrival of a welcome visitor.

It had been several sennights since she had last seen the lochagos, Darius, and his absence had her thinking he might have left the island.

What if he had left and never came back?

The thought had a sense of despair settling over her. There was no one else like him. No one else who seemed as interested in her as she was in him.

"I should not wish to ever displease you," a deep voice

said from her left. Stella grinned and turned her attention on Darius, her arms dropping to her sides.

"Nor I you," she replied, her eyes rounding as she noticed the leather armor he wore on his chest, wrists, and shins. An oval shield was gripped in one hand. His feet, normally clad in sandals, were completely covered in leather boots. And his red cape, secured around his neck with a bronze closure, hid his shoulders. Even Augustine sported a collar of leather, and the hilt of a sword could be seen protruding from its leather sleeve. "Is the island under attack?"

Darius allowed a shrug. "Only if you consider new recruits to the coastguard as enemies," he said as he dismounted. He attached the shield to his saddle and then approached her, shocked by how much she had grown since the last time he had seen her—only two months ago.

What was she now? Thirteen summers? In only a few years, he would take her to wife. "I have been training them for the past sennight, and despite their prowess with swords and bows, I fear for Strongili's future."

As was her custom, Stella reached up and kissed him on the lips before she fell into step beside him. Her thoughts about the old olive tree were forgotten when she noted how the tickle of pleasure in her head became more pronounced with their every meeting. She wondered if he noticed it, too.

She clasped her hands behind her back, hoping he might notice how her breasts had rounded. "I feared you might have left for Creta," she murmured, allowing the relief she felt at seeing him to sound in her voice.

"I did," he acknowledged, feeling a hint of relief that

she had noted his absence. "Apologies for not having paid a visit before I took my leave. I was summoned without warning by the king—"

"The king?" Stella repeated as she paused mid-step, excitement evident in her voice. "Do you know him?"

Allowing a chuckle, Darius nodded. "It was my..." He did a mental calculation. "Fourteenth time in his presence." He didn't add that he had been summoned by the prior king even more often—six times a year, always at the new moon. That had been because King Cydon understood the need for a strong defense. Pirates had been wreaking havoc around the Mediterranean for centuries, but their boldness had increased as the wealth of the Minoans multiplied.

Given the king was the administrator for trading activities with other countries—he had little power when it came to the governing of the islands once ruled by King Minos—King Tektamanos was determined to see to the safety of the trade routes and ports under his control.

"He must hold you in high regard."

Darius wondered at the hint of pride he felt just then. He had been alive far too long to think such thoughts, but now that he considered how he was received by Tektamanos, he decided Stella had the right of it. "I suppose," he hedged.

"Were you tasked with training his personal guards?"

Once again, Darius displayed his amusement. "Only some coastguardsmen," he replied. "New recruits for the two watchtowers the king ordered be built on the south side of Creta."

"To catch pirates?" Stella asked, giggling when Augustine moved up and nudged her shoulder. The horse had been following them as they made their way through the center of the orchard. She paused to smooth a hand along his neck before she dropped a kiss on his nose. "I have missed you, too, you big beasty," she murmured with a grin.

Darius bristled at the wave of jealousy he felt just then, before he reminded himself that Stella was but thirteen summers old. He couldn't be hoping for such attentions from her until she was older. Much older.

"To catch pirates, yes," Darius agreed, just then remembering her query.

"Why do you have new recruits here on this island?" Her eyes suddenly widened with excitement, and the slight tingle at the edge of Darius' consciousness flared into a bright, pleasant sensation. "Is there a new watchtower here, too?" she asked.

His grin widening until he was very nearly smiling, Darius finally nodded. "Indeed. On the north end of the island. Not far from my villa, in fact. It should be finished any day now."

Stella gave a start at how he referred to his home. Not an oikos, but a villa. *How grand it must be*, she thought, now that she knew he was an important man.

"And your new recruits... are they worthy?" she asked.

Not expecting her to be interested in his coastguardsmen—Darius had thought they might spend their time conversing about the upcoming harvest—he gave a nod. "They are. Ours here are better suited to the position than those I trained on Creta," he added, *sotto voce*.

"Why do you say that?"

He wondered at how he might explain the difference between the life of a young, unmarried man versus that of one who had taken a wife. Those without wives but with coin could afford to employ prostitutes to see to their sexual needs. Some were far too needy, though. They tended to be easily distracted by thoughts of who would next warm their beds and therefore made bad watchmen. "Our new recruits have all taken wives," he finally said. "While those on Creta are not yet betrothed."

"So our recruits have women to care for them when they are not in the watchtower," Stella reasoned.

Darius swallowed a guffaw. "Something like that," he agreed. "Which has me wondering why you were arguing with that olive tree back there," he teased.

Stella gave him a quelling glance. "I fear I have lost that argument," she murmured. "Again."

"You let an olive tree win an argument?" he asked in disbelief, trying to imagine how a conversation with a tree would go. Before her comment, he figured it would be a rather one-sided conversation.

"I did not *let* him," she countered. "We had what I thought was a reasonable arrangement. I would prune him, but not too much, and he would produce at least as much fruit as he did last year."

Darius nodded his understanding—not that he thought for a moment the tree and Stella could actually communicate with one another. He wasn't completely convinced Augustine and her could, either, even though the horse seemed particularly attuned to her. "What has happened?"

Stella rolled her green eyes and sighed in a most dramatic fashion. "I held up my end of the bargain, but he did not. I do not believe I shall even try to harvest a single olive from his branches next month."

Furrowing a brow, Darius remembered a time before he knew of Stella. Back when Andros had explained that some of his trees were over a thousand years old. "No unfurling the pearls from their strings?" he murmured in mock surprise, wondering if she was familiar with the way some on the island referred to the harvest. Although most simply beat the trees and let the fruit fall to tarps below, he knew Stella actually drew her fingers along the thin branches and dislodged the olives much like one would push the beads from a leather strip.

"That would require there be enough pearls," she replied, her gaze going back to Augustine.

The bleating of a goat interrupted their discussion, and Augustine's ears flattened. Stella giggled as the horse tossed his head. "You have no need to be frightened of a goat," she chided him. "Besides, if you are as thirsty as you claim, you will have to drink from the same water trough as he does."

A whinny of complaint sounded from Augustine at the same moment the goat lifted his head from the trough. The goat gave another bleat and bounded off, disappearing behind the oikos. "For a beast that has seen the number of battles you have, I cannot believe you would allow a goat to get the better of you," Darius said, just before he rolled his eyes. He was talking to his horse as if he expected an answer.

Augustine whinnied again and Stella let out a giggle as the horse hurried on ahead, eventually stopping at the trough for a drink. "He is a proud animal," she murmured. "But he fears other animals he does not know."

Darius realized the same could be said of most people. "I am sorry to hear about your miscreant tree," he said as he moved to take a seat on the stump of a tree. "Is he the only one?" He had hoped to learn what she thought the harvest might produce, remembering the news he had from King Tektamanos. Given the increasing number of people who occupied Creta, it was doubtful there would be enough in their olive harvest to meet the demands of the island.

Could the nearby island of Strongili be counted on to make up the difference?

Stella shook her head. "My father does not believe me, but I think the ground grows hot at the northern end of the orchard."

Darius furrowed his brows. "The ground?" he repeated.

Nodding, Stella replied, "Yes. And I have seen clouds of vapor appear and disappear. The odor is most foul."

Remembering how his men complained of noxious fumes from a mineral spring near the western shore, Darius angled his head. "This odor you speak of. Have you smelled it before?"

Stella nodded. "Many times. The first time was when you found me in the tree. The day I met Augustine. The steam nearly burned his leg, and you did not even notice." She gave a start then, her gaze going straight up.

Alarmed, Darius noted how Augustine had stopped drinking, his head lifted as if he were listening. He whinnied softly and was about to resume drinking when he suddenly reared. Darius was up and reaching for the leather reins when the ground seemed to shift beneath him. He managed to capture the reins before Augustine could bolt.

Her eyes wide, Stella was staring up at the trees, and Darius followed her gaze. The tallest branches on the two nearest to them swayed, the trunks bending back and forth in wide arcs. If they hadn't grown in the presence of the ever-present winds, which helped to make their trunks more flexible, the trees might have snapped in two.

"What did you notice?" Darius asked, relieved that Augustine seemed to have calmed down. "Just before the ground shook? What made you look up?"

Stella blinked as she turned her attention on the lochagos. "The birds. They stopped singing." Even as she made the comment, birdsong resumed, and the air around them seemed to come back to life.

"That was an earthquake," Darius stated. Although the ground's movement hadn't felt too violent out in the open, he feared what damage might have been done inside Andros' oikos. He was about to suggest he go inside to determine if it was safe when he saw how her attention had turned to the north. To the olive orchard. "What is it?"

Stella sighed and gave her head a shake. "With every earthquake, the ground grows hotter at the edge of the orchard," she murmured. "The oldest trees are dying. I am sure of it."

Darius saw her eyes brighten with tears, but she quickly blinked them away. "Everything dies, Stella," he said in a quiet voice. "Everything and everyone," he added. Just because he had lived for six-hundred years didn't mean he was invincible. One day, he thought he, too, would die and not come back to life.

He remembered the body he had had as a youth. Underfed and gawky, that body had succumbed to a blow from a rider wielding a spiked club.

A *mace*, he now knew. He could wield it with cunning precision when necessary. Back then, though, he was unfamiliar with weapons. Back then, he had never seen so much as a stone dagger.

With the blow from the mace, his descent into the Darkness had been quick. Almost painless, despite comments from some suggesting it was otherwise. He recalled wishing it had taken him when his hunger was so great he could barely go on. When he knew not when or from where his next meal might come.

Had he died from hunger, he now knew he would have come back to life, just as hungry and just as desperate.

Dying from a blow delivered by another Immortal had been a blessing. For when his body went to the Darkness, his Essence went into the other Immortal. A man whose own Essence was barely there. Untested by hardship, unchallenged by life's lessons, the other's Essence simply gave way to his, for when Darius had come back to life, he had done so in the other's body. With his Essence quickly subsuming the marauder's Essence—his memories, his personality, his limited intelligence and lack of good sense —Darius was left with the brute's body and its muscle memory.

The muscle memory had been another blessing. The ability to ride a horse. To wield weapons. Combined with his desire to defend himself and those he cared for, Darius soon gained notoriety, and later, earned coin for his work on behalf of those who could not defend themselves.

Work as a mercenary kept his belly full.

WHEN DARIUS SHOOK himself from his reverie, he found Stella regarding him with an expression of worry. "Where did you go?" she asked in a whisper.

Darius immediately understood her meaning. Her awareness of him was as evident as the tingle her presence set off at the edge of his consciousness. "Into my past." The simple words didn't exactly answer her query, but she straightened and allowed a nod.

"Because you prefer it?"

He shook his head. "Because I do not. Sometimes, I must remind myself that living now is preferable to the way things were back then." *Preferable because I have you to look forward to,* he almost added.

Stella allowed a wan grin, an expression he found made her appear far older than her thirteen summers. "It gladdens me to hear it."

A shout had the two turning to see Andros and Helena cresting the hill to the south. The path on which they walked led to Akrotiri. They were breathing heavily as they carried sacks of goods from their day at the agora.

Darius stood up and hurried to relieve them of their burdens. "Did the earthquake do damage in town?" he asked as he hefted the four bags in his hands.

Andros and Helena exchanged looks of confusion. "If there was an earthquake, we were unaware of it," Andros replied.

Helena had already hurried to the oikos, though, her expression of worry evident to Stella.

"Mother, no!" Stella called out, just as Helena made her way through the door. Stella was behind her as quickly as she could run, sure her adoptive mother would find the household in disarray.

Darius cursed and followed them in, depositing the bags just inside the door so that he could navigate the close confines inside.

A wail erupted from Helena even before she made it to the kitchen, and Darius winced when he noted the wide crack in the ceiling and the overturned jars of oil and water in the storage room.

Andros followed them in, but at a much slower pace. His eyes were hooded as he surveyed the damage.

"I do not know if it will be safe for you to stay the night here," Darius remarked, his hand easily reaching the ceiling so he could test its strength. When the open edges along the crack didn't move, he allowed a shrug and moved farther into the oikos. He pretended to survey the damage when he was really just curious to see where Stella spent her nights.

"We are honored by your concern," Helena said as she watched him move from room to room, watched as he studied hairline cracks in the concrete.

"Of course I am concerned," Darius remarked. "From where else will I get my olives and olio, if not from you?" The words were meant to sound light, but in truth, Darius was more worried about Stella. Especially when he found her bedchamber at the back of the oikos.

Small and hosting only a low cot and a table bearing a

few idols for worship, it hardly suited a girl he intended to eventually wed.

One wall featured what appeared to be a partial fresco, though. A scene depicting the olive orchard with a large white space left undone. "Is this your mother's doing?" he asked, noting the detail that had gone into painting the leaves and the trunks of the trees.

"No," Stella replied, giving her head a shake. "Please do not judge it, as I have not yet finished it."

Darius' eyes widened. "You did this?" he half-questioned, admiring the art. "And what will you paint here?" he asked as he waved to the white area. His gaze then went to the adjacent wall, where a sheet of papyrus was pinned to the plaster. Despite the evidence of it having been painted in a child's hand, he knew the horse was Augustine.

Stella dipped her head, her face turning a crimson shade. "I have not yet decided."

Darius pulled the papyrus from the wall and then held it over the white void in the fresco. "I believe Augustine would be honored to have such a prominent place in your fresco," he said, stepping away from the wall as he held out the painting and angled his head.

"I painted that when I was but a child," she said, hurrying to take the papyrus from him.

"And yet it is done well enough that I recognized my horse," Darius countered. "Did you mix the plaster for the fresco by yourself?"

Deciding he wasn't going to chide her for the primitive skills displayed in the painting, Stella set the papyrus on her cot. "Helena helped, at first," she replied as she pointed to the middle of the wall. "Once I knew how much to mix, then I did the rest."

Darius thought of the number of walls in his villa. Walls that were void of any decoration. "You have skills, Stella. If you lived closer to my villa, I would hire you to do one similar to this in a bedchamber."

Stella's eyes widened.

He tore his attention from the art and turned to see a crack running down the corner. Frowning, he hurried up to it, one finger following the jagged tear.

"That was already there," Stella said as she joined him in the close confines. "From the last earthquake."

Darius nodded his understanding and wrapped an arm around her shoulders. The slight tingle flared into a sensation he wished he could hang onto for a long time. He closed his eyes in an effort to concentrate on it. To memorize how it felt. When he opened his eyes, he found Stella watching him with a look of awe on her face.

"You feel it, too?" she whispered.

He gave a nod. "Every time you touch me," he murmured.

Stella stared at him for a time. "Why?"

The query was so simple, and yet he had no answer for her. That is, unless he told her she was an Immortal. He had no intention of doing such a thing until she was older. Much older. "Because you are special. Because you were a foundling. Because you are not like the others on this island."

Dipping her head, Stella knew he spoke the truth. Being special wasn't necessarily a trait that earned her friends, though. Or perhaps it was merely her red hair that had other girls her age avoiding her. "I do not like being special," she whispered with a shake of her head.

"Why not?" Darius asked as his fingers traveled the length of the crack in the corner. He was tempted to use those same fingers to stroke her face, for her smooth skin would have felt like velvet. He struggled to keep his attention on the damage.

For the concrete to crack meant an excessive force had acted on the oikos. The houses down below, in Akrotiri, were mostly made from stone blocks. This oikos had been formed by a combination of stone blocks and a mixture of lime, volcanic ash, and seawater. The thick mixture made it possible to form walls and a floor that should have been impervious to the earth's temperament. Cracks in the concrete were proof it could suffer in an earthquake.

He had a brief thought as to how his villa might have faired.

"What of your villa?" Stella asked, as if she could read his mind.

Darius gave a shake of his head. "As long as my servants were not injured, I care not," he replied.

Stella stared at him. "But... it is your home," she said in a whisper.

"True," he acknowledged. "But if there is damage, it can be repaired. As can this," he said as he motioned to the crack. "Before the winter rains do it more damage." His gaze went from where the ceiling curved into the two walls, grimacing at the thought the crack might make it that high.

"I do not believe my father will spend coin on a crack," Stella replied.

Darius tamped down the anger he felt just then.

Although Andros was a good businessman—he grew a product that was in demand, and he did it well—he was a fool when it came to other concerns. "I will see to it the repairs are made," Darius vowed. "I will not have you suffer this winter, nor allow this fresco to get wet."

Stella's eyes widened. "Gratitude, Lochagos," she said in a quiet voice.

"Darius," he countered. "You shall call me Darius."

At the sound of a bleating goat and an answering whinny from Augustine, Darius thought he best get his horse away from the water trough. He gave Stella a quick kiss on the lips and took his leave of the oikos with the promise he would see her again soon.

11

A THREAT FROM THE NORTH

A few days later

Darius allowed his housekeeper to lead him through his villa as she pointed out the damage from the island's latest temblor. He had expected worse, given what he had seen in Andros' oikos. Here, there were only a few cracks in some interior walls.

"Did anything break?" he asked, once they had completed their tour. The nine rooms that made up the sprawling villa were far more than he required, but the king had insisted he have quarters suited to his position.

Iris gave a shake of her head. "I had Pietros check the columns out front, and he said they are still upright." The entire portico on the front side of the villa was held up with red painted columns made from the trunks of cypress trees.

"I meant did anything break inside?" Darius asked. He thought the villa in good shape considering the reports he had heard from some of his men. The extent of the damage seemed to depend on where people lived on the island. Buildings in the south had obviously suffered more than those at the north end of the island.

Shaking her head, Iris said, "No," not adding that there was little that could have broken. Despite his wealth, Darius didn't display much in the way of decorative vases or trinkets in the villa.

"And the stables?" When Stella had first informed him that Augustine was lonely, he had seen to acquiring a mare from one of his ypolochagoi. The two seemed to get along, but just barely. He had hoped to have a colt from the union, but it was apparent the mare wasn't breeding.

Or that Augustine didn't yet know what to do with a mare.

Although, he thought his mount was quite interested in Glaukos' mare. When near one another, the two seemed to exchange greetings, their soft nickers and whinnies eliciting a crude comment from his ypolochagoi. He would have to ask if the mare was breeding when he next saw Glaukos.

"The stables are fine, sir," Iris assured him, the old woman rolling her eyes. "Melanie is fine," she added, referring to the mare. "As high-strung as ever, according to Pietro."

Darius nodded. "And the trees. How do they fare?"

At this query, Iris allowed a shrug. "I do not know. They are all alive but the one that did not take root," she said, one hand waving in the air. "As to whether or not they will bear fruit will be up to the gods."

Glancing out the window to the east, Darius could just make out the first few trees in an olive orchard. He had ordered they be planted the day after he had made the arrangement to take Stella to wife, deciding she would require her own trees to look after once they were wed. The plot of land just east of the villa would only support twenty trees, but he thought it enough.

As his wife, Stella would be expected to perform other tasks besides seeing to a garden and the orchard. He had already ordered a loom be set up in one of the well-lit rooms. Now that he knew she liked to paint, he thought about what she might require to practice her craft once they were wed.

He turned his attention back to the olive grove. The gardener had argued the north winds might be too much for the young trees, but Darius had seen to the installation of a row of thin poles on the north edge of the orchard. Not quite a fence—there was nothing connecting the vertical posts together—the poles broke the wind before it could damage the young trees.

Since olive trees didn't start bearing fruit until they were at least ten summers old, Darius hadn't needed to hire anyone to see to the harvest. He thought Stella could do so after they were wed, sure she would want full control over the care of the trees.

"Have the cracks plastered, and...," Darius started to order and then stopped. He moved to a room adjacent to his own bedchamber, pointing to the long wall. "And hire an artist to create the beginning of a fresco here."

Her eyes widening in surprise, Iris regarded the blank wall and then her master. "What shall I have him paint?"

Darius allowed a shrug before his face brightened. "An olive orchard. With a horse," he murmured as one of his hands swept over one section of the wall. "One that looks like Augustine. And yellow flowers here." He pointed to a lower corner and then stepped back, nodding in satisfaction.

Iris looked at Darius with an expression that suggested he might be mad. She crossed her arms. "What have you done with my master Darius?" she asked, her lip quirking in a tease.

None of the other servants would ask such a thing, but Iris had been in his household since the day he had agreed to accept the gift of the villa from the king. He crossed his arms. "I will take a wife in a few winters," he replied, one brow arching up as he wondered how she might respond to this bit of news.

The housekeeper regarded him a moment. "Ah, you are waiting for a woman to become widowed?" she half-asked, implying he had his eye on another man's wife.

Darius shook his head. "No," he replied, making sure she knew he was disgusted by the suggestion. Men on the island—any of the Minoan islands—knew better than to covet another man's wife. "I am waiting for..." He stopped and allowed a sigh. "Time to pass," he finished, deciding it better he not tell her his intended was many years younger than he was.

The thought of Stella had him wondering why she hadn't mentioned their eventual union. Surely Andros would have told her he had made arrangements for her future. Even if Andros hadn't, Stella always seemed pleased to see Darius. To greet him with a kiss on his lips and questions as to his health. Questions about his work. Questions about his horses and life on the north end of the island.

Nearly every night, he fell asleep trying to imagine what she would look like on the day he took her to wife.

Imagine how her red hair would be dressed—or not. How her lips might feel beneath his own. How her soft body would feel as he impaled her with his cock. How she might cry out with her ecstasy as his seed filled her womb. How she might beg for him again in the middle of the night.

Could she be the one who would give him a child or two? Ten or twenty? They might have hundreds of years together, maybe thousands.

When he was done being the lochagos of Strongili, perhaps they could start their own island paradise. Rule over peoples who shared his principles of fairness for all. Slavery wouldn't be allowed, nor would those who indentured others to their cause or to their purse.

He was still deep in thought when Pietros burst into the villa. "There is smoke, my lord. To the west."

Darius allowed a quiet curse and was nearly at a run when he passed the servant on his way out the front door. "Ready my horse," he shouted as he came to a standstill in front of the villa. He watched as a cloud of smoke rose above the western horizon. Another followed almost immediately. "Damn pirates," he murmured, annoyed his thoughts of Stella and their life in the future could be so easily interrupted.

He hurried back into the villa to don his armor and his cape. A few minutes later, he was mounted on Augustine and headed west at a full gallop.

12

FRIENDS OR FOES?

"Mycenaeans," Adamaos murmured when Darius' mount pulled up next to his.

"How can you be so sure?" Darius asked in alarm, bringing a magnifying glass to his eye. The white sails of the low-slung vessel gave away nothing of its home port. There wasn't even a pennon floating at the top of the main sail.

"It was my home at one time," the ypolochago replied, finally turning his attention on the lochagos. "One I do not miss."

Distant thunder had Darius giving a glance to the north, where a series of gray clouds, pregnant with rain, threatened to put out any warning fires. He nodded his understanding, remembering the tale the man had told when he first arrived on Strongili. His scarred flesh was evidence of frequent whippings at the hand of a slaver, and his muscled body was evidence of a life of hard labor.

Adamaos still bore those scars as well as the muscles, although he did so as the ypolochago overseeing the watchmen on the west side of the island. Before he had been pressed into slavery, he had captained an army of soldiers in Thrace.

"Where do you suppose they plan to dock?" Darius asked, scanning the horizon for other ships. Perhaps this was merely the first of many. King Tektamanos had warned him Mycenae had its eyes on the islands of the Minoans. *They will defeat us one day unless we remain vigilant,* he had said during Darius' last trip to Creta.

"I have men posted at all the possible landing sites," Adamaos replied. He shoved a finger toward the one in the middle, a small port town of only a few hundred people. Even as he pointed, his eyes squinted at the sight of a wisp of white that rose from the land in between them and the port. "What is that?"

Darius followed his line of sight, spotting the cloud with ease. "A steam vent," he murmured, his eyeglass aimed in that direction. "Many of them," he added when another appeared next to the first, and yet another several feet away. The ground around where the steam rose was nearly white. Any vegetation that had grown there was gone. "How long has this been going on?" he asked in a hoarse whisper.

Adamaos gave a shake of his head. "I have not seen such clouds from the ground before," he murmured in wonder.

"Has anyone complained of poor crops?" Darius pressed.

His lieutenant gave him a sideways glance. "It is why the village has diminished in size this past year," he replied. "The ones who remain rely on the farmers of Fira for food other than fish."

Darius nearly cursed. He had paid witness to similar steam vents farther inland. What would happen when Fira no longer produced enough food to bring to this village?

There wouldn't be a village, though, unless they could vanquish the invaders who were nearly close enough to put down an anchor. "How sure are you they are Mycenaeans?" he asked, nodding toward the ship.

Adamaos gave a one-shouldered shrug. "I am positive." As if to punctuate his claim, the sound of thunder once again rolled over the island.

Darius sighed. "Have your men load their arrows with fire. When the ship is close enough, have them shoot all at the same time. No warning. No mercy. See to it the ship burns, and be sure no one makes it ashore unless they are accompanied by one of your men."

Nodding his understanding, Adamaos had his horse in motion in seconds, and he raced to the nearest watchtower in an effort to beat the rain.

Darius raised the glass to his eye once more, still unable to see anyone on board the vessel. What if Adamaos was wrong? What if this ship carried friend rather than foe? Gold to trade for goods?

But the king's words had been clear. If any ship—other than those of the king's navy—came to trade on Strongili, they would do so from the south by way of Creta or from the east at Perisa. Those from the north and west were to be treated as invaders unless they flew pennons indicating their affiliation.

Since this craft was void of flags, Darius felt comfortable with his orders.

He continued to watch the ship make its way to the small port, wondering when Adamaos' men would begin firing. Although only two men appeared on the deck, they busied themselves with lowering the sails. At no point did any pennons crawl up a rope to indicate from where they hailed.

All at once, the shoreline seemed to light up as series of fires appeared. A moment later, and those fires were arcing through the air, the faint sounds of a *whoosh* making its way to Darius.

Darius knew he was too far away to hear the hiss of the lit arrows as they hit the deck of the ship, but he could imagine what it must sound like to anyone aboard.

Through his glass, he saw a crewman dodge an arrow, and another dive overboard. A few seconds later, and the sails that hadn't been taken down were cast in an eerie glow of yellow-orange flame. Loud booming sounds made their way to his ears as jars exploded, their contents spreading fuel and fire over the deck. When the booming sounds continued, Darius' gaze swept up. The thunderheads that had merely threatened earlier that morning were now overhead, and large drops began to pelt the area around where Darius waited.

At no point had Darius seen an anchor fall overboard. The ship continued on its path, although its speed had slowed considerably. Still, the flaming hulk would either hit the port and set it afire, or be caught in the sands and continue burning at sea.

Darius hoped it was the latter. He knew there were areas around the island where the Aegean was deep—too deep for a dock to be built. But he was sure this wasn't one of those.

Just as he was about to fear for the port, the ship seemed to come to a stuttering halt, its hull finally stuck in a sandbar. The fire continued burning, although he doubted it would sink the vessel given its position in the sand. And the rain, now coming down in sheets, was doing its best to put out the fire on deck. Clouds of steam briefly rose from the hot planks, and after a few minutes, any evidence of fire was gone.

Even as he wondered if the locals would attempt to claim whatever cargo it could, several packets left the dock. Powered by oarsmen intent on salvage, they converged on the smoking hulk. Men were soon clambering up the sides, weapons at the ready, and then onto the deserted deck.

Darius watched with fascination as those who boarded made their way below deck. He was sure there would be survivors on board. Crewmen who had retreated to the lower decks to get away from the fires. Crewmen who hoped they might be spared.

Thinking the villagers would dispatch any remaining survivors, Darius was stunned when several men emerged on the wet deck, one man poking them with a spear. They soon made their way down ropes to the packets below, and the oarsmen had the packets heading back to the port.

Darius cursed and put his mount into motion, deciding he had better be on the dock when the survivors were brought ashore.

13

SLAVES FROM AFAR

Finding Adamaos amid the chaos on the small beach was easier than Darius expected—he was the only other man on horseback. "Where are they taking them?" Darius shouted, noting how several coastguardsmen had intercepted the packets as they reached the shore. Most of the men from the ship wore shackles around their wrists, and some were still chained together.

"Just to the edge of the beach. Until this rain has a chance to wash them clean," Adamaos replied as he had his mount pull up alongside Augustine. The ypolochago used his shield as a sort of umbrella, and the rain hitting the metal made a thunderous roar.

"Covered with soot, were they?" Darius guessed, raising his own shield above his head to stave off the rain.

Adamaos shook his head. "No. The stench of a slave ship."

Darius hissed. In all his years as lochagos on Strongili, no slave ships had come to the island. "Were they lost?"

he asked, studying the faces of some of the men as they were led past them and then directed to stand in a line. Out on the ship, still more men were emerging from below deck, most simply content to make their way overboard and into a packet. A few actually jumped overboard, and Darius wondered how they expected to swim given their heavy shackles.

"Since we have not found a crew, I suspect there was a revolt," the ypolochago replied. "But let us find out for ourselves." He nodded toward those that had been assembled and did a quick survey. None of the men displayed unusual features that immediately made their country of origin evident. "From where do you come?" he asked in his native Thracian tongue.

A few of the men remained glassy-eyed while some merely stared straight ahead. Two spoke, almost at the same time.

"Thrace," they called out, their words barely heard above the rain.

"All of you?"

The two shook their heads.

Darius repeated, "From where do you come?" in the three languages that came easiest to him. The half-dead men seemed to come alive at hearing the query in Akkadian. A number of city names were called out in answer, only a few familiar to Darius.

"What are they saying?" Adamaos asked.

"They are from the east. From Akkadia," Darius replied, his brow furrowed in confusion. He raised his voice once again and asked, "Where is the ship's crew?"

No one offered an answer, at least, not right away. But

another group from the packets that had just landed joined them. Most looked just as bedraggled as the first group, but one stood out due to his broad size and height —and the fact that he didn't sport any shackles.

Definitely not Akkadian, but possibly from somewhere in the east.

"From where do you come?" Darius asked in Gutium.

The large man frowned and seemed to think a moment before saying, "Assyria," in a language Darius recognized as similar to Gutium.

"Were you part of the crew?"

Large man regarded him a moment, his brows furrowed. "Will I be put to death if I admit that I was?" he countered.

Darius inhaled slowly, beginning to understand what might have happened. "Was that the fate of the rest of the crew?"

At this point, one of the shackled men stepped forward and said, "He is the one who helped us," in the Thracian tongue.

"Helped you how?" Adamaos asked, relieved he finally understood some of the conversation.

"We were rounded up on the island of tin and forced onto the ship. They loaded the tin and copper meant for Creta—"

"Tin Island?" Darius repeated, recognizing the word even though he wasn't well-versed in Thracian.

The man nodded. "He was on the crew, but he is not a slaver—"

"I can speak for myself," Large Man interrupted, his muscled arms crossing over his chest. When he straightened, he was as tall as Darius and just as imposing. "I abhor slavery," he added, and then went silent.

"And?" Darius prompted, just as another group of men joined the ragged line.

"Theft," Large Man stated. "The tin was not ours to take."

Nodding, Darius aimed a glance at Adamaos. Even if the ypolochago didn't understand Assyrian, he had figured out some of what had occurred.

"So was your mutiny successful?" Darius asked, thinking if the interrogation went on much longer, Stella would be old enough to take to wife.

The thought had him blinking. Soon, he would have her to look forward to at the end of a day.

He wished today could be one of those days!

Large Man's black eyebrows furrowed. "I do not know this word... mutiny," he replied. "But it sounds as if it is without honor."

"The mutiny was successful," one of the Gutians said from farther down the line. "He tossed most of the crew overboard, and he strangled the rest."

Darius gave Large Man a look of appreciation. "Your actions are to be commended. Do you have a name?"

A grin appeared on Large Man's face, which showed he was missing one front tooth. "I am called Adad Zah Eil Yomadan Lebario Shimmokeen," he replied, pride evident in his voice.

Blinking, Darius thought of the meaning of one of the names—lionhearted—and decided he shouldn't be too frightened of the man. He leaned toward the man and asked, "What are you *called*?"

"Adad."

Darius turned to Adamaos, who was struggling to hide a grin. "You are of no help," Darius whispered, struggling to hide his own amusement.

"What are we to do with all these men?" Adamaos asked. "There must be...." He turned to find yet another group joining the others. If they hadn't been shackled or half-starved, they might have overcome Adamaos and his men.

"Offer refuge? Or, if the ship is not too badly damaged, perhaps Adad Zah Eil Yomadan Lebario Shimmokeen can return them to Tin Island," Darius suggested.

The word 'tin' had him remembering what Adad had said about a shipment of tin. "If we buy the tin that you have... *appropriated*,—" he dared not use the word 'stole' with the Assyrian—"would you take command of the ship and sail these men back to Tin Island?"

Adad considered this option before his gaze took in his surroundings. "No," he replied with a shake of his head.

Darius frowned. "Why not?"

Regarding Darius with an arched brow, Adad said, "I wish to stay on this island. Perform honorable work. Guard the coast?" he half-asked. He nodded to Adamaos' men, who had been keeping what could have been a chaotic situation well in hand. "Shoot flaming arrows at pirates. Kill enemies."

Adamaos inhaled sharply, knowing almost immediately how his lochagos would respond. "He led a mutiny," he whispered hoarsely. "What is to prevent him from doing the same within my ranks?"

Darius winked at Adamaos before turning his attention

back to Adad. "You would make a welcome addition to the men who guard the east coast of Creta," Darius stated. "But you must take that ship and any of these men who wish to live on Creta with you."

Adad angled his head. "Is this not Creta?" he asked in surprise.

Darius shook his head. "This is Strongili. Creta is another seventy milion south of here," he said as he pointed with his right hand.

"There are no stores aboard," one of the slaves said in a quiet voice. "No water. No food."

"We will trade water and goods for some of your tin," Darius offered. "And gold."

The slaves straightened as a group, their slight gasps sounding loud when joined together. Despite the language barrier, the word 'gold' was obviously well understood. Then one of them asked, "How much gold?"

Darius sighed. "Only enough to compensate you what you would have earned on Tin Island," he warned. He waited for translations to take place down the line, until he noticed how several shrugged and most nodded. "You must decide where you wish to go after Creta."

"And if we wish to remain on Creta?" one of them countered.

"Then let us hope you have a skill that is of use on the big island," Darius replied.

"And if we wish to return to Tin Island?"

A murmur of dissent made its way down the line, and the one who put forth the question merely shrugged. "Mining is all I know," he said in Akkadian.

"There is mining on Creta," Darius called out. "So there are frequently ships bound for Tin Island from

Creta. You will have transportation there should you wish to return."

Adamaos leaned toward Darius and whispered, "They are unloading the tin now, Lochagos," referring to the men who continued to row the packets out to the ship. "From where are we to get the gold to pay these men?"

Darius allowed his gaze to sweep over those from the village who had remained, as if watching the spectacle of Darius bargaining with slaves might be the highlight of their day.

None of them would have gold for tin. Those who made bronze were either at the north or south ends of the island.

"I will see to it from my own stores," Darius replied. "Which means I want the tin delivered to my villa."

Adamaos gave a start. He glanced at some of the villagers, deciding at least a few would have carts for hire. "What about food and water?"

"See to it they are fed," Darius replied. He turned his attention on Adad. "Since you only have one sail that has not burned," Darius said, knowing at least one had been taken down prior to the fire, "it would be best if you depart this evening. The winds are greatest at night," he explained. "You can make it to Creta on the morrow."

Adad seemed to think on this option for a time before he nodded. "And the gold to pay these men?"

Darius allowed a nod of his own, realizing the Assyrian was an honorable man. "Since there is none here, I must take my leave to get it. I will be back before the sun is on the water."

"You will not cheat us?"

Shaking his head, Darius said, "I will not."

Mounting Augustine in a quick motion that had a few of the slaves murmuring in appreciation, Darius dug his leather-clad heels into his mount. The horse was off on a run to the north.

After standing around on the beach for so long, Augustine was up for the gallop back to Paradisos. A promise of food and water had the horse negotiating the well-worn paths, his hooves making quick work of the trek over the slight mountain and around the northern end of the island to the villa.

Pietros was ready to take the horse to the stables, but Darius warned him he would be in need of his mount. "Give him some grain and water," he ordered. "I will not be long."

Darius rushed into the villa, almost ignoring Iris' query about a supper. "I will not be here to eat it," he said as he made his way to his bedchamber. When he opened the trunk containing his weapons, he gave a sigh and pulled out the ancient mace. He set it aside, wincing despite the fact that it had been that very weapon that had laid waste to his original body and made it possible for him to be here now.

To be here to raid his stash of gold coins.

He knew the king would reimburse him once he took the tin to Creta, but he was having second thoughts about sharing the metal. The nearby foundry might buy it from him, saving him the trouble of having to arrange transport for it.

He pulled out a purse laden with gold, the coins bearing the profile of King Cydon. They would still be honored on Creta—honored anywhere that took gold for products and services.

He thought of the men from the slave ship, deciding two such coins per man would go a long way toward keeping them fed until they could either return to Tin Island or find work in the mines on Creta. Spilling out some of the contents into one palm, he counted out enough and added a few more for Adamaos' men and more for whomever fed the slaves. Then he returned the rest to the trunk.

The heavy purse had him wishing he didn't have to make the trek back to the village so soon.

Lifting the mace and then placing it into the trunk, Darius regarded the weapon for a time before finally closing the lid.

Had he kept the weapon for sentimental reasons?

He thought not.

It was an effective weapon in battle, although it could do as much damage to the man who wielded it as it did to those who it was used against. He was about to allow his thoughts to wander back to the day it had brought his original body's death, but that day was best left in the back of his memories.

At least for now.

Realizing the sun would set within the hour, Darius got to his feet and made his way to the front of the villa.

"Supper, Lochagos?" Iris asked again.

"Not this evening. I must return to the village before the sun goes below the water," he replied, noting her worried expression.

"You will stay the night there?"

Darius winced at the thought of trying to find a bed in the small fishing village. "I will return here," he replied. "Do not stay awake on my account, though."

He didn't wait for Iris' acknowledgement, but took his leave of the villa and mounted Augustine.

The newly watered horse whinnied, as if in complaint, but Darius felt relief when Augustine did his bidding and galloped all the way back to the village.

14

A COMMENT BRINGS CONSTERNATION

Meanwhile

Stella stared at the corner of her bedchamber, stunned to discover the crack caused by the earthquake was patched. The work had been done by someone skilled with concrete. She could barely tell where the new met the old.

"All of the cracks are fixed," Helena said from behind her.

Whirling around, Stella found her mother leaning against the arched doorway of the small room, the fabric covering pulled to one side with a hand. "Did Father do this?" Stella asked in awe.

Helena had to suppress a laugh, as if she found the question amusing. "A man from Akrotiri came to do it. Said he was paid by Darius of Agremon," she replied, an eyebrow arching up. "I thought perhaps you might have known something of the arrangement."

Stella considered the comment. "He did not say he

would do such a thing," she replied. "But I will be sure to thank him when next he comes here." She certainly remembered how concerned he was after the earthquake. Concerned that the cracks would lead to leaks and larger cracks.

Perhaps he thought the oikos would crumble around them.

Her mother allowed a nod. "We are indebted to him. I fear we will always be so." She straightened suddenly, turning to find Andros directly behind her. "I did not hear you. Going to bed so soon?" she asked him, obviously embarrassed that he might have overheard her comment.

"I tire easily these days," Andros admitted. "Come, join me on this night," he whispered to her. Then he leaned into Stella's bedchamber, his gaze going to the repaired corner. "It is as your mother says. We are fortunate the lochagos favors us, but her fear of my always being in debt to Darius is unfounded."

Helena furrowed a dark brow. "Are you trading olives for his generosity?"

Andros shook his head. "There will be no need. One day, when Stella is older, he will come for her, and then all our debts will be paid."

Inhaling sharply, Helena was about to reply when Andros simply gave a sharp shake of his head. "We will not speak of it again. Good night, Daughter."

"Good night, Father. Good night, Mother," Stella replied absently.

For she was experiencing a moment of elation at hearing Darius of Agremon would one day come for her. The thought of spending more time in his company had been almost all she could think about as she prepared for the upcoming harvest. She thought she was too young to think she might be in love with the lochagos, but she was certainly infatuated with him.

I want nothing more than to be his woman.

She might be only thirteen summers old, but Stella was sure of her attraction to Darius. Despite his age, she felt a connection to him that she had never experienced with anyone else on the island. He seemed to understand her, and she knew she could read him in a way that didn't require words.

She watched as Helena allowed the doorway's fabric covering to fall back into place. Then her parents disappeared into her father's bedchamber, acting as if her father's words hadn't been spoken.

Climbing onto her cot, Stella replayed them in her head until she remembered the very last words.

All our debts will be paid.

Darius would come for her, but in order for their debts to be repaid, didn't that mean he would be paying coin to her father?

She was sure it wasn't supposed to be like that, though. Wasn't Andros supposed to provide a dowry to Darius to take her as his wife? A dowry in the form of coin? Or valuables? Animals and olives?

If Darius paid coin to Andros, then that would mean he was buying her.

Buying her.

That meant she would be his slave.

Crying softly, Stella tried to imagine what life as a slave would be like in Darius of Agremon's household.

Despite thinking he would treat her well—she could not imagine he would be a cruel man to his servants and slaves—she still felt despair.

When sleep finally took her, she was still weeping softly.

15

FREEING SLAVES HAS A COST

About an hour later

Upon his return, Darius found the slaves mostly unshackled and finishing the remains of meals made up of whatever the locals had been able to pull together on short notice.

"I suppose I owe gold to everyone in the village?" he half-asked of Adamaos.

The ypolochago gave him a wan grin. "Only two. They knew you were good for it, so they were generous with their catch and with their bread. I got the impression the baker will be making extra bread for days to replace what has been consumed on this beach."

Darius nodded, glad he had brought extra gold. "Is the ship seaworthy?"

"Indeed. Just a bit scorched, according to one of my men. The hull was never breached."

Nodding his understanding, Darius sighed. "I am unsure of how best to distribute the coins," he murmured.

Adamaos gave a start when he noted the purse Darius

held cradled in one arm. His eyes widened. "How much is there?" he asked in awe.

"Fifty men, so one-hundred coins, plus a few for those who supplied food," Darius replied. "I am of a mind to give the purse to Adad. Let him see to the disbursement to his men." He pulled out a handful and offered them to his ypolochago. "Give these to the villagers who helped you," he instructed, and then he pulled a pennon from a saddlebag. "Keep one for you and one for each of your men. I will be sure Adad flies this on his highest mast," he added as he held out the bright yellow pennon.

At the offer of the purse, Adamaos gave a shake of his head. "I cannot take your gold," he argued.

"You can, and you shall. Emptying a ship of slaves and its cargo was not what your men should have been doing on this day. They are coastguardsmen," Darius reminded the ypolochago. "I will request reimbursement from the king."

"You expect Tektamanos to repay you?" Adamaos asked in a hoarse whisper.

"He will when he sees how much tin I have for him," Darius replied, one eyebrow arching up. "That is, if the foundry at Tholos does not wish to buy it first. You did leave some tin in the hold, I hope?"

The ypolochago allowed a shrug. "As I suspected you would request, there is enough that they will be welcomed, but not so much they bring suspicion on themselves."

Darius grinned. "I cannot help but think that Adad will be one of the recruits I must train when I am next on Creta."

Adamaos matched his grin. "As long as he is not assigned to Strongili."

Allowing a guffaw, Darius allowed his gaze to sweep the beach and the slaves that were now free men. "I will see to it he remains on Creta," he replied.

"Very good, Lochagos." Adamaos paused a moment. "If you leave now, you can make it back to your villa before dark."

Darius narrowed his eyes. "But then I shall miss Adad and his exit from this island," he countered with a grin.

Allowing a laugh, Adamaos set about distributing coin to the villagers who had helped feed the slaves and then to his men.

When Adad was about to leave on the last packet to the ship, Darius gave him the purse and the pennon and then bid him farewell.

Adamaos, seeing the Assyrian waving from the packet using the yellow flag, gave a wave of his own.

Despite the growing darkness, Darius remounted Augustine and made his way back to his villa. He didn't hurry, though, and allowed Augustine to determine their pace.

And instead of thoughts of Adad and his band of freed slaves, he thought of Stella, wondering what she might be doing on this night. Although only fourteen milion separated them, there were times he felt as if they were separated by far more.

Time was a cruel mistress it seemed.

DETERMINED to see Stella again as soon as possible, Darius rose early the following day and made his way south by way of the watchtowers on the eastern shore. Augustine seemed to sense his urgency, but the horse struggled on some of the footholds between beaches.

Fearing he would come up lame, Darius slowed his mount and decided that making it halfway to Akrotiri would be enough on this day. Somewhere between the towers at Kamari and Perisa, near where he would normally find the path that led up to his tent, the hairs on the back of his neck prickled.

Sure he was being followed, Darius directed Augustine to the tower at Perisa. He found Klumenos and his men descending the tower, their voices excited about something.

"Darius!" Klumenos called out as he emerged from the door at the base of the tower. "You are early. Has something happened?"

The lochagos shook his head. "I fear my schedule has changed over an incident on the other side of the island," he replied.

"Pirates?" one of the other men asked.

"Slaves," Darius replied, noting how the young man seemed disappointed at hearing his response.

"Going where?" Klumenos asked, his brows furrowed.

"Creta. They had a shipment of tin in the hold and fifty slaves aboard, most of the men taken from Tin Island."

Those who overheard his comment winced. "What happened to all the slaves?"

"The Mycenaean crew was overcome. All but one were killed. The remaining man is seeing to it the ship gets to Creta..." Darius looked up to find the sun just past the zenith. "With luck and last night's winds, they have arrived. I sent him with a pennon and some gold for the men in the hopes they can find employment in the mines on Creta," he explained. He nodded towards the tower. "What has you out on the beach?"

Ypolochago Klumenos turned his attention north. "One of my men spotted someone on the beach. Near the caves. We have seen as many as three of them on occasion, but when we investigate, they are not there." His eyes widened. "Did you see them?" he asked.

Darius shook his head, wishing he had paid more attention to his surroundings than to his horse's hooves. "I was sure I was being followed," he admitted. "Which is why I did not go up to my tent. That, and I think my horse may have a rock in his hoof."

Waving for one of the men to join him, Klumenos ordered him to look at Darius' mount. The lochagos recognized Aries, the sentry from when they had found the grain traders in the caves. The young man had aged a bit as well as grown larger, more imposing. "I will see to your horse," Aries said as he took the reins.

"Come. Let us eat," Klumenos said as he motioned for Darius to join him. "If he cannot go on, you can have your pick of our newest arrivals," he offered.

"Arrivals?" Darius repeated. "New horses?"

"Indeed," Klumenos replied. "Orestes brought them on his latest trip from Creta. Said they were a gift from the king. I thought you would know."

Darius hid his initial reaction—surprise—and merely nodded. "They are here earlier than I expected," he said. "Have you enough grain to keep them until they can be claimed?"

"May we keep two?" Klumenos asked, as if he were bargaining for the extra mounts.

"How many are there?" Darius asked, expecting only a few.

"Five. All from Iberia, or so Orestes said when we met his ship."

Tempted to laugh—he had thought his latest request of the king had fallen on deaf ears—Darius nodded. "You can keep two."

Klumenos grinned. "I asked that first, for I do not believe you will find the king's query a welcome one."

Darius frowned. "What has the king asked?" He thought he had answered all of Tektamanos' questions on his last trip to Creta.

"Orestes says he is to bring back word of your betrothal," Klumenos replied, his voice kept low. "Seems the king learned of an agreement you had with Cydon. That you would take a wife once she was old enough to wed."

Rolling his eyes in disbelief, Darius realized he would be the brunt of many a jest over the next year. "Then tell me, how old was your wife when you wed?" he asked, just as they stepped into the watchtower.

"Sixteen summers," Klumenos replied. "It was the same for Glaukos, and most of the others, I suppose, given the priest is finished with them." After a pause, he arched a brow. "So, it is true then. You are betrothed?"

Sighing, Darius realized he could no longer keep his impending marriage a secret. "I am."

"How old is your betrothed?"

Darius stared at his ypolochago. "Fourteen," he murmured. "But the agreement I have with her father is to take her when she is seventeen." He gave his head a shake. "What is this about a priest?"

Klumenos offered him a hunk of cheese. "The girls must have their time with the priest before they can wed. Usually on the eve of their sixteenth year," he explained.

"To do what?" Darius asked, absently taking the goat cheese.

Klumenos allowed a shrug. "He is their first in matters of mating. Prepares them so their husbands can take them more than once on their wedding nights. Increases the chance a man can get a child on his wife right away."

His flippant words had Darius bristling. None of his other wives had been taken by another man before he took them to wife. All had been virgins.

The idea of Stella losing her virtue to a priest had Darius scowling. "And if I want my betrothed to remain a virgin until I take her to wife?"

Klumenos gave a start. "I do not know that there is a choice, Lochagos," he murmured.

"There must be a choice," Darius argued. "To whom must I speak about this strange ritual?"

Giving his head a shake, Klumenos said, "It may be strange to you, Darius, but it is our way here."

"For all Minoans?" Darius countered in alarm.

His ypolochago allowed another shrug. "For those on this island, yes."

"And you would have your own daughter lose her virtue to a... to a priest?"

Klumenos furrowed his brows. "You may think it strange, but we would have it no other way. My daughter will visit the priest in just a few years, and three days later, she will be wed to one of Glaukos' sons," he explained. "A day my woman and I look forward to with great anticipation."

Darius very nearly seethed. "To whom must I see if I do not wish this fate on my own betrothed?" he asked again, concerned about Stella. If anyone was to take her virtue, it would be him and no one else.

"The priest at the temple in Akrotiri," Klumenos replied. "But do not be surprised if he denies your request."

"What can I use to bargain with him?" Darius asked.

Blinking, Klumenos realized just then there was no changing the lochagos' mind. "Coin, I suppose. Gold."

Darius nodded, not at all surprised a priest might be bribed. "Gratitude," he whispered.

The ypolochago regarded him for several seconds before he asked, "Were your wives virgins when you took them the first time?"

"They were. Virgins are highly valued where I come from," Darius replied.

"And this woman to whom you are betrothed... does she know you expect her to be a virgin?"

Dipping his head, Darius realized he needed to arrange an audience with the priest when he was next in Akrotiri.

Tomorrow, should he make it that far.

"I will see to it her parents both know," Darius answered.

"Am I acquainted with your betrothed?" Klumenos asked in a whisper.

Shaking his head, Darius said, "I doubt it. She lives near Akrotiri. And you will say nothing of my betrothal to anyone."

Just then, several coastguardsmen entered the watchtower, their animated discussion suggesting something had just happened.

Aries stepped forward. "They escaped into the sea," he said. "Two of them. Just dived under the water. We waited for them to come up for air, but neither did," he said with a shake of his head.

Darius exchanged glances with Klumenos before they turned their attention back to the men. "So they swam away. Came up for air somewhere else," he suggested.

"We had men guarding the beaches on both sides of the caves," Aries countered. "Neither appeared above the waves. Neither came onto the shore."

"Underwater caves?" Darius asked, his attention on Klumenos.

"If there are, we are unaware of them," the ypolochago murmured. "But there must be, if what my men say is true."

"When the sun is high, send your best swimmers into the sea at the same place where these men disappeared," Darius ordered.

"I will, Lochagos," Klumenos agreed. "In the meantime, let us enjoy our midday meal." He turned his attention to Aries. "What news of Darius' horse?"

The coastguardsman nodded. "It was a rock, as you said. It has been removed. He has been fed and watered and will do your bidding."

"Gratitude," Darius said.

When he finished the meal with Klumenos and his men, Darius mounted Augustine and made his way to Akrotiri. Although it was too late to pay a call on the priest, it wasn't too late to visit Stella.

16

SLAVERY EXPLAINED

The sun was low in the sky when Darius urged Augustine up the goat path to Andros' oikos. At no point during the climb did Darius have a sense of Stella, and he worried she might still be out in the trees at the north edge of the orchard.

Just after he crested the hill, Darius dismounted and allowed the horse to make his own way to the nearby water trough.

The oikos seemed abandoned when he approached the door, but Helena appeared from the back and regarded him in surprise. "Lochagos?"

"Helena," he said. "Apologies for the interruption. Is Andros here?"

She shook her head. "He is in the orchard. Ensuring everything is ready for the harvest." Her eyes darted to one side, as if she was about to say something else and then thought better of it.

"And Stella. Is she with him?"

Helena nodded. "She is." When she didn't say

anything else, Darius furrowed a brow. "Is something wrong?"

The old woman allowed a slight shrug. "Stella has not been herself these past few days," she said. "She started weeping during her lessons this morning. She has not slept well. She will not tell me what is wrong..."

Her words trailed off as Darius jumped onto a startled Augustine, and he urged the horse into the growing gloom of the orchard.

Deciding speed was more important than stealth—he figured he would see Andros before he was aware of Stella's tingle in his head—Darius had the horse racing between the olive trees. He was't sure if it was the sense of Stella or Andros' shout that had him pulling back on the reins, but Darius soon found the two beneath one of the ancient trees at the north edge of the orchard.

Even before Augustine had come to a halt, Darius was off of the horse and hurrying toward Stella.

Usually, she would welcome him with a kiss, but tonight, she stepped aside and averted her eyes as he moved towards her.

"Darius of Agremon," Andros said with a nod. "You honor us with your presence."

"What is wrong?" Darius asked, ignoring Andros. He stared at Stella, sure he could see the evidence of recent tears.

Stella continued to stare at the ground. In his head, the pleasant tingle that was usually present when she was nearby could now best be described as sour. Angry.

When she didn't answer, Darius turned on Andros. "I ask again, what is wrong?"

The old man regarded him for a moment before

allowing a shrug. "Other than my trees are dying, I know not," he replied. Then he stalked off, mumbling in the manner of a man who had lost part of his mind.

Darius watched him go before he turned his attention back to Stella. When he moved to take her into his arms, she flinched, and he stepped back. "What has happened? Did he do—?"

"No!" she responded in a raised voice. "Yes," she added in a quieter voice.

Thoroughly confused, Darius lowered himself to the ground and sat cross-legged before her. "What did he do?"

She shook her head. "It is what he will do, apparently," she replied, tears seeping from her eyes.

"Stella," Darius whispered. He reached out with a hand and captured one of hers. Without much effort, he had her collapsing into his arms. Despite her tears and the slight headache they caused, he pulled her close and kissed her hair. "Please tell me what has you upset."

He felt her entire body shake in his hold and then finally relax. "Tell me about slavery," she whispered.

Darius blinked. "Slavery?" he repeated. Had she heard about what had happened on the west side of the island? "Is this about the ship of slaves I sent on to Creta?"

Stella's head lifted from where she had buried it, and she regarded him with an expression of confusion. "What?"

Frowning, he realized two things at once. She was asking about slavery, but apparently knew nothing of the Mycenaean ship. "A ship filled with fifty men who had been taken from Tin Island arrived on the west side of the island. All but one of its crew was dead."

"What happened to the crew?"

Darius sighed. "A man who knew they had done wrong —they were thieves—decided to set things right. He killed the crew and freed the men. After my men saw to getting them fed, I sent them on their way to Creta. Some of the men wish to stay there, while others will probably wish to return to Tin Island to resume their work in the mines."

Stella blinked several times. "How many slaves do you own?"

Darius frowned, his brows furrowing in confusion. "I do not own slaves," he answered, shaking his head. "I employ servants," he added, wondering if she was asking about those who worked at his villa.

"What is the difference?"

The slight headache at the edge of his consciousness faded, and Darius pulled her harder against his body. "I do not own my servants," he replied. "They are paid coin for their service. I pay them well so that they will remain in service to me." After a moment, he asked, "What happened to make you cry, Stella?"

He felt one of her hands press against his chest, and he inhaled slowly, reveling in the pleasant sensations that seemed to emanate from her simple touch. "My father said all his debts would be paid when you came for me."

Darius gave a start and stared down at her. "Debts?" he repeated. "I was not aware your father was in debt," he added, his brows once again furrowing.

"I think he gambles with the other old men in Akrotiri," she whispered, as if she feared being overheard. "He is gone all day, and comes home in poor spirits when it is time for the evening meal," she explained.

Wincing at her words, Darius wondered how deep in debt Andros might be.

Was the man referring to the coin Darius would give him to pay for men when Stella left his household? Counting on it to get him out of debt?

Or had he already lost those funds, too?

He briefly wondered if he should make inquiries. Ensure any debts were paid lest the old man suffer at the impatient hands of someone wishing to be paid.

Darius considered how much gold he had paid out this past few years and knew there was a limit to how much more he could afford to spend. Although King Cydon had been generous—he had given Darius a villa—he was not so free with his gold. King Tektamanos was better about seeing to it the coastguardsmen were paid for their services, and he had seen to reimbursement for Darius' expenses, but it would be years before Darius had saved enough to match what he had brought to the island.

Could he discover who owned Andros' debt and pay it off? Or should he let the old man see to his own fate?

He wanted to ensure there was enough coin for a good life with Stella. He wanted to be sure there was gold so that he might buy her everything she wanted. Wanted to be sure there was gold should they ever need to leave Strongili and begin a new life somewhere else.

"Do you want me to pay his debt?" he asked in a quiet voice.

Tears once again streamed down Stella's face, and she finally shook her head. "Not if it means I must become a slave," she whispered. "He is my father, but there are times I know he is not. Not truly."

"He raised you," Darius countered. "He loves you as he would his own daughter."

"And yet he would take coin for me," she hissed.

Darius wondered if she might have heard him wrong. If she had overheard Andros say something and misinterpreted the words. He was about to suggest it when the ground to the left of him shook and cracked open. Steam erupted, sending a cloud of white vapor shooting up with a 'hiss'.

Darius struggled to get to his feet, holding onto Stella as he moved back from the steam vent.

Meanwhile, a startled Augustine reared and whinnied. Darius grabbed for his reins and missed. Cursing, he swung Stella over his shoulder and managed to capture the reins on the second try. He hoisted her onto the horse and followed her up, hoping Augustine would settle himself when he realized Stella was on his back.

As he expected, Augustine immediately calmed down and had them well away from the cracked ground in only seconds. His steps were tentative, though, as if he expected the ground to open up and swallow him whole.

"Are you hurt?" Darius asked, an arm wrapping around her waist so that he could pull her against his front.

"I do not think so," Stella whispered, her brows furrowing as she looked up. "Is something burning?"

Darius followed her line of sight and furrowed his brows. Gray ash rained down, fluttering on the slight breeze and forcing Augustine to snort and shake his head in protest. "I do not smell smoke," he said as he surveyed what he could see of the horizon.

He had Augustine head for a clear line of sight, thinking perhaps a watchtower had sent up a plume of smoke in response to a ship. But when they reached the edge of the cliff overlooking Akrotiri, there was no sign of an invasion from the south. The ash was settling on the village, though, and from their vantage above, he could see confusion on the faces of those who milled about, their hands held out as if they thought it might be raining.

"The volcano," Stella said, her attention on something beyond Darius' shoulder.

He glanced back and managed to get Augustine turned around. Cursing in a language Stella didn't recognize, Darius had the horse heading north at a gallop. "Hang on!" he called out, the ride requiring he hold onto both reins.

When they had cleared the orchard and the branches of taller trees, the conical mountain near the center of the island came into view. A combination of gray smoke and white steam hovered over its peak.

"Is that what an eruption looks like?" Stella asked in awe.

Darius blinked, not sure how to respond. Although he had seen the effects of a volcano, he had never been in the presence of one when it was erupting. He had heard tales of hot, melted rocks flowing down the slopes, consuming anything in their wake. He had smelled the gases such an eruption belched into the air, the sour and putrid fumes causing him to nearly gag. But he had never seen what he was seeing now. "I am not sure," he replied, deciding Stella would know if he was lying.

They watched for a time, mesmerized by the view. After a few minutes, though, the wind wiped the steam and smoke from the top of the cone, and blue skies prevailed. No more ash fell from the sky. No more steam erupted from the ground around them.

"Are the gods displeased with us?" Stella asked in a whisper.

Brought out of his reverie, Darius was stunned to find Stella clinging to his body, her arms wrapped around his back as tightly as he held her against the front of his body. The tingling in his brain was a combination of pleasure and pain, calm and chaos. He dropped a kiss on the top of her head and said, "I do not think so. But perhaps they have simply reminded us of their presence," he murmured.

Stella looked up at him then, her gaze seeming to search his. Darius hesitated only a moment before he dropped his lips to hers. He kissed her, the touch merely a peck at first. When her lips opened in surprise, he opened his mouth and took her lips completely.

A flare of pleasure replaced any sense of calm. Any sense of chaos. The moan he heard might have been his own or it might have been hers, he knew not. He just knew he had to hold onto her as long as she would allow it. Brand her with his lips. Sear her body with the heat of his. Make her understand that she was his and would always be his.

Her name came on the breeze, barely heard above the sound of the wind and the slight moaning that surrounded them. When it came again, Stella gave a start and pulled away, her breathing labored and her eyes glazed with want.

"Helena," she whispered.

Darius struggled to understand her simple word until he heard Stella's name. A distant cry. Desperate. Pleading.

Augustine responded even before Darius could think of what to do. The horse had them turned around and headed back toward the oikos at a quick walk just as Stella's name sounded once again.

Urging his mount to go faster, Darius gave his head a shake in an effort to clear the lust from his thoughts. Had he spent another moment kissing Stella, he was sure he would have stripped her of her tunic. Dismounted and undressed and covered her body with his own in an attempt to become one with her.

Make love to her until their shared ecstasy set off earthquakes around them.

Their joining would be that powerful, he was sure.

Now he felt only embarrassment. Shame. He hadn't intended to kiss her so thoroughly. To pour every thought of want and need into the simple act of touching his lips to hers.

Had it really been that long since he had been with a woman? Was he really so in need of a woman's touch that he would do such a thing with his innocent betrothed? When he was only a year or two from making her his wife?

Helena's shout of Stella's name was cut off when she spotted them. Her hands clasped in front of her body as if she was praising a god, and she ran towards them.

"Thank the gods," she said as she came up alongside Augustine. The horse had slowed at her approach, Darius barely in control of the reins. "I feared the worst when I saw the ash fall from the sky," Helena said as Darius lowered Stella from the horse.

"I am fine," Stella said once she was on solid ground. "Darius saved me from a steam vent at the north end of the orchard. Or, rather, Augustine did," she amended, taking the horse's head between her two hands. Augustine lowered his head as she pressed her face to his until their foreheads were touching.

Even Darius could sense the relief and gratitude that passed between them. Although he might have felt a bit of jealousy at how easily they communicated, he couldn't deny his own relief that Stella said nothing of what he had done to her.

With her.

For she had returned his kiss with as much passion as he had given it.

"I must check on my men," he said, wincing when he realized how his words must have sounded. "Will you be all right?"

Helena nodded, pulling Stella into her arms. "We will. I think the gods have spoken enough on this day," she said.

Darius allowed a nod and caught Stella's gaze. Tempted to dismount and give her a quick kiss, he resisted the urge and merely held her stare for a few seconds before he had Augustine heading northwest.

When he dared a glance back, he managed a wave when he found her watching him.

Turning around was one of the hardest things he had ever had to do.

17

AN IMMORTAL LEARNS OF
MORTAL WAYS

The following day

"You wish to do *what?*"

Darius dipped his head, as if he regretted having spoken the words to the priest. The query as to how he might ensure Stella was absolved of her obligation to visit the priest on the eve of her sixteenth birthday had the priest displaying a combination of anger and disbelief.

"I do not want my betrothed to have lain with another before I take her to wife," Darius explained, realizing it would be wise to treat the priest as one of higher standing than himself. Used to commanding men and only showing supplication to the king, Darius found the situation in the temple awkward.

"But ..." The priest gave his head a shake. "This is the way it is done. So a husband can lay with his new wife without causing her pain. So he can get a child on her as soon as possible."

Remembering just how obsessed the Minoans were when it came to fertility and childbearing, Darius understood what the priest was saying. But his nearly six-hundred years of having lived among other cultures that valued virgins for wives meant this particular practice was unacceptable to him.

Besides, the idea of another man being intimate with Stella was unthinkable. He would be forced to kill anyone who violated her as he thought the priest would do.

"I do not wish to share my betrothed with anyone else," Darius said.

"But, I am a priest—"

"Even a priest."

"It is one of my duties to our people," the priest said in a quiet voice, although he didn't say the words with much conviction.

"What must I do to ensure she is excused from having to lie with you? Must I take my request to the king?" Darius hadn't intended to mention Tektanamos, but he was prepared to do what he must so that Stella was spared from having to spend time in the priest's bed—or wherever it was the priest took young girls' virtues.

The priest furrowed a brow. Although he knew Darius was the island's lochagos, the two hadn't met before this day. "You understand that you will cause her pain?"

Darius winced. "I do. I have had wives in the past," he added, thinking the priest was about to give in to his request.

Nodding, the priest turned from Darius and regarded the altar near the back of the temple. The remains of a sacrificed bird were being removed by one of the priest-esses. "Your request will be granted, but... you may fall from favor with the gods," he warned.

Resisting the urge to roll his eyes, Darius was ready to

claim he *was* a god by driving one of his blades into his chest just so he could come back to life in front of the priest. Instead, he waited for what he was sure would be a demand for gold. "How then may I remain in good stead with the gods?"

The priest pointed to the altar. "Make an offering. An item of some importance to you. It does not have to be great."

"Why not?" Darius asked in surprise.

Dipping his head to one side, the priest hesitated before saying, "You do me a favor with your request."

Darius gave a start. "How so?"

The priest glanced around the temple before leaning in closer to the lochagos. "Your betrothed is not... not like the other girls on this island," he whispered.

Darius had to choke back the guffaw he nearly allowed. Stella definitely wasn't like any of the other girls on the island. "What makes you say such a thing?" he asked, pretending to be intrigued by the man's comment.

The priest raised a brow. "She speaks to the animals. As if they speak to her."

Surprised anyone other than he knew about Stella's penchant for speaking to animals, Darius was about to agree it was an odd trait. About to mention that Stella had carried on conversations with his horse, Darius was struck dumb when the priest said, "And surely you have noticed the color of her hair?"

Darius blinked. And blinked again, as if he were trying to remember. "Red, is it not?" he countered, curious as to what the priest might say next.

"Indeed. A sure sign she is not one of ours."

"Ours?" Darius repeated, his alarm growing.

The priest dipped his head again. "She is like you."

Darius struggled to keep an impassive expression on his face while his thoughts were in turmoil.

Did the priest know he was an Immortal? Did he know Stella was an Immortal? Or would be, once she died for the first time? "In what way?" Darius finally asked.

"Like you, she is not of this island. But while you were brought here by boat, she was brought to Akrotiri by a large bird from the north. When the bird tired and could fly no further, it settled its burden beneath a tree. And when it was sure she would be found and taken in, the bird flew away."

Once again, Darius blinked. Andros hadn't mentioned a large bird when he told him about how Stella had been found in a basket beneath an olive tree. Was this just a story the priest was making up to explain how a red-headed babe could end up on Strongili? Or had someone paid witness to her delivery to the island?

Darius was almost tempted to ask, but the priest was regarding him with a half-smile. "A wise bird," Darius murmured.

"Indeed. So it stands to reason you two should be wed. And then, when you leave this island, it shall be by the same way you came. By boat," the priest concluded, giving a nod to reinforce his last words.

About to remind the priest there was really only one way to leave the island—by boat—Darius realized the priest was implying that he and Stella wouldn't be leaving the island the same way most Minoans did.

By dying.

Perhaps the priest was aware of their immortality.

"Would five gold coins be a suitable offering?" Darius asked then.

The priest angled his head to one side. "Three, I should think. The other two you should give to your betrothed on your wedding night, along with your apologies as to the pain you will cause. Your other sacrifice will be the two days you will have to wait until you can claim her again, for if you do not, you will not be welcome in her bed."

About to put voice to a protest—Darius had every intention of ensuring Stella suffered as little as possible in the marriage bed—he instead bowed his head to the priest before making his way to the altar.

Later that afternoon, the priest allowed a grin when he found four coins on the marble block.

18

THE CRUELTY OF THE YOUNG

A year later

Stella made her way down the goat path to Akrotiri, an empty sack tucked under one arm and her hand clutching a purse. Helena assured her there was enough coin to purchase the items she wanted from the agora. Should there be any left, Stella was given permission to use it for the purchase of dyes or plaster. She had begun a new fresco in her bedchamber.

She had finally completed the first one, the white spot in the middle of the olive trees now filled in with a painting of Augustine. Depicted with his head held high and free of a saddle, he looked proud. Almost wild.

He had felt that way when she had finally ridden the beast by herself. Darius had allowed Stella the brief stint, agreeing to let her have full rein when he found her speaking to the aging beast after Darius had completed negotiations with her father for the next year's olives and olio.

Darius had watched her every move, his thick arms crossed over his chest in an attempt to seem nonchalant.

Stella knew better.

He was tense, as if he expected Augustine to bolt or rear up. Instead, the horse had cantered around the trees, responding not to commands from her knees but from words she spoke as she leaned over his neck. She might have gripped his mane to hang on, but she was careful not to pull it.

When Augustine came to a halt in front of Darius, the lochagos uncrossed his arms and gave her a nod. "I wish training new recruits was this easy," he commented.

"Are they vexing you?" she asked, her attention still on Augustine. She leaned over and whispered a command, and the horse stepped sideways. She beamed in delight.

Darius had a hard time suppressing a grin. "Vexing is a good word," he agreed. "They are eager to vanquish pirates, but they lack the fighting skill to do it to the best advantage."

"Best advantage?"' Stella repeated, just before she once again leaned over her mount and whispered something. Augustine stepped sideways, but in the other direction.

"It does no good to be killed by a pirate whilst in the process of vanquishing him," Darius replied. "The men here believe it is a great honor to die in battle."

Stella blinked. "Is it not?"

Sighing, Darius gave a shake of his head. "It is far better to live so you can fight again another day," he explained. "And it saves me from having to train another recruit."

Nodding, Stella said, "I understand." She stared at him a moment, and then Augustine stepped sideways, turned around in a circle, and seemed to bow before him.

It was Darius' turn to blink. "Did you command him to do that?" he asked, when Augustine had straightened and lifted his head.

"Of course," Stella replied. "He is very eager to please. I think he fears you may have a replacement in mind for him, although he is not yet old enough to be put to pasture."

Replacement? Darius gave a shake of his head. "I do not have a replacement in mind for him," he claimed. "What gave him that idea?"

Stella put a hand on her hip as she shifted to one side of the saddle. "Perhaps you should ask him."

Once again, Darius was forced to hide a grin. "I will when we are on our way back to my tent."

"Tent?" she repeated. "I thought—"

"It is where I stay when I am too far from my villa," Darius explained. He motioned to the north. "A milion or so north of here, atop the next mountain."

Stella's gaze went to the mostly flat rise that prevented a clear view to the north. "Is there a stable for Augustine?" she asked, one of her hands smoothing Augustine's mane back into place.

Darius shook his head. "No, but there is water and grain."

The horse once again bowed before him, and Darius wondered if Augustine had made the move on his own or if Stella had commanded him to do so with a hidden signal. "Perhaps I shall have you train the next one," he said, his expression serious.

"Perhaps you should," she replied with a grin. Darius

lifted her off the horse, kissed her on the lips as she did to him, and then easily mounted the horse.

"Be well," he had said as he gave her a wave. "I shall think of you often." And then he was off, riding through the middle of the orchard and headed for his tent on the next mountain.

STELLA HADN'T SEEN him since that day. She wondered if the king had once again summoned him to Creta, or if something awful had happened to him. Perhaps he had been injured in a fight, or wounded by a pirate.

Once at the agora, she tried to concentrate on the foods Helena had requested. Fruits and vegetables, ground grain and flat bread. Honey.

The giggles of a number of girls her own age pulled her attention from the fruit cart, though, and she grinned. About to call out a greeting, she was stunned when one of the girls—one she had never seen before—pointed a finger in her direction and said, "What hideous hair!"

The gaggle of girls surrounding the one who spoke lifted their hands to their mouths as if they were shocked, but their sounds of amusement were still evident.

The grin on Stella's face disappeared as she regarded the new girl.

Had she heard correctly?

"Hello. Who are you?" Stella asked in a meek voice, dismayed when she recognized all four girls who stood with the newcomer. Girls whom she had known her entire life. Girls who were now laughing and giggling—at her expense.

The girl, rather tall and willowy, wore her blue-black

hair adorned with an expensive looking lisette, and she was dressed in a brightly-colored skirt. Despite her age, she wore a jacket that displayed her breasts.

She lifted her chin and regarded Stella with a look of derision. "I am called Mina, and I am the daughter of Aramus, the commander of the newest watchtower," she proclaimed.

Stella furrowed a brow, remembering Darius' comment about new recruits trying his patience. About the new watchtower and the difficulty he had with training its personnel.

About to say something, Stella couldn't when one of the girls said, "She has always had hair that color."

"I should hope she would not choose to dye it such a shade," Mina replied, as if Stella wasn't standing directly in front of her. "As it is, she cannot hope to make a good match when it comes to a husband unless she does. What man would wed a girl with red hair?"

The question brought a fresh round of giggles from her friends, and Stella could feel her cheeks flaming with embarrassment.

Never before had the color of her hair had her friends displaying such amusement. Had they been laughing about it behind her back all these years? Or had they decided to follow the lead of the new girl? "I am Stella of Akrotiri," she announced with a slight nod. "It is good to make your acquaintance, Mina. Welcome to Strongili."

With that, she turned and tossed a coin to the fruit vendor before she stalked off toward the goat path leading up to her oikos. She had only acquired half of what Helena had requested, but she couldn't continue to shop given the presence of the girls who continued to laugh at her retreating back.

A series of jumbled thoughts had her trying to stave off tears. A number of rejoinders she could have said came to mind.

As for a husband, I expect I shall make a better match than any of you, given I will be in possession of this island's largest olive orchard, was one such thought, but not something she would ever say out loud. Or *given your flat chest, I imagine it will be hard for you to procure a husband as well*. Or *I am good friends with your father's lochagos, and he will suffer a demotion for your insolence*.

She nearly stopped in her tracks at this last thought. Darius hadn't been to the olive orchard in several sennights. Longer, in fact. Perhaps he had found someone else to spend time with on the occasions he came to Akrotiri.

If Mina's father was the newest lieutenant, perhaps Darius was spending time at his oikos. Sharing the evening meal with the family.

Which meant he was in Mina's company.

Tears filled the corners of her eyes. Before Stella even reached the top of the cliff, they streamed down her cheeks. Her breathing, already made difficult with the steep climb, was made more labored with her sobs.

She dropped the sack of produce at the door of the oikos and rushed to the nearest olive tree, climbing only high enough to sit on the lowest branch.

Her body wracked with sobs and tears blinding her, she was completely unaware of the man who stood before her.

That is, until she was suddenly being lifted out of the tree.

She wouldn't have cared if it was a man she had never met before. Wouldn't have cared if he was a pirate or worse. She was so bereft, she would welcome whatever was to come.

Anything was better than thoughts of Darius with Mina.

19

RESPITE

The strong arms that lifted Stella from the tree branch wrapped around her shoulders and pulled her close. Stella would have given a start had she not been so bereft, so blinded by tears and heartsick she could barely breathe.

"I have only seen you cry one other time," Darius said as he tightened his hold on her. He could feel her tears dampen his bare chest, feel how her heart thudded against his torso, hear her slight gasp when she heard his quiet voice close to her ear.

He had known something was wrong from the moment he had entered the orchard. The sensation in his head was entirely different from how he usually knew Stella was nearby. Her distress had him experiencing a headache that was worsening by the minute.

For a moment, Stella's sobs increased before he heard her sniffle. He finally looked down at her when she pulled her face from his chest. "What has happened to distress you so?" he asked in a near whisper. Alarm shot through him when he thought something might have happened to Andros or Helena.

Stella blinked several times, wondering if she had conjured the lochagos into existence. She had been thinking of him only moments ago, her despair amplified by thoughts that she had not seen him in a very long time. That he might be spending time with Mina or some other young woman on the island.

"Nothing," she replied, a hand quickly wiping away the tears from her cheeks. She stepped away from him, her gaze going to Augustine so she wouldn't have to look at Darius.

Arching a brow, Darius knew immediately her parents must be well, or she would have answered differently. "You are a poor liar," he replied. He used the crook of a finger to lift her chin. "I ask again, what has happened?"

Stella sniffled just before a sob had her body shaking. "My hair," she managed, just before a hiccup sounded.

Darius lifted a lock from where it rested on her shoulder and regarded it a moment before doing the same with the other side, rubbing it between his thumb and forefinger with unexpected reverence.

Although she had brushed it out that morning, she hadn't dressed it, electing to simply let the wavy curls fall where they pleased. After the incident at the agora, she wished she had dressed it. Secured it into loops at the back of her head with gold bands and then topped it with her very best lisette.

Her only lisette.

She remembered the one that Mina wore, and jealousy replaced some of her sorrow. Mina probably didn't have to perform chores or otherwise earn the trinkets she displayed on her costume or in her hair.

"Your hair is beautiful, as always," Darius remarked, just before he bussed her on the lips.

Stella gave a start, which was reinforced with another hiccup. No one had ever said that about her hair before.

"I was reminded it is red," she replied.

Darius couldn't argue, so he tried a different tack. "Did another girl make the observation?" he guessed, struggling to remember how old Stella was now. *Fourteen summers?* He supposed it was the age when petty jealousies made it difficult for girls who were not yet betrothed.

Stella nodded, finally lifting her head so their eyes met. "Mina, a daughter of the commander of your newest watchtower," she said with a sniffle, emphasizing the *your*.

The tone of her voice suggested she might be blaming him for what had happened. Darius had a difficult time hiding his initial reaction—humor—and had to cover his mouth with a hand as he pretended to think on the matter.

"If you order it, I shall see to it he is relieved of his command," he offered, just to pay witness to her reaction.

He wasn't disappointed.

Stella's red-rimmed eyes widened in shock, and she gave her head a quick shake. "No. You must not," she said. "It is not his mouth that called my hair hideous."

Darius noted how his headache had subsided, but now his hackles were rising at hearing exactly what had been said about her hair. "Hideous?" he repeated. "Hmph. Mina must be blind. Or she is unfamiliar with our language and used the wrong word," he mused as he indicated they should head to the oikos. Stella fell into step next to him, her gaze directed at the ground below.

Darius knew of the girl Mina. He had met her as well as the other members of Aramus' large family. They had just come from Creta so that Aramus could take on the new watchtower at the southwest edge of the island. Used to life in luxurious quarters on Creta, the oldest daughter was probably none too pleased to have found herself living on the western edge of Akrotiri on a small island.

"In some countries, a father and his entire family are put to death because of the actions of just one of them," Darius explained, wanting Stella to understand why he had made the offer, even if it was in jest. "Especially if others have paid witness to the crime."

Stella gasped. "Even if they did nothing wrong? That hardly seems fair."

Darius gave a shrug. "Much of what happens in the world rarely is," he countered. Although he had never lived in Egypt, Darius had heard tales of familicide. Rather than live with the shame of a crime committed by one family member, fathers killed all their children and wives and then themselves. "Where exactly did this insult occur?"

Closing her eyes as she remembered all too clearly the crowds at the agora, Stella allowed a sigh as she walked alongside the lochagos. "At the agora." She glanced at the bag she had left at the door of the oikos. Only about half of what Helena had ordered her to buy was in that sack. The purse she had been given, now hanging around her neck, was still heavy with coin.

Helena would be furious with her for not completing the simple chore, especially when she was spending the day at the bathhouse. The older woman rarely had an opportunity to enjoy such an outing, given the work she did around the oikos. Meanwhile, Andros spent more of his days with men who were no longer able to work. They played knucklebones and discussed the latest gossip brought by sea captains and sailors.

"Before you finished your shopping," Darius guessed, as he reached over and pinched the purse between his thumb and forefinger.

The move had the back of his fingers brushing against the bare skin at the top of one breast, and the touch set off a frisson in him.

Would the simple act of touching Stella always set off such pleasant sensations beneath his skin? Or was it merely because her breasts weren't covered? He had never seen her wear the traditional garb of a Minoan woman—the short-sleeved open jacket cinched at the waist with a brightly colored skirt that flared at the bottom. The costume, mostly in greens the color of leaves, set off her red hair to good effect.

Stella nodded, and tears once again welled up in her eyes. Before she could reply, she noticed how he winced, as if in pain. "What is it? What is wrong?" she asked as she stopped to regard him with worry. Realizing the lochagos was bothered by her crying, she managed to blink back the tears.

"Come. Let us finish the shopping you were sent to do," Darius replied, ignoring her question. Before he could turn to summon Augustine, the horse hurried up and nudged Stella on the shoulder. "Would you like to ride him into town?"

Stella blinked and nodded, lifting the back of her hand

to wipe the remaining tears from her cheeks. "I would," she replied, a grin finally lighting her face.

Darius wondered at how the tingle at the edge of his consciousness brightened. He no longer experienced the strange headache. "Take inside what you have already bought. Wash your face. Brush your hair, and be quick about it," Darius said, not intending to sound like he did when he ordered his men about.

"Yes, Lochagos," Stella replied with a slight bow, and then hurried off to do as she was told.

Darius took the opportunity to study the exterior of the oikos. He noted how simple maintenance could improve its appearance. One window shutter hung crooked, no doubt loosened by the northerly winds. Finding one of the fasteners on the ground, he set to repairing the shutter and then stepped back to survey his work. Then he noticed a simple crack in the wall, and wondered how it had happened. Surely Andros would want to fill the crack, especially before the winter rains started.

He was pondering a crack in the bone-dry ground when Stella emerged from the oikos, an empty burlap sack clutched in one hand. Darius couldn't help but grin. Her glorious hair, bright red under the midday sun, was now topped with a modest lisette. The shape of the front formed a sort of diamond with the longest point at the center of her forehead. Even without jewels, the metal ornament reflected golden light in several directions.

Someday, he would have to see to a more ornate hair jewel for her. One made of gold with gems that would capture the green of her eyes and the pink of her cheeks and lips. Perhaps another studded with rubies to match her hair, with obsidian and onyx stones surrounding the red gemstones.

He thought of how he might tease her by saying she could only wear them in his presence. An image of her sharing his bed whilst wearing only a lisette and nothing else had his loins tightening.

Silently cursing, Darius wondered how a fourteen-year-old could have him aroused, and then he realized he hadn't been imagining her as she was now, but rather how she would be in a couple of years. After she was seventeen summers and he had taken her to wife.

In a few years, she would be taller. Her rounded cheeks would become defined by high cheekbones. Her mouth would form smiles easily, prompted by his occasional teases and the pleasant tingles she would feel whenever he was in her presence.

Her breasts, already round, would be fuller, her nipples hardening into tight buds with a bit of help from his lips and tongue. Her skin, made golden from the sun, would feel like velvet beneath his touch as he prepared her body for his cock. Her warm, wet cocoon would welcome his invasion, surround him and tighten on him as he brought her to ecstasy.

Her cries of delight and moans brought on by intense pleasure would send him into that same ecstasy. Her soft body would then cradle him as he drifted off to sleep, and he would find her tucked against his body when he awoke the next day.

For the rest of his days, she would be his.

Giving his head a quick shake, Darius moved to where his horse was helping himself to water in the goat's trough. He mounted Augustine, and then pulled Stella onto the horse. She sat sideways as Augustine picked his way down the goat path and into Akrotiri. He covered the rest of the trip to the agora in only a few minutes as Stella's mood lifted and she giggled at being bounced atop the beast.

Darius halted the horse at the edge of the marketplace and tossed a coin to a young boy who stood holding the reins of two other horses. "I will not be long," he told the boy, lifting Stella from where she was perched. He took longer than normal to lower her to the ground, his gaze searching the agora for the tall girl he had met only a sennight ago.

Invited to join Aramus' family for dinner, he had agreed only because he had not been successful in his hunt for a small animal for that evening's meal. The table had held a number of dishes, including two kinds of fish and hot bread with olio. Darius had sat near Aramus so they might easily converse, but he spent most of the meal listening to the five children speak about their recent move to the island. The oldest, Mina, had kept quiet through the dinner, speaking only when asked a question and otherwise sulking.

When he learned Aramus' wife was a niece of King Tektamanos, Darius wondered if the king had assigned Aramus to Strongili as Darius' eventual replacement.

Or had Aramus been sent to spy on Darius?

Since Darius had no intention of giving up his position as lochagos of Strongili—death or a better offer would have to take him first—he hoped Aramus wasn't counting on the promotion.

Darius' roaming gaze finally stopped when he spotted Mina. A number of girls about Stella's age stood clustered together, happily chatting with one another and occasionally turning their attention to the shoppers, as if they were looking for people to tease. None of the girls carried sacks or purses or any other indication they were there to buy anything.

He made sure he was spotted with Stella before he placed a protective hand at her back and escorted her to the first stall.

Pretending not to notice Mina and her friends, Stella stood straight as Darius masterfully negotiated the best price for fruit. She watched in wonder at the next stall, where Darius haggled over several vegetables. His manner with the beekeeper was familiar—he apparently purchased his honey from the man on several occasions, and he managed to secure a larger pot than Stella had ever purchased for far less than she usually paid.

He even carried the bag of goods as they made their way.

When they had completed an entire circuit of the agora, Stella watched as Darius' gaze swept the area. She secretly thrilled when she noted how Mina's gaze quickly turned from his, as if she had been caught staring at them.

When Stella seemed reluctant to leave, Darius regarded her a moment. "Have you forgotten something?" he asked.

She shook her head, her fingers judging how much coin was leftover in the purse. "Helena said I could use any extra coin to buy pigments and lime," she said. "For plaster."

Darius frowned before a look of understanding appeared. "To paint frescoes?" he guessed.

Stella nodded, a slight smile coming to her face. "I have never before had this much coin left."

"And you have a fresco to paint?" he half-asked.

"To finish, yes," she agreed. "I think there is enough to buy lime," she said with widened eyes. "Gratitude."

His brows furrowing at her word of thanks, Darius realized just then that she had probably never been able to negotiate for the best prices at the agora.

Had her youth been the reason? Or was it the color of her hair?

Were Minoans really so closed-minded as to find her red hair offensive? He wanted nothing more than to comb his fingers through it. To wake up to find locks of it tickling his cheek, or sliding down his chest, or...

He squeezed his eyes shut in an attempt to block out the image of Stella making love to him.

Another two years, he thought in dismay. He wondered once again why his body seemed so hungry for her. After this many years without a wife, surely he could wait another two years!

"Come. I will take you to the shop where they sell pigments and lime," he said, once again placing a possessive hand at her back as he guided her to Augustine. His gaze fell firmly on Mina, who was staring at them with wide eyes and a look of worry. Nodding in her direction, he made sure not to smile. In fact, he hoped she took note of his look of disapproval, and was sure she had when her eyes quickly averted his gaze.

Darius grinned as he took the reins from the boy and made a show of lifting Stella onto the saddle. Instead of joining her atop the horse, he led Augustine away from the agora, making sure they passed in front of where the group of girls stood. A few watched, as if in confusion, and he noted how they quickly turned away before he could make eye contact. Meanwhile, Stella allowed a grin of satisfaction as she proudly rode Augustine to the shop.

As he had done with the vendors at the agora, Darius saw to it Stella had more colors than she had thought possible. When it came to the lime for the plaster, she shook her head at the size of the bag he intended to buy. "However will I get it home?" she asked in alarm. "I cannot carry all of this!"

Darius couldn't decide if he was offended she would think he wouldn't provide assistance, or charmed that she would have such concerns. "Augustine will carry it for us," Darius countered. "And I am not leaving you until I know you are home safe," he added. He paid the shopkeeper and lifted their latest purchases into the crook of one arm.

Stella dipped her head and said, "Gratitude," to the shopkeeper before following Darius. When she joined him next to Augustine, he was loading the day's purchases into large bags attached to the back of the saddle. She fingered the purse, stunned to discover there was still one coin left inside. "How is it I still have a coin?" she asked in wonder.

Darius grinned as he turned to regard her. "I am good for more than just fighting off pirates," he replied, his humor evident with the white teeth he displayed as he smiled.

Inhaling sharply, Stella noted how young he appeared just then. She thought she even saw a dimple at the base of one of his cheeks appear, if only briefly. "I never doubted it," she replied in a quiet voice. "You would make a good husband," she added, at the same moment Darius moved to give her a boost onto the horse.

He paused and regarded her for a moment. *Would* make a good husband?

Not *will* make a good husband?

Hadn't Andros explained to her that she would one day be his wife?

"In a couple of years, I shall," he finally replied, deciding he might have to have another discussion with the olive farmer. Then he set Stella atop Augustine and followed her up. "In the meantime, if Mina should make any more derisive comments about your red hair, do inform me," he instructed as he gave Augustine the command to move.

"What will you do to her?" Stella asked, quite sure Mina would never dare say anything more to Stella for the rest of her life.

"I will not *do* anything to her. I will, however, have a word with her father," he warned.

Stella couldn't help the combination of fear and admiration she felt for the lochagos just then. Perhaps he sensed it, for he once again allowed a boyish grin. "I will not dismiss him from his position," he assured her. "But I shall make it clear I have no intention of taking *her* to wife."

Jerking her attention to regard him directly, Stella gave a shake of her head. "Had you been considering her for such an honor?"

Darius frowned, realizing just then that Andros hadn't said anything to Stella about his plans to take *her* as his wife. "I have not," he replied. "I think Aramus wishes I would, but... I have made it clear I am betrothed to another," he replied, eager to hear Stella's response.

He sensed her unease at hearing his words, and he silently cursed himself for having said them. Meaning only to tease her, he realized now he couldn't tell her he intended to take her to wife.

Andros hadn't told her of the plan.

But why not?

Perhaps he had changed his mind and hadn't informed Darius. If so, Darius intended to have a word with the farmer.

The lochagos considered this and more as Augustine picked his way up the goat path.

20

A MOTHER KNOWS

A moment later

Betrothed to another.

The words would have been a relief to hear if Stella hadn't felt such jealousy just then. Jealousy of whomever would one day be Darius of Agremon's wife.

She was sure she was in love with him.

How could she not be, after what had happened at the agora?

Darius had seen to it the other girls paid witness to how he appeared to favor her. Had he done so because he truly favored her? Because he might one day make her his woman?

Or had he only done it for show? As a means of putting Mina in her place?

Or perhaps he really wanted Mina, and thought to make her feel jealous so she might admit she favored him.

Stella felt her heart clench at this last thought. Mina was the daughter of one of his men. Perhaps an arrangement had already been made.

Surely that cannot be, she thought as tears collected in the corners of her eyes.

She couldn't even think on the situation when shouts from above had her lifting her attention up the steep hillside.

Helena stood watching them from the top of the goat path, her hands on her hips. Stella thought she looked angry for a moment, but then the expression on her adoptive mother's face softened.

Stella waved, as did Darius, and soon Augustine crested the path and came to a halt near where they had started a couple of hours earlier. Even before Darius could dismount, Helena had hurried up to join them.

"Apologies if she has been a nuisance to you, Lochagos," Helena said as she bowed her head.

Darius regarded the woman for a moment, his brows furrowed. "She has not," he replied, and then turned to lift Stella from the saddle.

Helena gave her head a shake. "She was supposed to be shopping—"

"I was," Stella interrupted. She removed the purse from around her neck and offered it to Helena. "We owe gratitude to Darius for his negotiating skills. We were able to buy far more than I would have on my own."

Helena continued to eye Darius with concern, but when he moved to retrieve the bags from behind his saddle, her eyes widened in surprise. "What is all this?" she asked.

"Everything you wanted me to get, and pigments and lime, too," Stella replied happily, as she led Augustine to the water trough.

"Where would you like me to put this?" Darius asked

of Helena as he hefted the full bags in his arms to adjust their weight.

"Gratitude, Lochagos," Helena said as she led him into the oikos. "Right here is fine," she said as she indicated a wooden table just inside the door. Her nervousness at being in the presence of the important man was evident when she asked, "May I offer refreshment? An... an ale or... or water?"

Having ignored his thirst, the mention of ale had Darius deciding to accept a cup. He quickly downed it in a few gulps. "I must be going," he said as he watched Stella see to putting away that day's purchases. "I am expected at the next watchtower by nightfall, and I should not wish to be mistaken for a pirate."

Stella hurried over to stand before him. "You will not be so long in returning next time?" she half-asked.

He shook his head, heartened by her query. "I shall not," he assured her. "I do not return to Creta for almost two moons." Then he bent down and kissed her, well aware Helena stood watching them. "I expect you to show me your finished fresco when I return," he added.

Grinning, Stella nodded and watched him as he mounted Augustine. A moment later, and the lochagos had the horse galloping off to the east.

When Stella turned to go back inside, Helena was standing at the door, an odd expression on her face. "How long were you with him?" she asked in a quiet voice.

Stella allowed a shrug. "Long enough to make the purchases and then return here."

"You left hours ago," Helena argued. "I just now returned from the bathhouse."

Sighing, Stella dipped her head. "I did go shopping

when you told me to. But something..." She paused and realized she had to tell Helena what had happened. She would learn of it from one of her friends, no doubt, given how many people were in the agora. "Someone at the agora took exception to my hair, so I came home with only half of what you wanted." She proceeded to tell Helena what had happened with Mina, surprised when Helena's brows furrowed.

The old woman took a seat and regarded Stella with a sympathetic expression. Stella wasn't like the other girls on the island. She kept to herself, spending her days in olive trees rather than with other girls her own age. She communed with the animals, talking to them as if they could understand her—and her them.

As for her bright red hair, Helena had known for some time it would one day be a source of contention. From the day she had discovered Stella in a basket under one of the oldest trees, as if she'd been deposited on the ground like the fruit during the harvest, Helena always wondered if Stella had been left there because her hair was so red. There wasn't another girl on the island with the same coloring.

Helena gave an audible sigh. "If you do not like the color of your hair, we can dye it," she suggested.

Stella shook her head, remembering what Darius had said about it. "No. I like it very much this way."

A bit surprised by the remark, Helena lifted her hand to the hair ornament. "The lisette is a nice touch," she said, a wan smile appearing to soften her expression of worry. "It makes you look... older."

Dipping her head—she would never think to wear such an adornment except for a special occasion—Stella blushed. "I only wore it because..." She stopped, remembering she had put it on because Mina had been wearing one. "Because I wish to look my best when I am with Darius."

Expecting to be teased for her comment, Stella was surprised when Helena grinned. "Does he always greet you and say farewell with a kiss?" she asked.

Stella could feel the blush continue to heat her face. "Is it not the way of our people?" she countered.

Deciding not to discourage the relationship—if he didn't change his mind, Darius would one day come for Stella to make her his wife—Helena allowed a nod. "It is." She glanced over at the pigments still on the table. "And it seems you have a painting to finish before he next comes to see you."

Following Helena's gaze, Stella nodded. "I do, and I look forward to it. If I am allowed, I will work on it tomorrow, when there is enough light in my bedchamber."

Helena gave her a nod. "Then I shall not spend time teaching you tomorrow," she replied. "But know this, young lady," she added with a hint of warning. "You will learn to weave," she said as she pointed toward the loom that took up almost an entire wall of the central room.

Stella followed her mother's gaze and grimaced. "If I must," she replied.

For if it were up to Stella, she would always spend her days out of doors, and should she have to be inside, she preferred to paint.

21

A GRAIN TRADER RETURNS

Meanwhile

Having left Stella with her mother and determined to learn if Andros had changed his mind about his daughter's betrothal, Darius returned to Akrotiri.

Finding the old man was easy.

A game of knucklebones was always going at the edge of the agora. Flanked by men just as old or older than him, Andros was shaking the bones in his gnarled right hand and was about to toss them onto a tabletop when he spotted the lochagos. "Darius of Agremon," he said, just as he released the bones.

The other players ignored the interloper, choosing instead to watch as the bones settled into place. Quiet complaints and sighs of disappointment prefaced Andros' race to collect several coins.

"A word," Darius said as he stepped to Andros' side.

The olive farmer seemed torn, as if he couldn't decide between giving up control of the knucklebones and speaking with the lochagos, or ignoring the man. He finally placed the bones on the table and swept his coins into one hand. "Another day," he said to his opponents, and then he slowly stood up.

"Apologies. I did not mean to take you from your game," Darius murmured, when they were several steps away.

"No apologies are necessary. In fact, I am glad you did. My luck would not have lasted," Andros replied as he opened his left hand to display a number of coins. Then he frowned. "Has something happened?"

Darius shook his head. "It is about what has *not* happened," he replied. "Why have you not told your daughter of our arrangement?"

Andros' expression betrayed shock before his slumped shoulders straightened. "I thought you had changed your mind," he said in a quiet voice.

"I have not."

His words had Andros furrowing a bushy, gray brow. "But... I heard your newest watchtower commander brought with him a daughter—"

"He did, but she is none of my concern."

"And yet there are those who say you are to be wed," Andros continued, his face displaying disbelief.

At seeing Andros' widened eyes, Darius realized the local rumors must have had him betrothed to Mina.

No wonder she had looked so stricken when he had accompanied Stella to the agora. Given how many had paid witness to his time with Stella, surely that rumor would no longer be on a gossip's tongue. "I will wed your daughter and no one else," Darius stated. "I will pay you as we agreed when the arrangement was first made," he added.

"Yes, Lochagos," Andros said with a nod.

Darius held out his right hand, and Andros moved to shake it. He winced as Darius gave it a firm shake and then stood and watched as the lochagos mounted his horse and hurried off to the east.

Glancing down at the coins he held, he grinned and made his way back to the agora. Even if his luck turned bad, there would be coin in his future.

AN HOUR later

Despite the uneven terrain, Augustine quickly covered the ground between Andros' orchard and the watchtower at Elefsina. The sun had just started to set when he led his mount to a water trough and corral that had been built nearby. Even before he made it to the lookout, his gaze went to the coast.

A familiar ship was anchored just off shore. Darius struggled to remember the name.

South Winds.

At one time, he had thought the ship was manned by pirates, and his men had treated Perakles and his crew as such until Darius arranged to buy Perakles' grain for his coastguardsmen and their families.

Now, in the waning light of day, the ship looked abandoned.

"You are to be commended for your reliability," Glaukos said from where he stood next to the watchtower, his arms crossed over his chest. "But perhaps not your timing."

Darius dismounted and led Augustine to where several other horses were hobbled and helping themselves to grain in pots and water in a huge bronze tub. "Apologies. I had business in Akrotiri," he replied. "What has happened?" He motioned toward the ship.

Glaukos moved to join the lochagos. "Captain Perakles is here again."

"I recognized his ship," Darius said. "Does he bring more grain?"

The ypolochagoi shook is head. "Unfortunately not. He sold it at his last stop, but then it seems some of his crew decided they did not agree with the way he distributed the profit."

Darius winced, knowing almost immediately what had happened. Besides being boarded and robbed by pirates, mutiny was a ship captain's worst nightmare. "Did he kill them all?" he asked in surprise.

Glaukos shook his head. "He had some who remained loyal and then died for it. At least three managed to escape the ship before they could be mortally wounded."

Frowning, Darius glanced back out to the ship, now barely visible in the twilight. "Did you dispatch them?"

Shaking his head, Glaukos audibly sighed. "Had we known they were out there, we would have. Unfortunately, the three who lived jumped ship before it was even visible to us. We saw the pennon on the mast and knew it was a friendly ship once it cleared the horizon. We had no reason to suspect there was a problem."

"The men have probably drowned," Darius remarked.

Glaukos allowed a sigh. "Perakles is in the watchtower. He claims they can all swim, and he fears they will cause problems here on Strongili."

Darius grunted, realizing that individual men swimming onto shore would be difficult to spot from one of the island's watchtowers. "I will speak with him," he said, before asking, "Does he have enough crew left to make it back east?"

The ypolochago shook his head. "Only a few who hid in the hold."

"Does he have any cargo?"

Glaukos shook his head. "He sold all his grain on Creta. Said he shared the take with his men, and that's when the mutiny started. They accused him of cheating them. The three that jumped ship took far more coin than they were entitled to—"

"Weighed down by gold, they would have surely drowned," Darius remarked.

"Perhaps," Glaukos replied. But he didn't look convinced.

Darius sighed. Once he was sure Augustine was happy to remain with the other horses—his mount seemed particularly enamored with Glaukos' horse—he made his way into the watchtower.

The base of the stone structure offered a large room in which the men on duty could take turns sleeping and preparing meals. Now it was crowded with sailors from the *South Winds* and the coastguardsmen who weren't in the tower above, keeping watch for other ships.

Darius recognized Perakles, although he nearly winced at seeing how the captain had aged since their last encounter.

How many years had it been?

"Perakles," he said as he held out his right hand.

The captain regarded him with surprise. "Surely you are not the same man who bought my grain..." He paused before saying, "Six or seven years ago," in a quiet voice.

Although time had aged Perakles, other concerns seemed to have added to the effect.

"I am," Darius replied. "Tell me of the men who escaped your weapons."

Eying Darius with suspicion, Perakles said, "There were three who swam to shore. With my coin." He continued to stare at the lochagos, as if he couldn't believe what he was seeing. "How is it you look exactly the same?"

Darius ignored the query. "You are sure they would have made it despite being laden with gold?" he asked. The crew who escaped must not have taken much—gold would weigh them down in the water and make swimming difficult.

Perakles allowed a shrug. "We have seen no bodies on the shore," he replied.

About to remark that any purse filled with much gold and tethered to a body would have kept them from washing up on shore, Darius merely nodded. "I will be sure my men on the south side of the island make queries in their villages. Strangers are easily noticed."

"My humblest apologies for whatever they intend to do on your island," Perakles said then. "I suspect they will behave in a most unwelcome manner, especially if they can find the others they once sailed with, or so this is what they said as they took my gold."

Darius furrowed a brow. "Others?" he repeated.

Perakles gave a shrug. "I know not of whom they speak. They have sailed with me for four years."

Were the 'others' the men who seemed to disappear under the sea, perhaps into underwater caves or lava tubes?

Darius had barely finished the thought when Glaukos asked, "What of the rest of your crew?"

Perakles allowed a shrug. "Three were killed in the skirmish for the gold. Three hid in the hold. I survived only because they had locked me in my cabin."

One of the coastguardsmen stepped forward. "He speaks the truth. We had to remove a brace from across the door to get him out."

"And the cargo holds are empty?"

"There is little of note. Nothing that would allow a crew to survive a trip to the eastern shores of the Mediterranean."

Darius turned his attention back to Perakles. "You still have your ship. What do you intend to do?"

The sea captain's shoulders slumped in resignation. "I have no coin. No gold. No means to hire a crew. But I also no longer have the stomach for the life of a trader. I am old."

Frowning, Darius regarded Perakles as if he doubted his word. "If you sell your ship, you can return to your homeland and live the rest of your days in relative comfort," he suggested.

The words had him suddenly yearning for Stella. Wishing she were older so that he might take her to wife. She would be the reason he would spend more time at his villa. Spend more time enjoying the life on such a paradise instead of always hunting for those who would take it from the islanders.

From the time he had accepted the position of locha-gos, Darius had thought he would be satisfied to serve the king for the rest of his days. Now that he was speaking of a different life for another, he saw that he, too, could adopt a different life.

But how long would a peaceable existence satisfy him? How long would it be before he would yearn to return to battle? To command men in the never-ending wars that were their past and their destiny?

His immortality ensured he would survive such battles. That he would live on in whatever capacity he was ordered to serve by the victor.

Any capacity but that of slave, though. He knew he could not abide such a life. That meant he had to choose well when choosing sides. To be owned was to give up on life. And the fact that he seemed to have so much of it would raise suspicions over time.

Perakles' comment was proof enough that he had noticed Darius' lack of aging.

Darius glanced at Glaukos. Another three children in his brood, and the ypolochago's dark hair was streaked with gray. His face, weathered from the wind and sun, had taken on the appearance of leather. In only six years, Glaukos had gone from looking younger than Darius to looking at least as old. Maybe older.

"Or I could settle here, if I would be allowed such an honor," Perakles said in response to Darius' suggestion of returning to his homeland.

Several of the coastguardsmen exchanged nervous glances. Although some newcomers were welcomed on Strongili, it was because they were Minoan and came from the other islands. It was rare when an outsider was allowed to join a village on the island.

"The people that live here are hard workers," Glaukos replied. "They would look upon you with suspicion and distrust. They will not share their harvest with you if you have no coin. Is that really how you wish to live?" he continued, noting how Darius seemed lost in thought.

Perakles nodded his understanding. "If I am not a burden to a village—because I have coin with which to buy what I need in the way of food and shelter—what then?"

"You must first find a buyer for your ship," Darius countered, just then coming out of his reverie. "It can remain anchored where it is until then. In the meantime, you will stay here. Spend your days in search of a buyer and your nights under our watch."

Perakles realized almost immediately he was being given a chance that might not otherwise be offered to someone else in a similar circumstance. "May I enquire as to why you would do this for me?"

Inhaling slowly, Darius glanced around at the other men, noting how most of them had been the beneficiaries of the grain Darius had bought from Perakles. Despite the distrust that many of them had had of the trader and his crew back then, the grain had been good. "Let us say your history with us is honorable, and leave it at that. But believe me when I say this—your welcome will only last as long as your word is good."

"And your gold," Glaukos put in. "I will escort you to the docks at Akrotiri in the morning. Introduce you to those who may be in the market for a ship."

"Gratitude," Perakles replied.

"As for a meal," Glaukos said as he regarded the cluster of men in the watchtower, "we are fortunate to have had good fishing on this day. You and your men are welcome to join us."

Even as his lieutenant said the words, Darius inhaled the scent of grilled fish and heard his stomach grumble at the same time. Like those around him, his thoughts went from his future life to the camaraderie of eating as a group.

Thoughts of Stella would no doubt return when sleep was upon him.

22

A MYSTERY CONTINUES

The following year

Word that Perakles had secured a buyer for his ship reached Darius when he was next in Perisa. Klumenos had just come from having fought off a band of marauders from the west—their deaths came before word of their origin—and had been joined by a few of Glaukos' men in the heated battle.

Although none of the coastguardsmen had died, one who commanded a watchtower had suffered a deep wound and would be unable to perform his duties for a sennight or two. Aries agreed to take on the task, convincing his father he was old enough for such an assignment.

"It is past time you let him be a man," Darius remarked, after Klumenos had briefed him on what had occurred.

"If he fails, I shall—"

"He will not fail. Even if something should happen, you have experienced men that will assist him," Darius assured him. "Now, you must tell me of the other men you spoke of?"

Klumenos hissed, his gaze going out to the sea before he turned his attention back to the lochagos. "They are like ghosts. My men claim to see them on the beach, or in the water, and then they are gone for sennights at a time."

Darius always left Perisa concerned that the "ghosts" were simply biding their time until they had a chance to take command of a ship or ambush the watchtower.

When he had last made his way to his tent from this particular watchtower, Darius was sure he was followed. Repeated attempts to determine who was following him proved fruitless. Every time he paused to look—he pretended to appear as if he were enjoying the view from the elevated path—he was instead surveying the lands below, sure he could spot whoever had the hairs on the back of his neck rising.

Instead of spending the night at his tent—it wasn't well hidden, although it also wasn't along one of the paths that led over the mountain—he instead doubled back on the trail and headed north. Although he was sure he had lost his follower within a milion of Perisa, he had Augustine take him the entire ten milion or more to his villa.

He had spoken with the servant in charge of his stables, Pietro, and asked that he keep a lookout for any strangers. So far, the stable master hadn't reported seeing anyone new to the area.

"When was the last time you were aware of them?" Darius asked, wishing the ghosts would make an appearance that night. He was anxious for a fight. Ready for action.

"Three nights ago. One of my men spotted a man in

the sea, apparently swimming. Then he disappeared beneath the waves."

"He probably swam beyond your man's vision," Darius remarked.

"My man followed the shore until the watchtower was beyond his vision. At no point did the swimmer reappear above the water," Klumenos countered, an eyebrow cocked to reinforce his words.

Darius furrowed his brows. If the swimmer drowned, a body would have washed up on shore. If he didn't come up for air, perhaps there was a reason he didn't have to. "Did you ever have your men explore what's beneath the water out there?" he asked, remembering a time when other men had disappeared beneath the water, never to be seen again.

Klumenos nodded. "I sent my best swimmer. He found a cave, but it was filled with water," he replied. His brow furrowed as he regarded the lochagos. "What are you thinking?"

Darius dared a glance at the sea. "Perhaps there is an underwater cave that leads to one above water," he suggested. "One that also has an outlet on land." A lava tube left from past volcanic activity would explain how the ghosts were managing to stay hidden.

"A lava tube?" Klumenos queried, excitement evident in his voice.

"Indeed. Perhaps your best swimmer can discover its opening under the water."

Klumenos' eyes suddenly widened. "It would explain much," he murmured. "We may even know who they are," he added, his attention no longer on Darius.

"What are you saying?"

"Remember when Perakles said his mutineers escaped with gold?"

"They disappeared at sea," Darius replied, nodding. "Probably drowned."

"Or they were excellent swimmers, and have been biding their time, hiding in caves," Klumenos suggested.

A shiver went up Darius' spine. "Biding their time?" he repeated.

Klumenos allowed a shrug. "Waiting until they can take a ship, perhaps. One..." His eyes suddenly widened. "One they are already familiar with."

Darius shook his head. "If you are thinking of the *South Winds*, then you must believe the new owner would give in easily to being boarded. Are you truly thinking they are waiting to take it?"

Screwing his face into an expression of frustration, Klumenos said, "It would explain much."

"Then why did they not take possession of it when it was moored on the south side of the island?" Darius asked.

The ypolochago straightened. "Because it was docked right next to a watchtower. Anyone attempting to pirate a ship located next to a watchtower would certainly be caught and executed on the beach," Klumenos explained.

Darius had to agree. "Then where is it docked now?"

Klumenos gave a shrug. "Orestes bought it, so I expect he will dock it at Perisa once he completes his current run to Creta."

Darius inhaled sharply. "Orestes?" he repeated. How is it he wasn't aware that the island's most successful ship's captain had purchased Perakles' ship?

"He is seeing to creating a fleet of ships from which he

can run his trading operations," Klumenos explained. "He has other captains under his.command now, so that he does not have to leave his wife on Creta for two sennights at a time." The ypolochago thrust his hips forward as he finished the last comment, a clear sign he was implying sexual intercourse.

A few years ago, Darius would have easily ignored the motion, but now, it had him remembering that he would be taking a wife soon. That he would once again be sharing his bed with a woman. That his cock would have a home on most nights–and hopefully some mornings, as well.

Once he finally took Stella to wife, he wondered if he would have to change how he commanded the ypolochagoi and the men under them.

Would he be able to spend six days traveling around the island and only one day in her company? Or would he have to take her with him, so that he might keep her close? Sleep with her every night in his tent or at an inn?

He was pondering this and more when Klumenos passed a hand in front of his face. "Do I have you thinking of taking a wife?" he asked in a teasing voice.

Darius allowed an impish grin. "I will do so within the next two years," he replied. "My betrothed will finally be of age."

Klumenos blinked, his expression growing serious. "You jest," he accused.

The lochagos shook his head. "I have been betrothed for nearly six cycles," he countered, and then mentally kicked himself for having admitted something he had only shared with the king. Stella's father knew, of course, but

Andros hadn't shared the information with anyone else, as far as Darius could discern.

Not even Stella.

"You will remain our lochagos, though," Klumenos half-asked.

"I will," Darius agreed. "For as long as the king wishes me to be."

"Is your betrothed living on Creta?"

Darius dipped his head. "She lives here on Strongili. Has lived here for her entire life."

Klumenos' eyes widened. "You honor us," he murmured. "I would have thought only a woman of Creta would suit you."

Frowning, Darius was about to ask why when one of Klumenos' men sought his counsel. "I must take my leave of you now," the ypolochago said. "Duty calls."

Lifting his head in acknowledgement, Darius watched as Klumenos conferred with the man, his thoughts of Stella and how he might live during the next chapter of his life.

So engrossed was he in his thoughts, he did not notice that a man followed him at a distance as he made his way up the mountain to his tent.

23

A MAN TAKES A YOUNG WOMAN

A few months later

With everything she owned stuffed into the satchel her mother had hastily assembled, Stella clambered onto a midnight-colored Andalusian horse. The mount was unfamiliar to her, and she sensed the horse's distrust in her.

Or maybe he sensed her fear.

When she was younger and she and Darius rode Augustine, she had sat between the lochagos and the small pommel at the front of the saddle. Now that she was older, he had her sit in front of it until he hefted his large body onto the horse and swung one leg over. Once he was settled at the back of the leather saddle, he would wrap an arm around her middle and pull her hard against the front of his body. He did so now, and for the first time in her life, she stiffened in his hold.

The tingling at the edge of her consciousness flared as it always did when he touched her. But now that sensation was accompanied by a sense of desperation. Of a need so primal, she almost feared him.

That is, when she wasn't allowing her anger with him to dominate her thoughts. Anger and betrayal. Hate, perhaps, although the emotion was foreign to her.

Whatever had happened to cause the lochagos, mounted on a black horse that was not Augustine, to thunder up to her parent's oikos and ask—nay demand—that "Stella of Akrotiri" be made ready to join him?

Her parents had both appeared thunderstruck, as did she. But Helena recovered her wits and went about preparing Stella for her departure from the only home she had ever known.

Stella wondered at the soft sigh that seemed to emanate from Darius just then. She could feel the breath of it against her hair, the warmth spreading around her at the same time his arm provided heat at her waist. Despite the layer of fabric at her back—after her quick bath, she had pulled on a short-sleeved jacket and her most colorful skirt at Helena's insistence—she felt the heat of his body permeate her skin.

Never had she been held so close and so completely in her life. Even Helena, when she hugged her on occasion, did not press her entire body to hers.

"She will be allowed to visit?" Andros asked once Darius was settled on the saddle. His expression betrayed his worry, and perhaps his guilt at having accepted the payment Darius had offered for taking Stella nearly a full year before the original agreed upon date.

"Of course," Darius replied, annoyed the farmer thought him heartless. "My tent is but five, perhaps six thousand paces from here. Near Mesaria. My villa is near Tholos."

Assured Stella would remain on the island and could

come back to the orchard when she wished, Andros gave a short bow. A glimmer of tears showed in Helena's eyes, and Stella caught the frown her adoptive mother aimed in her husband's direction.

At least Helena shared her annoyance with her father. Did she also despise Darius as much as Stella did at this moment?

Only once before had Darius seen her dressed in a traditional Minoan skirt and short jacket, with her breasts bared. That had been the day he had accompanied her to the agora. But he had never seen her hair done in the elaborate manner favored by all the women on the island. Never seen how mature she could appear when dressed the same as the other girls her age. The girls whose skin was far lighter because they spent their days indoors working looms and dyeing fabrics or creating beautiful pottery.

Stella knew all this and more because she had never before been garbed like this, nor had her bright red hair been dressed quite like the other girls. From the brief reaction Darius displayed when her mother brought her to him, Stella thought he approved. Then his expression hardened, and he was once more the lochagos of the Minoan coastguardsmen.

"MESSARIA," Andros repeated. "It is not so far," he agreed. "Tholos is... a day's ride."

Darius nodded. From his tent's vantage atop the second highest hill on Strongili, he could scan the horizon to the east and the west, watching for the ships that brought goods for trade as well as those that brought trouble. His men could be counted on to defeat any marauders, as long as they, too, spotted them in time.

His villa was much farther away—at the other end of the island—but he didn't intend for him and Stella to go there just yet. He wanted her all to himself for at least a day. A day of what he had been dreaming about for over a hundred years. A day when he took an Immortal to wife, so that he might have a companion for far longer than just the twenty or thirty years a mortal wife might live.

Besides, the king had ordered that he take a wife, and he had been determined to do so before Tektamanos took his last breath.

Now that he felt the warmth of her body, his heart ached with yearning for her, as did his cock. She smelled of lemons and something floral. He pressed his nose against the crown of her head and inhaled, closing his eyes as he did so. He straightened when she turned her head sideways, sure she was about to speak. When she remained mute, he murmured, "You will not be far from them. You only need tell me you wish to see them, and I shall see to bringing you back."

Her acknowledgement was a slight nod. He wondered at her quiet manner, expecting she might say something— anything—when he appeared earlier that afternoon. A greeting, at least. Maybe the wide smile she usually afforded him on the days he found her in the olive trees.

A kiss.

But her response to his appearance had been one of hesitance, as if she didn't want her parents to know she had frequently spent bits of time in his company since he discovered she existed. As if she suddenly regretted having made his acquaintance. Regretted having shared her secrets with him.

Surely she would realize he meant her no harm. Return his warm smile. Resume her easy rapport with him.

Kiss him.

Once he made her his wife, made the promises of providing protection and shelter, pledged his troth, and kissed her, he would take her virtue. Even now, his cock was hard with anticipation within his codpiece. His loin-cloth would not hide the evidence of his erection if he had been standing.

Darius had told her nothing of his plan to make her his wife, thinking her father had seen to that detail. The betrothal had been in place for nearly six cycles, after all. So her surprise at his appearance on this cool day had unnerved him a bit before he remembered he was an entire year early in claiming her.

Hence the extra coin he had given Andros.

The farmer would have to hire someone to see to the trees in the spring, hire more than the usual number of laborers to see to the olive harvest in the fall. Perhaps he would need to hire someone to prune the trees as Stella had been doing.

Then Darius had waited patiently for Stella to pack, unaware Helena had insisted she bathe before changing her clothes. He had never seen her wearing the traditional garb of most women on Strongili. She was usually just dressed in a full, tattered skirt that allowed her to climb the olive trees with ease, a light-weight, long-sleeved tunic providing some protection against scratches from tree branches.

The jacket she wore now, its full sleeves displaying a series of decorative cut-outs to provide airflow when it was warm, was cinched tight at her waist and left open above. Her bare breasts, not yet fully developed, were round and pale but for their rosy nipples. He imagined how they might feel beneath his lips—he could feel them resting on the arm that held her—and absently lowered his lips to her red hair once more.

"Ride safe, Lochagos Darius," Andros said, interrupting his reverie.

Helena moved to stand next to the horse, and she lifted a hand to Stella's arm. "Do as he says, and do not be frightened." Her cheeks were red, as if she had stayed out in the midday sun too long, and tears threatened at the corners of her eyes.

STELLA FROWNED, not sure what was happening. But she had paid witness to the exchange of coin between Darius and her father.

She remembered her discussion with Darius about slavery. Remembered his assurance that he did not own any slaves. Her concerns over the comment about her father's debts had been put to rest.

All our debts will be paid.

But now, thoughts of slavery were again consuming her, as were thoughts that she was leaving the only home she had ever known.

To live in a tent.

"Yes, Mother," she managed, keeping her tears at bay as she clutched the satchel to the front of her body.

Before she could say anything else, Darius dug his

heels into the strange, black horse, and they were off, riding north along the western edge of the olive orchard.

Stella glanced down at the city of Akrotiri. She thought of the number of times she had made the descent on the winding path from her father's oikos to the island's largest southern city to procure foodstuffs for the pantry.

At the *agora*, she would see other girls her own age and wonder at their beauty and light skin. Wince at their apparent disapproval of her tanned skin and red hair. Feel jealousy when she overheard them tell of their upcoming appointment with the priest at the temple. She wondered why it was she had to wait until her seventeenth birthday before she might be welcomed in the temple. Then she'd had to climb back up the hill with her bags full and nearly dragging on the ground.

Except for the one time Darius had accompanied her. Put her on display as he shopped with her. As he put on a show meant only for Mina and the other girls to watch, as if he wanted to be sure they understood he approved of the red-haired girl.

Her mother would be forced to do the shopping now, although Stella hoped her father might hire a kitchen servant who could make the frequent treks to Akrotiri.

He has coin to do so now, she thought with a combination of spite and sorrow. From the size and apparent weight of the purse she had seen change hands, she was sure Darius had given her father enough coin to pay for a number of servants.

As for what her duties would be in Darius' household, she had no idea. She was about to ask when she was suddenly aware of how she was being held, of the scents of musk and horse that filled her nostrils, of Darius' labored breathing as he managed the large horse over the uneven terrain.

She glanced down at his arm, her eyes following the strange, dark patterns that colored his tanned skin. She had wondered at them in the past—thought they were painted on, perhaps for battle—but she had never seen them so close. Now she realized the markings weren't paint at all, but a dye that stained his skin.

"What do they mean?" she asked, her voice raised so it could be heard over the hoofbeats. She ran a fingertip over his forearm, tracing one of the patterns until it reached his elbow. A shiver seemed to passed beneath his skin as she did so, and she quickly pulled the finger away lest he let go his hold on her.

She wasn't sure she would be able to stay on the horse if he didn't hold her as he was doing. This beast was much larger than Augustine, but when she pressed her hand to its neck, she felt the essence of a gentle but proud animal.

A chuckle burbled up from Darius as his hold tightened on her. Stella was sure she felt his lips touch her head for at least the third time since their ride had begun. Although her mother had dressed her hair in the traditional manner, securing sections in a series of bands that started at the back of her crown and ended at her neck and then adorning it with her simple lisette, she had done so in haste.

She complained several times of not wishing to keep the lochagos waiting.

"They are the markings of a warrior," he said as he slowed the horse to a trot.

Stella angled her head so she could glance back at him.

"Have you always been a warrior?" For the last six years, they had spoken of many things, but rarely about his past.

Darius gave up his hold on her for a moment as he switched the reins. His left arm was now around her midriff, its markings entirely different from those on his right arm. "For almost my entire life," he replied, memories of his early existence on the giant land mass to the east coming back to him in waves of nearly forgotten images. "I have commanded men in many lands."

"But you live here now," she said, hoping he wasn't about to take his leave of Strongili—and her with him.

"I do. I like it here," he said, hoping she wasn't imagining a future of frequent travels to other islands. He had finally found what he hoped was a mate for life, and he had no intention of giving up his comfortable life on Strongili—an island with a rather advanced civilization—for the barbaric countries to the north and east he had once called home. Besides, war was practically unknown here. Slaves could only be kept if an owner was wealthy enough to keep them in the same manner in which he kept his own family. Those who were responsible for the trade with other lands were masters at negotiation.

Minoans were just a peaceful people employing their skills at creating beautiful fabrics and pottery and excellent wine and olive oil for trade with other countries. Builders of ships and well-crafted sailing vessels that were perfectly suited to the waters of the Mediterranean. Darius could almost imagine a life of domesticity, except he had never learned the skills that were valued here.

He had only ever known war.

Barbarism.

Death.

"Do you like it here?" he asked then, wondering at her silence. Usually their conversation came easily, although Stella was the one asking the questions, her inquisitive nature a source of amusement for him. A reminder that those who were young didn't know what had come before. She might be an Immortal, but she didn't yet know it, nor had she lived longer than the sixteen years that her young body displayed.

"I do like it," she replied, once again angling her head to regard him. "But unlike you, I have never been anywhere else."

"Trust me when I tell you this is a better place to live than most," he remarked. "Much better, in fact. The wine. The olive oil. Even grains grow better here."

Stella furrowed a brow, wondering why he would say the words, *trust me*. She had no reason not to, except that now she found she was his property. Sold to him by the man she had called father for as long as she could remember.

"This place where we are headed," Darius started to say when he spotted the top of his tent on the horizon. "It is only temporary. I ask that you not judge me based on what you think of it."

He found the large tent a comfortable respite from his sprawling villa, but he suddenly doubted Stella would see it that way. She was already used to a rural lifestyle, though. "In a few days, I will take you to my villa in Paradisos. Near Tholos. You will have your own bedchamber there, of course," he added, secretly hoping she would only use it as a place in which to dress for the day and prepare for bed at night.

Frowning, Stella wondered at his words. During a

discussion they'd had in the olive orchard just the year before, she was under the impression slaves were not always treated well by their owners. She had also understood he didn't find slavery agreeable. "Gratitude," she murmured, not sure what else she could say to his mention of her having her own bedchamber.

The barest hint of his hold tightening on her was his only response until he said, "This is my tent. We will stay here this evening and the next. Head to Paradisos after that."

Stella stared at the structure, a mixture of surprise and disappointment keeping her from saying anything in response. Made of a heavy fabric dyed in dark green, it was protected on the north and the east side by a grove of trees while open land spread out before it to the front and to the west. She wondered if water soaked the insides during the winter rains, and then decided he probably lived in his villa during the wetter season.

The sun was just beginning to set, its yellow glare slowly changing the colors in the sky above it to peaches and aquas.

Stella had to resist the urge to cry out when Darius suddenly lifted her from the saddle. Managing to bend and pull her legs together, Stella allowed him to lower her to one side of the horse until her feet touched the ground.

She clutched her satchel in front of her, as if she feared he might take her only possessions from her. Then he dismounted and led the horse to a wooden barrel filled with water. He undid the straps that held the saddle on the beast's back and easily removed it. With a flick of his wrists, he had a thick fabric unfurled and settling over the saddle, apparently to protect it from rain.

"Where is Augustine?" she asked, thinking his other horse might be nearby.

Darius straightened and finally turned his attention to her. "He lives. He enjoys the large pasture next to my villa," he replied finally. "But he is old. Too old to climb the mountains."

Stella dipped her head, wondering if she would ever again see the only other horse she had ever known. "And this one? What do you call him?"

Giving his head a shake, Darius sighed. "I was hoping you might have an appropriate name in mind," he replied.

A brow furrowing at hearing this bit of news, Stella regarded him for a moment before turning her attention to the black horse. "Is he from the same place as Augustine?"

Darius shook his head. "Not exactly. This one comes from a land not far from where Augustine was born, though. Across the large sea and to the west. Iberia." He watched as she approached the horse. Watched as one of her hands rested on the beast's withers and then on the side of his head. A pang of jealousy shot through him as she leaned the side of her head against the horse's neck and her hand slid over the black hide of his back.

"Well?" he asked, not intending for his impatience to sound in his voice.

"Arion," she announced when she finally stepped away from the beast.

The horse must have agreed, for he responded with a loud whinny and then nickered several times before returning his attention to the water.

"Arion," Darius repeated. "I like it." He hoped his

words might have Stella giving him a modicum of a smile, but her expression remained sullen.

He was sure she would be happy to join him. Happy to give up her life living in the olive trees in exchange for one where she would be the mistress of a large villa, in charge of a phalanx of servants and free to do as she pleased every day for the rest of eternity.

So what had happened to change her usual happy manner? She seemed so depressed.

He pulled back the flap on the front of the rectangular structure, its slightly slanted roof higher than he stood.

Gingerly, Stella stepped into the dark space and quickly moved aside. In the gloom of impending nightfall, she couldn't make out any details until Darius lit a candle from a central fire pit that had been banked. The golden glow of the lit flame bathed the interior in a soft light.

Her gaze flitted from the fire to a pile of cushions to a bed draped in diaphanous fabric.

Darius placed the candle on a table near the bed and then moved towards her. "Is this truly everything you own?" he asked as he reached for the satchel.

Stella reflexively tightened her hold on the fabric bag. "It is," she replied in a quiet voice. "My clothes and pigments." There were a couple of idols, as well, the small carvings of two goddesses given to her when she was ten. Helena hadn't included the lime, probably due to its weight. Stella had barely had to use any of it to finish the fresco on her bedchamber wall. The thought of never seeing it again had a sob threatening deep in her throat.

The reality of her circumstances had started setting in, and she was on the verge of panic.

"I only wish to put it in a safe place," Darius replied, wondering at her hesitance.

Reluctantly, Stella gave up her hold on the satchel and watched as Darius took it to a large box. Leather strip hinges allowed him to open it and place the satchel inside. "This is yours," he said as he indicated the trunk. "You may put whatever you like in it," he added when he noted how she still frowned at him.

Stella merely nodded before she crossed her arms over her bodice. Unaware she was shivering, she gave a start when she realized Darius was moving to rejoin her.

Noting her odd behavior—she had never before cringed in his presence—Darius said in a quiet voice, "There is no need to fear me." When he saw that she was shivering, he added, "Are you cold?" He was about to reach for her when she took a step back. He regarded her with furrowed brows. "What is it, Stella? Tell me what is wrong."

"You once told me you did not agree that people should be sold as slaves," she whispered, a tear escaping one eye.

"They should not," he affirmed. "It is one of the reasons I like these islands. There is no slavery," he said as he regarded her. "What... what is this about?"

"I hate you," she hissed, backing up another step so she was outside of the tent, her hands balling into fists. "I hate you."

24

A PUNCH IN THE GUT

The words were like a punch in his gut—*I hate you*—but the pain they caused in his head was far worse. "Stella," Darius murmured as he moved to join her, the hurt apparent in his eyes despite the fading light.

"I saw you pay my father for me." When he appeared about to respond, Stella added, "Do not deny it. I saw you give him coin," her voice rising with every word. "A heavy purse. How much did I cost?" she demanded to know, her clenched fists shoved down at her sides as her fear of him was replaced with anger.

She took several steps back, wanting to be as far from him as possible given the strange sensations warring at the edge of her consciousness.

Hurt, anger, confusion, dismay, lust and disbelief. She hardly knew which were hers and which were his.

Darius cringed, wishing she hadn't been in the room when he gave Andros the purse. "You cost me *nothing*," he replied with a shake of his head, taking another step toward her. "You are not a slave, Stella."

Her lips trembling and tears streaming down her cheeks, Stella stared at him in disbelief. "I saw you give him coin," she repeated, her chin rising in defiance even as her knees were giving out beneath her. She sunk to the ground, her knees bent in front of her as her arms wrapped around them. "I saw it," she repeated, although the words were garbled by tears and her efforts to catch her breath.

Darius finally nodded. "It is true, I did give him coin," he admitted, and then regretted his words when her tears began anew. "But not for you." Another attempt to reach out to her only had her cowering more. Not sure what to do, Darius allowed a heavy sigh and disappeared back into the tent.

25

AN EXPLANATION AND AN APOLOGY

Stella stared at the closed tent flap, stung at the thought Darius would simply leave her alone. The sun was setting, and the sky would be dark soon. Even if she knew the way back to Akrotiri—and she wasn't sure she did—she couldn't imagine walking the uneven terrain in the dark. The nights were cooler, too, and she didn't know if her mother had packed a cloak in the satchel.

A satchel that was in a trunk in the tent. She would have to go back in there to get it.

She was already shivering, despite the warmth of the air around her.

Everything had happened so fast!

One minute, she was cutting small branches from the inside of an olive tree, and the next, she was being ushered into her parent's oikos, told to bathe and to dress. *Today is an important day,* Helena had said while she folded nearly every piece of clothing Stella owned.

Which wasn't much. A few skirts, two of which were

torn from tree branches, some *chitons*, a jacket and a pair of shoes. Her only pair of sandals were on her feet.

She was wearing the only clothes Helena hadn't packed.

She thought of the wooden trunk. *This is yours*, Darius had said. Well, if she had any intention of retrieving her satchel, she had to go back into the tent.

Lifting the flap, she expected to find Darius waiting for her. The tingling in her head was still chaotic, but at least there was no anger there. No thought that he might do her harm.

When she glanced around, she discovered he wasn't in the tent. How could this be? She was sure he had made his way back into the tent.

In the dim light, she discovered another opening at the back, a flap covering it, and realized he had taken his leave by way of it. Thinking she had only a few minutes until his return, she hurried over to the box, her hands smoothing over the lacquered lid. The leather straps were tooled in an intricate swirled pattern and held in place by metal fastenings. A quick glance to her right, and she discovered a similar box.

Older and much more worn, she knew it was his, a trunk worthy of a warrior. She lifted the lid and peered inside. In the gloom, she couldn't make out most of what was in the box, but she was sure the various leather pieces were meant to be worn in battle.

Beneath those, she found a garment she recognized as one of her own. One she had worn as a youth. One that was a bit tattered and torn from when she climbed olive trees. She held it to her face and breathed in, sure she could detect the scents of home and hearth under the prevailing odors of leather and musk that permeated his trunk.

Why does he have my skirt? she wondered as her fingers separated the folds of several other garments in the trunk. They were mostly loin cloths and *chitons* made from rough spun wool and linen. Although some were brightly dyed in the familiar manner of Minoans, most were not.

Her gaze went to the other items in the tent. A wooden table on which there were several urns. Leather shoes beneath a wooden bench. The colorful cushions piled to one side of the fire.

The bed.

She pushed aside the fabric curtain, marveling at how finely woven it felt in her hands. The covering, dyed a deep purple, was unlike anything she had felt before. Soft as a hare's fur, but its pile very short, the fabric displayed the sweep of her small hand as if in shadow. She quickly pushed her hand back in the other direction, hoping to erase the evidence of her having touched it. As if by magic, the pile was once again restored and showed no evidence of her hand.

Several pillows were arranged at the head of the bed, each one covered in a different dyed fabric. She thought of the pillow on her own bed, its covering threadbare and its stuffing of feathers having been flattened from years of use. These appeared as if they had never been used.

Of course the lochagos would have items of luxury, she thought then. He was a man of importance. He probably had great wealth. The fact that he had given her father gold coins was a testament to it.

But not for you, he had said.

Stella wondered at the words, her gaze once again going to her old skirt.

She wanted a return to the kind of easy manner she had enjoyed with Darius since the day she had first spotted him in the olive grove. She wanted to speak with him the same way she had become accustomed to over the years. As if he were a friend, and not some marauder—a slave owner—come to steal her away in the night.

She wanted to go home. She wanted things to be the way they had been her whole life. But she also wanted answers, and she knew they wouldn't be found in the torn fabric of a skirt she could no longer wear.

The tingle she felt when he was nearby was still at the edge of her consciousness. *He couldn't have gone far,* she thought as she closed his trunk and rose to her feet.

About to make her way out of the tent through the same flap in which she had come into it, she nearly fell over him. Darius was sitting in front of the entrance, his knees pulled up and his thick arms wrapped around them.

"Apologies," she said as she struggled to regain her balance, her hands coming to rest on his bare shoulders. The simple touch had a frisson shooting up her arm, had her gasping in shock. A memory of how he had felt the first time she had ever touched his bare skin flitted through her mind.

An old soul, she remembered thinking. Weary with age, but determined to remain living, as if he thought the future might offer him a better life than the one he had been living. Old in spirit, as if the life of constant warfare was no longer providing the excitement—the sense of purpose—it once did.

And at this moment?

Sorrow. Sadness.

Loss?

One of his hands moved to cover hers before she could pull it from his shoulder, and the sensations were magnified. As was the tingle that seemed to surround him. A pleasant tingle that she used to equate with the trees she pruned and the olives she harvested. The horse he used to ride when he first came upon her that day in the olive grove.

"Why are you sad?" she whispered.

He allowed a sound much like a grunt as Stella lowered herself to the ground next to him. He held onto her hand though, his thumb on the back of her knuckles and his large fingers wrapped around her palm.

A shiver shot through her entire body as he lifted it to his lips and brushed a kiss over the back of her fingers. About to jerk her hand away—the shock of the intimate touch might have been a lightning strike, except this one resulted in immense pleasure rather than the pain of a burn. She let him continue to hold onto her hand even after she had settled herself next to him.

"I didn't want it to be like this," he murmured, in answer to her query. "I want us to be... to be like we have been."

Stella wondered if he could read her mind and turned to regard him. "As do I," she replied.

He inhaled then, and let out a long breath, once again kissing the back of the hand he held.

They sat in silence for a moment, their gazes on the western sky. The last rays of the sun had disappeared beneath the water, leaving streaks of purple and gold in their wake.

Darius reached an arm behind Stella's back, heartened when her head dropped into the small of his shoulder. "I have come to suspect you were not told of this day," he murmured in a quiet voice.

Of this day.

Stella closed her eyes and cursed her father. No wonder her mother had known exactly what to do, what with packing her satchel and dressing her. She had known Darius would eventually come for her.

"As have I," Stella replied on a sigh. "Is my father to blame for that?"

Allowing a shrug, Darius finally turned his attention to her. "I had thought he would have informed you long ago. I made the arrangement to take you to wife five summers ago," he explained.

Startled at hearing this bit of news, Stella straightened in his hold and regarded Darius for a moment. "Wife?" she repeated, staring at him in shock. "Not..." She was about to say 'slave' but remembered his parting words. *You are not a slave, Stella.* "Helena did not say a word of it, either," she murmured, feeling ever so betrayed by her parents. Had she known the lochagos would one day come for her, she certainly wouldn't have behaved as she did. She would have been more welcoming. Ready for his arrival.

Anxious for it, in fact.

"You must think me a spoilt child," she murmured.

Darius swallowed. Hard. He had assumed that by now, Stella would have been told of the arrangements he had made. Assumed she knew she was to one day be his wife. Assumed she knew what to expect in a marriage bed.

Especially after his discussion with Andros.

Now he had the unenviable task of explaining what he would be doing to her before this night ended, especially since he had made sure the priest wouldn't lay claim to her.

He had a brief thought that perhaps he should have allowed the priest to have her first, but he quickly shoved the thought aside. For the rest of his days, he would have regretted that decision. "I have waited a long time for you," he said in a whisper, his words reinforced with how he hugged her tighter. "Longer even than you have been alive."

Furrowing a brow at this, Stella was about to put voice to a protest—how could he make such a claim?—but one of Darius' fingers pressed against her lips. "One day I will tell you everything. I will tell you of my past and the other lives I have lived before this one. But not on this night. Tonight I wish to pledge my troth to you. Pledge my fidelity, as well."

Stella stared at him for a long time. How many days had she hoped to find him seeking her company in the olive orchard? How many nights had she imagined him doing exactly as he was doing this moment? Holding her against his body as if he truly cared for her? And not because she was a child in need of consolation? A young girl in need of reassurance? A young woman in need of a friend?

She finally allowed a nod. "Then I pledge my troth to you," she said. "And my fidelity." She sounded out the word, not sure of its meaning.

Dipping his head, Darius said, "It means you will not share a bed—or your body—with any other man but me."

Frowning, she gave her head a shake. "I wouldn't want

to," she argued, following her comment with a sound of disgust. She wasn't sure she wanted to share a bed with Darius, except that she knew she would welcome the warmth of his body on nights such as this. There was now a decided chill in the air.

He struggled to maintain an impassive expression and said, "I take you as my wife."

Stella blinked. "I take you as my..." She stopped, not sure what she was supposed to say. "Man?"

"Husband, but that works, too," he replied with a wan grin. From the ground next to his knee, he picked up a jeweled bracelet and slid it over her hand, gratified when he saw how her eyes widened in delight. Before she could say anything, his lips were on hers. They barely touched at first—much like they did when they greeted one another —but after a moment of testing and teasing, his finally took possession.

Stella understood what to do—she had only ever been kissed like this once before, when his lips opened for hers when they were in the orchard. But when she felt the tip of his tongue against her teeth, she nearly recoiled.

Sensing she was about to pull away, Darius ended the kiss but left his forehead pressed against hers. "Apologies. I should not have tried that so soon," he murmured.

"It was... it was just unexpected," she whispered, disappointed she ruined the quiet moment. "Perhaps we can try again—"

"It is getting colder. Let us go inside," he said. Despite his apparent age—he looked upwards of forty winters–he easily rose to his feet, holding onto her the entire time. When he was about to go through the opening in the tent, he lifted her into his arms. Ignoring her sounds of protest, he passed into the tent and then deposited her back onto her feet before turning to close and tie up the tent flap.

"Why did you do that?" she asked, a bit unsteady on her feet once he set her down.

"So you would not run away," he replied with a smirk.

"But... I was not going to," she countered, her brows furrowed in confusion.

"Then you know what happens in a marriage bed?"

Her cheeks blushed a bright red, and Darius angled his head. "Did Helena explain it to you?"

Stella shook her head. "I watched it happen once. When I was up in a tree," she whispered.

Frowning, Darius tried to imagine how that might be possible when he realized some amorous couple had probably decided to enjoy a fuck under the shade of an olive tree.

"And again when one of the priestesses in the temple at Akrotiri..." Stella paused and swallowed. "Ordered a man to... to worship her body on the altar."

Darius arched a brow, rather glad he had avoided going into the temples on Strongili as long as he had. "I suppose he did so willingly," he commented.

Stella's eyes darted to one side. "I think he was honored," she replied in a whisper, remembering that she was due to pay a visit to the temple for her own initiation.

She was of the age to have her virtue claimed by a priest. Helena had said she would go on the eve of her sixteenth year, but then she said later it would be on the eve of her seventeenth year.

What had happened to have the priest push back the time? Did he somehow know her monthly courses had not yet begun?

Attempting to hide his amusement, Darius regarded her for a moment before asking, "Does it frighten you? What a man does with a woman?"

Her eyes darting sideways, Stella finally shook her head. "No. Not really." She took a breath. "Maybe. But I have not yet been to the temple. I am expected by the priest. He will see to my first claiming."

Another moment, and Darius was sure she would weep again. "You will not be giving your virtue to a priest," he said with a shake of his head.

Stella blinked, her thoughts going between anger and relief. Every young woman on Strongili was betrothed to a priest until a marriage to someone else was arranged. Only priests were allowed to bed the virgins of the island. "I will not? But—"

"I have seen to it you are excused from the ritual," he said, not adding how much he had paid in the offering to see to it Stella wouldn't be expected at the temple on the eve of her sixteenth birthday.

"Excused?" she repeated in alarm.

"Is there another word I should use?" he asked, his brows furrowed in confusion.

"No one is exempted," she argued. Then her eyes widened in horror. "Except for foreigners. And slaves."

Darius nearly cursed out loud. He hadn't known of the island's customs with respect to young girls until just a couple of years earlier, when one of his coastguardsmen was bragging about how his daughter was to have her time with a priest in the temple. *Then she will be married to a tradesman in Akrotiri and no longer any of my concern*, he had said.

When Darius asked what might happen in the temple,

the fellow coastguardsman merely shrugged. *It is none of my concern.*

Darius could hardly believe the man's comment. Did he have no regard for his own daughter? No regard for how she would be treated by a priest who would no doubt see only to his own pleasure and leave the girl bloodied and bereft? Such a ritual wasn't practiced on Creta. There were only priestesses in the temples there.

Perhaps the inability to father a child had made him more conscious of what happened to those too young to defend themselves.

More protective.

So when he was next in Akrotiri, Darius had paid a visit to the temple and asked how much it would cost to exempt a young woman from the priest's bed. He paid the amount in gold coins by placing them on the altar. He had been left with the impression that if he hadn't held the position he did, he wouldn't have been granted Stella's virtue. Because she had red hair, his cost to secure her protection was probably double compared that of a typical dark-haired Minoan female.

Or maybe it was only half. Her red hair seemed to cause some to revile her while others were obviously attracted to it. He never had a sense of the priest's take on Stella, other than the story he had told of the large bird that had delivered her to the island.

Clearly the priest regarded her as a foreigner.

As did the young women who had held her in such contempt that day at the agora.

In order to ensure she wouldn't have to undergo the ritual by the cock of a man old enough to be her father, Darius moved up his plan to take her as his wife. Instead of waiting another year as he had originally arranged with her father, he decided to wed her two days before her sixteenth birthday—or at least the date her adoptive parents had determined was to be her sixteenth birthday.

Darius gave his head a quick shake when he remembered some might consider him old enough to be Stella's grandfather.

"You are not my slave, Stella," he whispered. "But it is true I paid the priest so you would not be expected at the temple on the morrow."

Stella's eyes widened. Her gaze darted in the direction of Akrotiri before she finally allowed a long sigh. "Gratitude." She said the word without wondering if she really should be grateful to him. To be in service to the priest—if only for an afternoon—was supposed to be one of the highlights of a young woman's life in Akrotiri. An honor. Assurance she might be blessed with a man's child after their first coupling. "But I cannot help but believe that I am your slave."

Darius shook his head, his brows furrowed. "Why would you think such a thing when I have given my word that you are not?"

"Because you have spent coin on me," she replied quickly. "Much coin, it would seem, when a dowry was not provided to you." She held out the arm that was now adorned with a gold bracelet. Colorful gemstones in purple and blues were set in small clusters all the way around the band.

Allowing a grunt, Darius regarded her a moment. The girl could be stubborn, although he found he wasn't bothered by it at the moment. "Even if it had cost me all that I had—and it did not—it would have been worth it to keep you safe from that priest," he said firmly. "As for the bracelet, it is merely the first of many gifts I intend to bestow on you."

Stella recoiled at hearing his initial words.

For the first time in her life, she wondered what the priest would have done to her. Taken her virtue, certainly, but would there have been more to the ceremony?

Although Stella was acquainted with a few girls her own age—she would speak with those who didn't openly shun her because of the color of her hair—none of them were old enough to have been summoned by the priest. No one shared what they knew of the ceremony. And no one seemed to think anything sinister happened in the temple.

"Then even if I am not your slave, it would seem I am still indebted to you," she argued.

Darius inhaled slowly, realizing there would be many arguments in their future. His betrothed was capable of reasoning. She possessed the ability to use logic. She might vex him to distraction.

And yet he found he couldn't help the grin that lifted his lips. "I believe I shall enjoy spending the rest of my life with you as my wife," he whispered.

About to reply that she might feel the same way about him, Stella was prevented from saying anything when his lips covered hers.

26

FIRST NIGHT

The rest of his life.

Stella's brows furrowed. On the one hand, she had to wonder how much longer that might be—he didn't look as if he might die in the immediate future. But on the other, she knew he was far older than he appeared.

Six-hundred years.

At least, that's what she felt in the tingle that was present at the edge of her consciousness, a sensation she had come to realize she would miss if it ever disappeared.

Stronger than the one she experienced when climbing the oldest olive trees, or the one she felt when she rode Augustine, Darius' tingle changed when she was in his presence. Sometimes vibrant and pulsating, sometimes calm and quiet, it seemed to call to her to pay attention. To notice its existence. To demand she acknowledge it and embrace it. When she did, she wondered if Darius was as aware of her as she was of him.

There had been times in the past she climbed an ancient olive tree or touched an animal, like a donkey, just to feel a kinship—a sort of connectedness—to something. When in the presence of Darius, she had no desire to seek out a tree or spend time with a beast of burden. She was satisfied simply to be near him.

She never felt a kinship with her parents. Once she had learned she was a foundling, she understood why.

So why did she feel such a connection to Darius? From the moment she was aware of him, she knew they were somehow similar. Despite their age difference, they seemed to share a common knowledge others around them did not.

Which had her once again curious about his age, especially at hearing his comment about spending the rest of his life with her.

How much longer might Darius live? And would she grow old while he continued to look as he did this moment?

Remembering the day she first saw him, deep in conversation with her father, she thought he looked exactly the same back then as he did on this day. His face was not lined with deeper wrinkles, nor had his hair grayed with age.

"The rest of your life?" she repeated, once he finally pulled away from the kiss and regarded her with hooded eyes.

Darius gave a start, and she noticed how one of his brows furrowed. "Yes," he replied.

"How long might that be?"

He allowed a chuckle, his face brightening with his mirth. Stella's eyes widened at seeing how he seemed to youthen. "Why are you laughing?"

Darius sobered and took in a slow breath. "I have no

idea," he said with a shake of his head. "That is to say, I have no idea how long I should expect to live."

Stella leaned away from him a moment.

"Do you think you will live forever?"

Giving a start, Darius regarded her a moment before asking, "Forever? Why would you think such a thing?"

Allowing a shrug, Stella said, "Because…" She reached out and placed a hand on his forearm, which sent frissons through them both. She held on despite how his arm jerked beneath her fingers. "I feel it when I touch you. I always have."

Darius blinked. Never having touched another Immortal besides Stella, he had been unaware of the possible sensations.

When she was younger, those tingles were merely pleasant—a brightening sensation at the edge of his consciousness. Now they were harbingers of pleasures far more carnal in nature. His cock, already excited at the prospect of intercourse, hardened even more. "I feel it, too," he murmured. "Not that I could live forever, of course, but you have the right of it. I have been alive a long time." When Stella moved her hand farther up his arm, so her fingers wrapped around the bulge of his triceps, he lowered his lips to hers. His touch was light, tentative, until Stella slid her hand up to his shoulder and over the fabric of his chiton.

Bereft at the loss of her touch on his skin, Darius wrapped an arm around her back and pulled her hard against his body even as he deepened the kiss.

Her slight moan had him finally pulling away. There was a more comfortable place where they could continue.

On the bed he had transported from Creta for this very night.

Their marriage bed.

He gathered her into his arms and held her a moment. "I will do everything in my power to see to it you are thoroughly pleasured before I take your virtue," he said as he once again dropped his forehead to hers.

Stella couldn't help the shiver of anticipation that shot up her spine. "Pleasured?" she repeated.

He nodded. "That is the point of making love," he replied with a grin, before kissing the inside of one of her wrists.

Sucking in a breath at the darts of pleasure shooting up her arm, Stella furrowed a brow. "I thought it was to make a baby."

Darius sobered. "That too, of course." Despite having had wives in the past, none of them had given him a child. His first wife, a young woman from a tribe near his homeland, had never conceived, but then she had also died before reaching her twenty-third season. His second wife, the youngest daughter of an army general, had lived far longer, but again did not bear him any children. When his third wife had not conceived after two years, he had come to realize he could not father a child.

Employing a surrogate had been tricky. A combination of a blindfold on her and a mask on a nomadic man who had fathered a number of children finally resulted in a son who they raised as their own.

He had never told his third wife of the deceit, nor did he make such arrangements ever again. Seeing his woman beneath another man had nearly proved his undoing. The desire to see the man dead had him banishing the nomad from their village for the rest of his life.

"You do not wish me to bear children?" Stella asked in a soft voice.

Pulled from his reverie, Darius gave his head a quick shake. "I want you to, of course. If you can. But I admit to fear of what can happen to you in the childbed." He had known far too many women who had died giving birth to heirs and daughters.

Could Stella even conceive a child?

"Have your monthly courses begun?" he asked as he reached down to undo the fastening of her jacket. Their bodies were so close, there was barely room for his fingers to work.

Stella's eyes widened for a quick moment before she directed them to the floor. "They have not." After a moment, she added, "If I am unable to conceive, will you then take a concubine to your bed?"

Sensing the hint of sadness in her voice, he lifted her chin with a finger. "I will not. Even if you never bear a child, I will still honor my vow of fidelity to you," he said as he removed the jacket from her arms. The backs of his knuckles brushed against the sides of her breasts as he did so, and he reveled in how her nipples puckered in response.

Stella stared at him for several seconds before she finally nodded. "I am honored," she murmured, one of her hands smoothing over the skin of his bare chest until it joined the other one at his belt. Her deft fingers undid the fastening, and the loincloth fell to the floor once it finally cleared the codpiece beneath.

Darius searched for the means to undo her skirt, its

tight fit at her waist hiding the button that held it secure. Once he pushed it through its slit, the band at the top loosened, and the skirt slid down her legs to form a colorful puddle around her feet. Naked but for the gold bands worn about her upper arms and the earrings that decorated her lobes, he thought her more beautiful than the depictions of the goddess of fertility that graced so many oikoi.

One of his hands cupped a breast, barely touching the nipple as he did so. He felt her body tremble as he slid an arm around her back to help keep her upright.

"I wish to spend the entire night learning every detail of your body," he whispered, just before he captured her lips with his own.

Stella had thought to answer that she would allow it, but she knew he wasn't asking permission. Instead, she concentrated on what his lips were doing to hers, on the sensation his tongue created when it delved into her mouth and touched her tongue and teeth, and finally on what his hands were doing as they grazed down her sides and cupped the globes of her bottom.

At this, she jerked in his hold, and he ended the kiss.

"May I do the same to you?" she whispered.

Darius blinked. "The same?" he repeated, not sure of her meaning. The tingle at the edge of his brain had flared into an intensely pleasurable sensation, and he wanted it to go on as long as possible.

"I wish to spend the entire night learning every detail of your body," she said, her words breathy.

Her own hands had been smoothing over his body, feeling the warmth of his skin. With their bodies so close, the codpiece was pressing into her belly. Her hands searched for the means to remove it, finally undoing the ties that held it in place. Unwrapping them from around his waist, she thought to simply pull the offending garment from his body when his hand stilled hers.

"Perhaps you can do that on the morrow," he murmured as he pulled the codpiece from his cock and tossed it onto the pile of clothes at their feet.

"Why do you cover it?" she asked, her attention on his erect manhood. She had seen cocks depicted in the statues that graced the squares in Akrotiri, but never were they as large as what was now pressing into her soft belly. She could feel his pulse through it, her own quickened heartbeat matching it.

"Protection," he murmured, the word sounding strangled. His eyes closed when one of her fingers touched the tip of it. A bead of moisture had already formed there, and she drew it down a bit before glancing up at him.

"Does that hurt?" she asked, noting how the cords in his neck seemed to strain against the skin covering them.

"Quite the opposite," he replied, one of his hands moving to cover hers. "I think it is time I took you to our bed."

Stella glanced over to the curtained bed. "*Our* bed?" she repeated. Even before she could make her way there, Darius lifted her into his arms and carried her the four steps to the edge of it.

"I am not going to run away," she protested, although she had given it half a thought a few moments ago. When he was stripping her bare. When his body was pressed against hers and she felt trapped. When his cock pressed into her belly.

Darius grinned as he used her body to push aside the

fine fabric. "Promise?" he countered. He set her down on the plush covering, but Stella quickly pulled her knees up to her chest and wrapped her arms around them. "What is it?" he asked.

Stella inhaled. "It is far too fine a covering to lie upon," she protested. "It must have cost a fortune!"

Frowning, Darius moved past her to yank the covering from the bed linens and the hides beneath, sending several pillows over the edge in his haste. "I thought you would like it."

"I do like it. Very much," she said as she scrambled beneath the linens. "Wait," she added, just before he was going to pull the entire velvet covering from the bed.

Darius regarded her with impatience as she used a hand to smooth the evidence of her bottom and feet from the soft pile. "I am not waiting another moment," he warned as he folded the covering back and then climbed onto the bed. "If we ruin it, I can always buy you another."

Stella's eyes widened. Her earlier thoughts were true. He had to be wealthy if he could simply buy another covering as fine as what he had folded back on the bed. "Gratitude," she said as she watched him, trying not to notice how his erection bobbed about in front of him. For just a moment, she thought it a weapon, clearly aimed in her direction and poised to impale her at any moment.

Darius regarded her with a quirked brow. "For what?"

She allowed a sigh. "For the covering. For the trunk. For... For taking me to wife."

Darius allowed a nod. "Gratitude for not running away."

Before she could respond, his lips covered hers once

more. As did one of his hands, smoothing over her suddenly heated skin and sending shock waves in its wake.

No one had ever touched her like this. She hadn't imagined being touched like this. Even in her daydreams, she hadn't imagined what it might be like to have his body so close, his hand cupping her breasts just before his lips moved to suckle her nipples.

She knew she was holding her breath, partly in anticipation and partly because she couldn't help herself. So she wondered if his next touch was a deliberate move to get her to suck in a breath. His hand moved between her thighs and pushed them apart, forcing one of her legs to bend at the knee. The flat of his hand was suddenly covering her most private place, the heel of it pressed into her mons as his fingers pressed against the swollen flesh surrounding her womanhood. At the same moment she wanted to push his hand away, his lips covered hers, and darts of pleasure shot through her body as the smooth skin of his chest rubbed over her nipples. Then the pleasure changed as a finger rubbed somewhere between her thighs, circling and teasing her entire body into a frenzy of sharp darts and rolling waves.

He must have known exactly when one of those waves crested, for he was no longer lying along her side. He loomed over her. Even before she knew quite what was happening, he pressed his finger harder against her womanhood, and her entire body seemed to break apart into tiny pieces.

That he had waited until that very moment to drive his weapon into her was a testament to his experience with virgins. Stella barely felt his cock enter her. It there was pain, he had seen to it there was pleasure to counter it, until that wave of pleasure had passed and all that was left was the feeling of fullness. Of being on the edge of bursting.

Her eyes widened when she realized what he had done. She watched as his body hovered over her, his arms straining with effort to hold himself still. His eyes were closed, but his face displayed an expression of ecstasy crossed with pain.

She was about to ask what she should do. Hold on, certainly. She moved her hands to grip his sides. Then she remembered what she had seen the other women do when they were impaled by a man's cock. She bent her knees and lifted them slightly, which had Darius sucking in a breath.

"Gratitude," he whispered as his cock drove further into her body.

Stella felt the change, inhaled sharply when she realized he was as far into her body as he could go. The hilt of his weapon rested on her swollen quim, pressing hard. She whimpered, hoping he would either move, or stay, or kiss her. She wasn't sure what she wanted.

And then he did move. Or attempted to pull out of her. Only a few inches, but Stella sensed he was about to leave her body entirely, and she clenched on him in an attempt to stop his retreat.

His groan was followed by a chuckle. "I will not last long on this night," he whispered. He thrust into her, thrilling at how she gripped him with not only her body but with her hands and her knees. The soft whimper had him doing it again and again. But on his fifth thrust, his entire body seized.

He thought of everything he had planned for that evening, the quiet moments he had thought to simply hold her and tell her of what they would do on this night. Of the dinner they would share. Of the jar of wine they would drink in a toast to their joining. But darkness took him before he could tell her of any of it, and his body collapsed atop hers.

27

AFTERMATH

Stella watched as Darius' face changed, watched as his body stiffened and his back arched and his breath ceased immediately after he emitted a guttural moan. The wash of warmth that filled her lower body was entirely unexpected, but even more surprising was when Darius simply fell onto her, his head ending up on the pillow next to her head.

She had a moment of panic when she thought he might have died, but then she felt the pounding of his heartbeat against her breast. Her own heartbeat was evident in her ears, nearly drowning out the sounds of his labored breathing.

Taking an experimental breath of her own, Stella was gratified to learn she could. Despite the weight of his body atop hers, the soft mattress provided a cushion of comfort.

The reminder of the bed beneath her had her hoping she might be welcome to remain on it for the rest of the night. Given Darius' large body, she thought he might request that she move to a pallet on the floor, although she hadn't remembered seeing one.

Our bed.

The words came unbidden, but the reminder had her mind quieting. Had her concentrating on the pleasant tingle that seemed to suffuse not only her mind, but her entire body.

How often might Darius wish to bed her like this? To pleasure her until she could barely breathe and then join with her so that he might experience his own pleasure? For surely that was what had happened just before he collapsed onto her. She could feel his ecstasy in her head, as if she had experienced the same. She had, moments before, although the sensations were quite different. Sharp and intense and quick instead of slow and rolling and all-consuming.

Which of those sensations had been hers?

Which had been his?

Stella allowed her thoughts to calm at the same time her breathing did. Perhaps she would dream of this night, and understand better what had happened so she could ensure it happened again.

Ready to simply close her eyes and allow sleep to take her, she was surprised when one of Darius' hands moved to the back of one of her thighs. Her body was suddenly lifted atop his as he rolled onto his back. Despite the move, his cock was still firmly inside her as her legs strad- dled his body.

"Apologies," he murmured in response to her cry of surprise. "I was afraid you might suffocate."

She stared down at him, barely recognizing him in the dim light. His face no longer appeared strained, nor did the muscles of his neck and shoulders. He looked years younger, an expression of contentment having replaced the one of intensity and concentration he had displayed only moments ago, just before he froze and then fell onto her. "Are you well?" she asked, her hands pushing into the mattress in an attempt to lift herself up from where she had been pressed onto his torso. One of his hands moved to her back and pulled her torso back down onto him.

"I am. More than I have been in a very long time." He wrapped his other arm around her back and simply held her for a moment. "And you? I tried not to, but did I hurt you?"

Stella settled the side of her face onto his shoulder. "I... I do not think so," she replied. His cock had filled her near to bursting, but at no point had she felt pain, exactly. She could still feel him inside her, although the sensation of being stretched had subsided, as had the wash of warmth that signaled the end of his thrusts into her.

"The next time will be better," he murmured.

Stella gave a start and lifted her head from his shoulder. "Better?" she repeated. "How is that possible?"

A chuckle erupted from Darius, vibrating through his body and causing hers to bounce atop him. "Because you will not be frightened, and because I will not be in such a hurry to take my pleasure," he whispered. "By the gods, I have missed this."

Stella wondered at his words. "Why is it you will not be in a hurry?" she asked.

Darius allowed a long sigh. "I tried not to be tonight," he replied. "But I fear my body betrayed me. It has been a long time since I had a woman in my bed." When he noted her look of consternation, he added, "A long time since my last wife died."

Furrowing a brow, Stella regarded him with surprise. "You have been a husband before?" Her eyes widened when she remembered how old she had thought he was when she first touched him. "How many times?"

Darius sobered. He supposed now was as good a time as any to tell her some of his past. "Three." He tightened his hold on her when he sensed she was about to pull her body from his. "Remember, I am *old*," he added, recalling how fascinated she had been when she had first touched him all those years ago. Back when she was but a young girl, and he was merely a curiosity who had invaded her olive orchard atop his noble horse.

At this reminder, Stella relaxed back onto his body. "Will you outlive me, as you did your other wives?"

"I will not," he replied, almost before she could finish her query. He hadn't expected they would speak of such serious matters on this night, but perhaps it was best he assuage any fears she might have of their future.

"You will leave me a widow?"

Darius blinked. "No," he answered. "At least, I have no intention of doing so." It was far too soon to be explaining immortality to her. To tell her of how he would see to arranging her first death once she was closer in physical age to him. Arranging it so she would stay that same age for the rest of time, no matter how many times she might die from the hand of a murderer or the whims of nature. "Will you let me hold you as we sleep?" he asked.

Stella stared at him, his query completely unexpected. "Of course," she replied. "Just let me know when I must move to the floor."

Another chuckle erupted from Darius, which had Stella attempting to angle her head so that she might determine what had him so amused. Before she could ask, he said, "If one of us must move to the floor, it will be me. I have no intention of allowing you to sleep there. Remember, I told you this was *our* bed." He was silent for a moment and then suddenly tightened his hold on her and asked, "Why would you think it necessary to move to the floor?"

Embarrassed, Stella thought to pretend she was asleep, but when she felt him lift his head from the mattress, she said, "Helena moves to the floor when my father is finished with her," she whispered. For a moment, not a sound could be heard in the tent. Then she felt Darius settle back into the mattress.

"Your father is a fool to treat his woman in such a way," he murmured.

Stella turned over in his hold so she faced him. "My father snores, which causes the bed to shake. Helena prefers the floor."

The bed once again shook with his chuckle. "I will be sure not to snore," he whispered, just before he kissed her on the nose. He closed his eyes and was asleep before Stella could turn over again.

Wondering if every night might be like this one, Stella decided she wouldn't mind the marriage bed. She would always know what was expected of her.

Not having considered a life outside of her work in an olive orchard, she found she was more concerned with how she would be spending her days as a wife.

28

MARAUDERS

The following morning

Awakening with a start, Stella wondered at the heaviness that had her pinned to a pallet far more comfortable than the one she was used to sleeping on. Warmth seeped into her back from something solid but alive. Another moment, and the events from the day before filled her consciousness. Caught between feeling relief at remembering where she was—and with whom—and missing what she found familiar, she knew she needed to pee.

Attempting to leave the bed, she soon discovered Darius' arm would not allow her an easy exit. Carefully maneuvering and lifting the bedcovers finally gave her a way to slide out of the bed. She was about to exit the tent when she was reminded of her nakedness.

Pausing to pull on the skirt she had worn the day before, she untied the tent flap and emerged into the early morning light to find Arion grazing nearby. She paused to slide a palm down his neck as he nickered softly before she moved to the trees behind the tent. She discovered a latrine, and decided she shouldn't have been surprised the lochagos would have such a structure built, especially given his tent seemed to have been here a long time.

Once she had relieved herself, she was arranging her skirt while on her way back to the front of the tent when she sensed she wasn't alone.

"Hello," she managed to get out before she realized those who stood before her were not citizens of Strongili. Her attempt at escape was thwarted when a beefy arm wrapped around her middle and lifted her so her feet flailed about. Her attempt at crying out was stifled when a large hand covered her mouth. And any thoughts of escape left her head when the tip of a dagger touched her cheek.

DARIUS OPENED his eyes at the sound of Stella's single word of greeting. He briefly wondered if she was talking to his horse. Shifting feet and a stifled gasp had him on full alert, though. He was off the bed and out of the tent before he could think to dress or grab his sword. Rising to his full height, he knew three things all at once.

Someone on patrol had either fallen asleep on the job or been overwhelmed by marauders.

Stella had managed to remove herself from the bed, despite how tightly he had been holding her to his body whilst they slept.

And he really regretted not having his sword at his side.

Three men, their skin dark with the sun and garbed in leather armor, stood in a semi-circle outside the entrance to his tent. The one to his left held Stella around her waist, apparently enjoying the fact that her bare breasts were brushing against his arm as he held a hand over her mouth. His shield lay on the ground, obviously tossed there when he needed both hands to hang onto Stella. The other two, both wielding swords, tall shields, and expressions of amusement, watched him as he came to a halt and straightened, naked, his morning tumescence on full display.

"Let me go," Stella demanded as she continued to writhe about, once she had pulled her face from her captor's hold. Darius thought she had probably bit the man's hand.

From the foreigner's single command, "Be still, whore," Darius realized the men were from the lands to the east. Not Assyria, but somewhere near there. Or perhaps they were from Hyskos.

DESPITE THE MAN'S strange language—at least foreign to Stella's ears—she stopped fighting his hold and lowered her feet to the ground. Her pulse pounded in her ears, and she thought she might faint. The odor surrounding her suggested the man hadn't bathed in a very long time.

Having a hard time catching her breath, she felt bile at the back of her throat and thought she might be sick.

Through it all, though, she was aware of the tingle at the edge of her consciousness. A tingle that now spread and promised safety. A sense of calm settled over her when she noted the expression on her husband's face. Saw how he stood, fists clenching and unclenching, his knees slightly bent as if he was preparing to move when an opening presented itself.

. . .

"YOU WILL RELEASE HER," Darius said in the language he deemed closest to the one they spoke.

"I think not," her captor replied with an evil grin. He pinched a lock of her hair between his thumb and forefinger. "Red-headed whores always bring much coin at the slave market."

Darius bristled, and for a moment he was glad Stella couldn't understand their language. "Release her, or you will die," he stated. Then a flicker of recognition had him thinking he had seen the man before.

The tallest one, who stood opposite Darius, allowed a huge grin, spreading his arms wide while he asked, "By what sword?"

At that very moment, a flaming arrow arced through the sky to the east, capturing the attentions of the marauders. Darius took the brief opportunity to duck sideways and sweep a foot against the nearest invader's leg.

Dislodged from beneath him, the leg's kick straight out from his body sent the man stumbling backwards. He landed hard on the ground, and as he did so, Darius helped himself to his sword. He plunged it into the invader's neck and quickly pulled it out at the very moment the leader lunged into action.

Aware the man holding Stella was moving backwards, Darius dared a glance in her direction before he met his attacker's first move. Stopping the sideways slice of his sword with his newly acquired weapon, Darius winced at the ineffectiveness of his counter move. Although the weapon was poorly balanced—the sword's slightly curved blade was thicker toward the end—Darius managed to adjust his hold on the hilt to compensate and he took another swing.

The leader jumped back, apparently surprised at the agility Darius displayed. "Your moves defy your age, old man," he said before beginning an attack.

Darius easily countered the man's moves, glad that he had only this man to fight and not all three at once. The one holding Stella seemed content to simply watch from where he was, although he was slowly making his way backwards.

Determined to see to the remaining invaders' deaths, Darius worried the one holding Stella would escape down the hillside—with or without her. Darius moved in that direction, deciding he wanted to get clear of the tent at his back. Get farther away from where Arion was tethered to a tree.

His sideways move worked. The taller man was forced to step laterally as Darius continued swinging his borrowed sword in downward arcs—a disadvantage for a taller opponent. The wide arcs used against Darius required him to counter the blows with his sword higher than usual, but it meant he could continue to move to his left.

When the taller opponent tripped, Darius found an opening and sliced the man across one forearm. Annoyed, the invader lunged at Darius, who stepped aside and brought down his blade onto the man's shoulder.

The sound of flesh tearing and bone crunching preceded the leader's howl of pain and anger. He moved back several steps, each one more unsteady than the one before it. He gave a nod to the one holding Stella before he went down on one knee and finally toppled over.

But Darius' attention was on the last man. He held a dagger at Stella's throat. For a fraction of a second, Darius forgot she was an Immortal. That even if she died, she would come back to life, although she would forever remain a young woman of only sixteen. Darius wasn't close enough to strike down the man, but if he threw down the sword, he might be able to prevent Stella's death.

He was about to do just that when the unmistakeable *whoosh* of an arrow was followed by the man's grunt of pain and widened eyes. Stella jerked free of his hold, stumbling as she hurried toward Darius.

Her captor toppled forward, an arrow in the middle of his back. Right behind him stood Glaukos, his bow already reloaded and aimed at the downed leader. The man had gone limp and was sprawled on the ground, though, the wound from his shoulder having bled profusely.

"Gratitude," Darius managed as Stella ran into him. He could feel her entire body trembling as he wrapped his arms around her, using her body as much to hide his nakedness as to shield hers from his lieutenant. "I have you," he whispered. "You are safe now."

"Apologies for my late arrival," Glaukos said as he tore his attention from Stella and surveyed the bodies, his breathing labored. "My men took down two of them as they crossed the beach, but these three made it past them." He paused to take a few breaths. "Name your punishment for their oversight, and I shall see to it immediately."

Frowning, Darius tried to ignore Stella's quiet sobs as he digested the ypolochago's words and wondered at the gray peppering Glaukos' hair and beard. "Did your watchman fall asleep?" he asked.

Glaukos shook his head, his breathing finally slowing. Given he hadn't arrived on a horse, Darius realized he had run up the side of the mountain on foot. "He did not. He sent up an arrow when he first spotted their boat coming from the southeast. My men on the beach were slow to respond, however. Thought they could take down the five who were in the boat with arrows, but these three evaded their weapons."

"By climbing the mountain?" Darius countered in disbelief, obviously annoyed by the comment. They should have been easy targets for anyone with a bow.

And a boat carrying only five?

Glaukos bent and then lifted one of the men's oval-shaped shields, holding it to his side to indicate how they had managed to accomplish such a feat. "I must have seen half our arsenal of arrows littering the path on my way up here."

Noticing the shape of the shields for the first time, Darius understood the ypolochago's comment. A barely crouched man could protect his flank while holding the shield at his side. "Effective defense," he murmured, thinking he would take one to the island's armorer and ask that new shields be designed for his coastguardsmen.

"Do you recognize these men?" Glaukos asked, his gaze going to the first one Darius had killed.

Darius shook his head. "Not this one," he murmured. His gaze went to the one who had seemed familiar. "This one, perhaps."

Glaukos used a leather-booted foot to nudge the leader's body. "The direction of their ascent was deliberate. They knew exactly where they were going."

"And where might that have been?" Darius asked. He absently dropped a kiss atop Stella's head, relieved that her sobs seemed to have subsided. The awareness of her distress had finally left the edge of his consciousness and her familiar tingle settled there. He didn't lessen his hold on her, though.

"Here," Glaukos responded as he waved to indicate the area around Darius' tent. "Are you sure you do not recognize them? I believe they came here seeking you." He dared a nervous glance at Stella. Despite seeing only her back, he recognized the daughter of the olive farmer known as Andros. She was the only girl on the island with bright red hair.

Understanding the man's point, Darius turned his attention to the first one he had downed. In death, the man's face was slack, and his neck was covered in blood. Glaukos kicked off his helm, though, and Darius furrowed his brows. "I thought him an Egyptian at first," he murmured. "Or from Hyskos. But he is one of those from the lands to the east. From the Zagros Mountains."

A chill went up his spine. Older but recognizable now that his helm was no longer hiding most of features, Tyrus had been one of the men with the sea captain, Perakles, who had sold them grain—and continued to do so until the mutiny.

Darius remembered the discussion he'd had with Klumenos about the ghosts who disappeared beneath the sea. Possibly using a lava tube to gain access to a cave. Laying in wait until they could take a ship.

"This is Tyrus. One of Perakles' crew. One of those who committed mutiny and took his coin," Darius explained. "Perhaps one of Klumenos' men finally discovered where they were hiding and forced them to make a move."

Glaukos cursed. "They have been on our island this whole time?"

Darius nodded and turned his gaze onto the leader. "But I am sure I have never seen *him* before. Or him," he added as he pointed to Stella's captor. "Which means they were either already aligned with another crew or they gained some cohorts over the past few years."

He felt revulsion at the thought of how the invader had been holding Stella. At his comment about how much coin she would bring at auction. Her red hair would always set her apart.

Two of Glaukos' men appeared behind Glaukos, both mounted on horseback. Another riderless horse was tethered to the back of one of the mounts, apparently meant for Glaukos.

"'Bout time you got here," Glaukos groused.

"Apologies. Another boat came onto shore."

Darius jerked his head in their direction, almost regretting having told his men he would be unavailable to join them in battle for a few days. Although the excitement of combat had abated, he could easily be ready for another match.

None of his ypolochagoi had asked why he had assigned them higher positions to cover his absence, although they all knew his villa was at the other end of the island. "Were they like these men?" he asked.

The two nodded. "Five more in a small boat. We saw a

warning shot from the watchmen a few milion north of here."

Five more? Only three of Perakles' original crew had escaped. From where did the other seven come?

"Where are they now?" Glaukos asked, his annoyance with this men having abated.

"On the beach. Dead."

"Anyone familiar?" he asked.

The two exchanged glances of surprise. "We have seen none of them before, although it is possible one of Klumenos' men know of them. He spoke of ghosts taking to the sea and disappearing into underwater caves when he was last at our watchtower."

Glaukos nodded his understanding. He turned his attention to Darius. "What are your orders?"

Darius regarded the invaders with an expression of disgust. "Take these bodies down to the beach to join their brethren in death. Help yourself to their shields and weapons and whatever other treasure you can from the bodies," Darius ordered. "Then burn them." He had considered ordering them buried, but the number of bodies would take the watchmen from their duties for too long as they dug graves.

The three men nodded. "You will go north?" Glaukos asked as his men dismounted and moved to lift the bodies onto the backs of their horses.

Darius sighed. "I thought to stay here with my new bride for another day, but now I think we shall not," he murmured, dropping another kiss on Stella's head. She had been so quiet, he wondered if he might have smothered her.

"Bride?" Glaukos repeated, before he managed a

crooked smile. The other two coastguardsmen paused in their work, their faces displaying their surprise at hearing the lochagos' words. "You might have said you were taking a wife," Glaukos scolded. "For a moment, I thought..." His mouth shut when he saw the glare Darius cast in his direction. "I thought you had simply rescued her from them," he managed in a quieter voice.

Stella pulled her head from Darius' chest and said, "He did that, too."

Although her voice didn't sound as if she was glad about what he had done, Darius felt a hint of relief when her head nestled into the small of his shoulder and her hold tightened on him. "A feat for which I wish to show my gratitude," she whispered. She allowed a wan grin when she felt his cock once again harden against her belly. "But first, there is a horse I must touch," she whispered.

Darius gave a start. "What?"

Before he could put voice to a protest, Stella was hurrying to the riderless mare that was still tethered behind one of the horses. She paused a moment before it, and then reached out with a hand to touch the horse's head. A brilliant smile appeared before she finally dropped her forehead against the mare's withers. A quiet knicker sounded, and the mare tossed her head.

A moment later, Stella had rejoined Darius and was regarding him with a look of expectation.

"I should like to see to my wife now," Darius called out, his words meant for Glaukos and his men. "I will return to your watchtower in a sennight and not before." With that, he lifted Stella into his arms and carried her into the tent.

Glaukos scratched his nose, curious as to what Stella

had been doing with his mount, but he dared not put voice to a query. He gave his men a grimace. "You heard the lochagos. Let us get these pirates down to the beach."

A few minutes later, the three horses with their burdens picked their way down the mountainside while Glaukos retrieved as many arrows as he could pick up along the way.

MEANWHILE

Darius had his mouth on Stella's even before he set her on the bed. "Apologies for what happened," he whispered, his breaths labored, and not from having carried her into the tent. "I do not believe I have ever been so worried and so angry all at the same time."

"You could not have known," Stella managed as she hurried to the tub and undid her skirt's fastening.

"What are you doing?"

"Washing off the stench of that barbarian," she murmured as she lowered herself into the cool water. She took up a cloth and began washing her breasts and belly, the memory of her captor's arm wrapped around her midriff making her movements far too fast and too hard.

Darius hurried to her, his larger hand covering hers in order to stop her frantic ministrations. He slowly removed the cloth from her hand and just as slowly drew it down her body, barely allowing the linen to touch her skin. "He is dead. He will never again touch you," he whispered.

"What about you?" she countered, her eyes bright. "Will you ever touch me again? Knowing that another has touched me so?"

Despite wanting to put voice to an answer, Darius had

learned long ago his actions were more effective than words. His lips had already moved to her neck, to her collarbones, to her breasts, and finally to her nipples, where they kissed and nipped before he pulled away to regard her with hooded eyes. He pulled a linen from a nearby trunk and wrapped her in it before lifting her from the tub.

She let out a squeak when he didn't set her down and allow her to dry her body. Instead, he took her to the bed.

As he hovered over her, his cock rock hard and ready to claim her, he said, "You are mine, Stella. For the rest of eternity."

Inhaling sharply, Stella didn't have a chance to answer, for he pushed part of the linen from her body and lowered his head to hers. His kiss was as thorough in its claiming, as was his body.

When the linen fell away beneath him, so did her legs as they spread open for him. A moment later, and he had his cock plunged into her, wishing oblivion and eternity could be one and the same.

29

TREK TO A PALACE

Later that day

"Why did you not tell your coastguardsmen that you were taking a wife?" Stella asked as she led Arion down the northeast side of the mountain. Darius walked beside her when the path allowed; otherwise, he was ahead of her as they made their way toward the well-worn road that would lead to Paradisos.

"I did not wish them to know. At least, not yet," he replied, wincing when he realized she might take offense at the comment.

"You are ashamed of me?" The thought of her red hair had her making the query, despite Darius having said he liked it.

Darius slowed his steps and turned around. "Never," he assured her. "I was worried about what they might do should they discover my plan."

Stella considered his words. "Do?"

Knowing he needed to explain himself, Darius said, "To me." He allowed a sigh. "The last time one of the coastguardsmen announced his betrothal, his team arranged a night at the brothel near the port in Akrotiri. Then they stood and..." He stopped, realizing his next words would make his men sound as barbaric as the invaders that he and Glaukos' men had vanquished.

"And?" she prompted. A grin teased the corners of her mouth.

Darius swallowed. "They watched while he was serviced by two prostitutes, and then teased him mercilessly for days after about his lack of prowess."

Stella dipped her head. "Surely you do not lack... prowess," she said, glad that the midday sun would keep her blush from showing too much.

"I should hope not. Remember, I have had three wives," he replied with an arched brow.

Even before he finished the comment, a stream of steam suddenly shot straight up into the air, just to the left of Stella. Hearing the hiss even before the white cloud appeared, Darius was quick to turn and lift her from where she had paused on the path, swinging her around and carrying her until she was well away from the geyser.

Arion whinnied in protest and appeared as if he might bolt, but Stella clung to the reins—as well as to Darius.

"Are you hurt?" he asked, even as stinging needles of steam fell onto his arms. He turned slightly so his cape shielded them both from the heat and the spray of scalding water.

Stella, her eyes wide with fright, shook her head. "I do not think so," she managed. When Darius didn't let go, she followed his line of sight and gasped at the plume of white, scalding hot water shooting into the air. The stench of rotting eggs assaulted her nostrils before a gust of wind blew the mist in the other direction. "That is far larger than any we ever had in the olive orchard," she whispered in awe.

His heart still hammering in his chest, Darius tightened his hold on Stella until she let out a sound of protest. "Apologies," he murmured. "But I cannot abide the thought of losing you."

Stella relaxed into his hold, closing her eyes so that she might relish his words. To think, only the day before, she was on the verge of hating him. Despising him for buying her from her father.

If only Andros had told her he had promised her to Darius.

"Exactly when did you speak with my father about taking me to wife?" she asked.

Darius blinked at the unexpected query, especially given their current circumstance. "The day after I met you in the olive orchard. You were... you were ten, you said."

Still pressed against the front of his body, partially wrapped in his scarlet cape, Stella sighed. "How could you know you would... want me?"

Darius dropped a kiss on her forehead, and the now-familiar tingle flared at the edge of his consciousness. "Do you feel that? In your head?"

Stella furrowed a brow. "You mean the tickle?"

Grinning, Darius felt a wave of relief. "Is that what you feel? Only a tickle?" he teased.

A blush suffusing her face, Stella said, "Sometimes it is far more than that, but I do not know the word to describe it."

His suspicions were correct. Darius was sure now she

was an Immortal. "I felt that tingle the first time you touched me. And I have felt it every time since."

"And with your wives? Did you feel it with them?" Surely he must have.

"No," Darius replied. "I have never felt it in another but you." His gaze went from her to the steam vent, where the geyser had ceased and now only a cloud of steam and a circle of mud marked where the eruption had occurred.

Stella followed his line of sight and allowed a sigh. She glanced down at her hand, the one that held the reins, and she winced. She had been holding onto the leather straps so tightly, her fingernails had dug into her palms. One had left a half-moon shaped cut where a dot of blood now appeared.

Arion tossed his head, impatient at standing still while the earth threatened to cast up another geyser of steam and boiling water.

"But you have felt it in a lover, surely," she said, even as Darius noticed the blood in her palm. He lifted it to his lips and kissed it, the intimate contact sending a frisson of pleasure shooting through her hand and up her arm. He gave his head a shake.

"I have not."

Stella blinked. For a moment, she thought he lied to her, but she didn't sense deceit in him. Confused, she stepped from his hold and led Arion back to the road. "Do you have a lover now?"

Darius frowned. "Lover?" he repeated. "No. I pledged my fidelity to you."

Stella regarded him a moment, realizing that if he did have a favorite bedmate, he wasn't about to share the information with her. "Surely you have had companion-ship since your last wife's death." When he didn't answer right away, she added, "Helena says all men have need of a woman, even if they are not bound to one." She resumed the walk on the road, Arion dutifully following her.

Remaining mute for several minutes, mostly in an effort to decide if now was the time he should tell her what he knew about her, Darius continued to stand where he had been holding her.

Would things change between them if she knew she would come back to life after dying? That for the rest of her days, her appearance would remain the same? No matter how many times Death took her?

Deciding he wouldn't tell her—at least, not yet, Darius finally allowed a sigh and hurried up to walk by her side. "There are times in my life when I have not been in need of a woman," he said in a quiet voice. He was about to say more. To mention the times when he felt such despair, he didn't dare seek the company of other humans. When his bloodlust was such that anyone near him might be in danger of dying by his hand. Time when blind anger would have seen him destroying anything and everyone in his wake.

But he didn't wish to frighten his new wife.

Memories from his very earliest days played back in his mind. Back before he had been hit with the mace. Back when, as a young boy, he had paid witness to the atroci-ties of men who had no regard for others. They had killed not because of hate, but because of indifference. Not because they were defending themselves, but because of greed. And he had somehow known it was wrong.

Who had taught him that? Right from wrong. Honor and dishonor. Good and bad.

He struggled to remember if he'd had a parent or a mentor who saw to his earliest days. Before the days of endless hunger had turned him into a scrawny adolescent.

A flash of a woman's face came to mind, a young woman who bore a slight resemblance to Stella, if only because her hair was red and her eyes were green, her face a perfect oval. Her skin was darker, though. Bronzed from the sun but smooth despite her being older. She was staring down at him with an expression of surprise and delight.

He remembered being held in her arms. Remembered running towards her when she called his name. Remembered her brightly-colored robes, and how her hair had been dressed in an elaborate style and adorned with chains of gold and flowers of gemstones. He remembered sleeping on a comfortable pallet. Wearing clothes of the finest woven linen and sandals of leather.

And then chaos reigned. Shouts and cries, thundering skies, heat from flames, and pain.

So much pain!

He winced when he remembered her death. The loss tearing at his heart as if it were happening right then and there.

Mother?

Darius struggled to hold onto the image of the first woman he ever remembered seeing, sure she must have been the woman who found him. For he knew she hadn't bore him. He had been a blessing to her, though. A foundling wrapped in swaddling clothes and left where she would find him. Find him and take him in, nurture him, and raise him as her own.

She told him the tale several times as he sat on her lap, and then later, when she took him by the hand to a place far from their home where a man of some importance had been buried. She had brought with her a small offering, and placed it on the grave. She said words of reverence and love as tears streamed down her cheeks.

And then they had returned to their home.

Mother.

The story the priest had told about Stella came to mind. That of a large bird who carried her over the water and delivered her to Strongili. To leave her at the base of an olive tree so that Helena could find her.

Had the same thing happened to him? Had a large bird delivered him to a woman who pined for a child?

Mother!

His throat threatened to close up, and he swallowed hard in an attempt to breathe.

"How often do you share her bed?"

The simple question didn't pull Darius from his reverie. "Never," he struggled to say, nearly choking on the word. The woman in his memory never shared her bed—she had no husband, no lover—and she always saw to putting Darius into his own bed for the night, kissing him on his forehead.

Then Darius remembered when and where he was.

He glanced around, anxious to determine just where they were. The question echoed in his head along with a tickle of her confusion. He realized then that Stella had taken his silence as confirmation that he had a lover. He cleared his throat. "Other than you, I do not have a lover. Nor will I ever."

Stella frowned. "But... you did once."

He finally nodded, deciding he could share that bit of his past with her. "There was a woman on Creta. Before I was made the lochagos of all the coastguardsmen of Strongili," he admitted, thinking of the nights he had spent in the widow's bed. Long nights made longer in that loneliness had finally caught up to him.

New to the island and to the culture of the Minoans, he was at once glad for a chance at a new life and sad that he had come from the north alone.

Meeting Katina had been a blessing. They were two lonely souls who never would have made a life together by day. But at night, when the hours passed slowly and his body yearned for the touch of another, he always knew she would welcome him into her bed.

Sometimes he merely spent the night holding Katina while she slept, while at other times, they would join as one and revel in an ecstasy he had never achieved with another woman.

At least, not until he had bedded Stella.

There was something about the thrum and tingle at the edge of his consciousness that had him convinced he would be joined with Stella for the rest of his life. The way it flared and brightened had his body reacting in an entirely different manner from the way it did when making love to a mere mortal.

The sheer intensity of his first climax with Stella had shocked him to his core. Spoiled him for the rest of time. For he knew he would never experience such pleasure with anyone but his new wife. Perhaps not even with another Immortal, should he ever meet one.

What might happen after Stella had died for the first time and her immortality was permanently established? What might their joining be like then? More intense?

His body gave a start that had him sucking in a breath.

"Do you love her?" Stella asked, her query absent of any jealousy.

Darius frowned as he shook his head. "I did not. I have not seen her in... in thirty winters or more?" he guessed. "Given her age back then, I doubt she is still among the living."

Stella stopped in her tracks, which had Arion tossing his head in protest. They had finally made it to the flat lands and the smoother road. "But you are," she murmured.

Tempted to tell her he was immortal—what else could explain his six-hundred years of living? His numerous deaths followed by resurrections—Darius thought better of it and allowed a shrug. "I have lived a long time and know not when I shall die." He mounted Arion and then moved to lift her to sit in front of him.

When she sucked in a breath, indicating her discomfort at straddling a horse, he quickly moved her to sit sideways in front of him. "Apologies," he said in a quiet voice. "I have been an inconsiderate husband," he added as he kissed the top of her head.

"But an attentive one," she whispered, secretly glad he understood why she preferred to walk over riding the horse down the mountain.

"*Possessive* would be the better word," he admitted, not

aware of how the term might sound after his claims that she was not his slave.

Although Stella had at one time bristled at the thought of being possessed by a man—just yesterday, when the word conjured slavery—Stella knew Darius meant something different. From the time she had first met him, she knew they were connected in a way far different from the way her father and mother considered themselves bound to one another.

"What else has happened to you in your six-hundred years?" she asked, leaning her shoulder against his chest as she raised her knees and rested her feet on Arion's neck, knowing Darius' arm around her middle would keep her from falling off the Andalusian.

Darius gave a start. "What makes you think I have been alive that long?" he asked, wondering if he might have told her and then forgotten, or spoken of it in his sleep.

Stella raised her head and gave him a quelling glance. "I have known of your age since the first day we met," she murmured, her hand lifting to his cheek much like it had done the first day she met him.

"I thought you were teasing!" he countered.

"I thought you were a god," she said over her shoulder, a grin causing a dimple to appear in her cheek.

Frowning, Darius wondered once again if he should admit he was an Immortal. He was fairly sure he wasn't a god. Other than coming back to life after times he had known he shouldn't have survived a blow from a weapon, he had never had a visit from an apparition. Never heard voices from above—or below, for that matter. "I do not know exactly where I was born," he said then. "Somewhere far east of here."

Angling her head so she could look up at him, Stella wondered why he didn't deny her claim. Perhaps he would be more forthcoming once they had spent more time together. "Then what is the first thing you remember?"

Darius closed his eyes, a parade of images passing through his mind. He tried not to think of the woman he now realized was his adoptive mother but rather of their surroundings. He allowed a slight grin. "Snow," he murmured.

Stella blinked. "What is... snow?" she asked before feeling a rumble rise in his chest. She grinned when she heard him laugh. He so rarely laughed, and yet his entire face lit up with such joy, he appeared years younger.

"Rain that is so cold, it has frozen into flakes," he explained. "It falls from the sky and does not seep into the ground, but rather piles up in white layers."

Stella tried to imagine what he described. "Does it go away?"

Darius nodded. "When the air warms with spring, it melts. Into water."

Stella furrowed a brow. "Where does it go?"

Shrugging, Darius said, "Into the ground. Into the rivers. Into the sea."

An expression of concentration had Stella's brows drawing together. Darius leaned down and kissed her on the top of her head. "Someday, you will see snow," he murmured.

Not exactly sure she *wanted* to see snow, Stella took a breath and asked, "What is the second thing you remember?"

Despite remembering a homeland with mountains, trees, lakes, and animals, Darius also remembered arid wastelands of sand. He didn't think they were the same locale, but he didn't know what they were called to be able to locate them these days.

That morning's encounter with Tyrus reminded him that he had at one time known the land of the Zagros Mountains. Perhaps those mountains were near his original home. They had certainly sported snow.

"Mountains," he finally said. "With snow on them. And a village at the base of the mountains." This last image had come to him in a flash. A large village where peoples who were weary from their nomadic lives had chosen to congregate. To work and to create products to trade with those who made their way toward the Mediterranean Sea. To offer respite to other traders before they continued their treks to other lands.

The language spoken by Perakles and his band of grain traders was a reminder of those days in that village.

"What was it called?" Stella asked, her gaze taking in the view of the Aegean, its waters stretched out to the west as far as she could see. She had never been this far from home before. Never this far north. And surely never this high up.

"Kunara," Darius murmured. "Part of Akkadia, I think," he added, sure she would ask. "A land far east of here."

His words had Stella turning her attention to her right. Traveling as they were on a ridge that bisected this part of the island, she could see as much of the island and sea to her right as she could to her left. Straight ahead, the island sloped down to the sea, although a mountain up ahead and to their left hid the northwestern most tip of the island.

"Was it on the water?" she asked.

Darius shook his head, remembering the long trek he had taken with a band of men intent on making it to Tin Island. The Mediterranean's source of tin for making bronze was located there, and he was after weapons better than those that traders offered with their wares.

He had been so young back then! Young and stupid, believing the life of a mercenary, of taking coin for killing on behalf of others, was somehow honorable.

It was better than killing for sport, which is what the beast in whose body he now resided had been doing before. Before he wielded a massive mace and flattened Darius with the spiked ball.

Darius remembered that mace well, for a few moments after it collided into him and sent his scrawny body flying against a rock so his bones shattered and his skull cracked, he was holding its handle. He remembered staring at the spikes, sure his own blood darkened them. He rode the horse on which the murderer had been riding. And he knew how to wield the mace. How to use his newly-acquired muscled arms to swing it to wipe out those who would see him vanquished.

He accidentally killed two of his own villagers before he realized what had happened. Before he had turned his mount around so he could stare at the body in which he had been living for the first twelve or so years of his life.

Dispassionate.

That's what he remembered feeling at that moment. He knew he was seeing a dead version of himself, but he felt no grief. No fear. Not even a need to burn or bury the body.

A hand waved in front of his vision, and Darius gave a start. Stella was staring at him, her brows furrowed.

"Apologies," he murmured, stunned at having remembered so much of that day he had first died. He hadn't revisited the memory in hundreds of years, and he couldn't recall it being so vivid.

"Where were you just then?" she asked, managing to turn her bent body sideways on the saddle. One of her arms, still wrapped around her bent knees, rested against his chest, and her head fell into the small of his shoulder.

"As a new husband, I would be a fool to be anywhere but with my wife," he replied, not sure he wanted to tell her of his days as a mercenary.

"Yet my query had you remembering something," she accused.

He nodded. "True. But it was a time and place I am not fond of remembering," he admitted. "I fear I have not always been an honorable man."

"But you have been since?" she half-asked. She felt him stiffen before he finally nodded. "I only kill when I must," he agreed. "To defend myself, or those I am charged with defending," he went on. "Or you."

Stella wrapped an arm around the back of his waist. "Although I was afraid for you this morning, I knew you would prevail," she murmured.

Darius allowed a chuckle. "Afraid for me?" he repeated, squeezing his eyes shut at the memory of how the pirate had been holding her. That man had been destined to die from the moment he put his hands on Stella.

"You were... naked. Without a weapon," she countered. "And all I could think about is that you might die because I had to..." Stella screwed up her face in a grimace. "Because I needed to pee," she finished. She felt his lips touch the top of her head, and she lifted her eyes to meet his, stunned to find him smiling. "You find it humorous?" she asked, incredulous.

"I do hope you finished before they discovered you," he said, reining in his amusement. Given the sheer terror he had experienced at what might have happened to her—for those brief minutes, he had forgotten she was an Immortal—he hadn't been able to think clearly for a long time after he had vanquished the pirates.

Lust for blood and lust for Stella were equally debilitating.

"I did," she replied. "They found me when I was making my way back to the tent. Your latrine is well done, by the way," she added. "I was expecting to have to squat amongst the trees."

"Gratitude," he replied. "It shall be the last time you have to use such antiquated means." Despite thinking they might spend some nights in the tent on occasion, after the events of that morning, he didn't think Stella would ever wish to go there again.

Stella frowned. "What are you saying?"

Darius angled his head to one side, so he could better see her face. "You have your own toilet in your bathing chamber, my love," he said. "A basin with running water. A bathtub with warm water. Your own bedchamber. A housekeeper you can order about as you see fit. Stables for our horses."

Arion nickered at this comment while Darius decided not to mention the olive orchard.

Stella's eyes widened in wonder. "How is this possible?" And then she realized he had said *our horses* and she gasped. "How many horses?"

Once again grinning, Darius decided he rather liked being in the good graces of the king. "Just three. I am the lochagos here on this island, and the king has decided I am worthy of a villa with such amenities."

"For how long?"

Darius gave a start, not expecting such a question. "As long as I am lochagos, I suppose," he replied with a shrug. Although Cydon had died, his successor, Tektamanos, seemed satisfied with his continued appointment. They still met on a regular basis, and Darius was still in charge of training new recruits.

Darius felt a twinge of guilt at never having introduced the former king to Stella. Over six years ago, he had promised the king he would take a wife, and then Cydon had died before he could see to taking Stella with him to Creta.

"Will you take me to Creta when you go to train new recruits?"

Not having thought that far ahead, Darius gave a nod. "I will. Until then, I must decide if I should take you with me as I make my rounds of the island."

"You should," Stella said, a grin betraying her amusement. "So that you can introduce me to all the men who protect the island."

"You do realize I spend most nights in watchtowers or at my tent," he countered. "I do not think I shall tempt my men with your presence in a watchtower." He glanced down at her as she looked up at him. "Or you with their presence," he added, his manner growing more serious.

"Because they are younger than you?" she teased, hoping to coax a smile.

But Darius remained sober. "Does my age—?"

"No," she interrupted, a finger going to his lips. "It is merely part of who you are."

"You do not mind that your husband appears old enough to be your father?"

Stella winced. She hadn't considered his age from that perspective. "Not if you do not mind your wife looking young enough to be your daughter."

Darius mimicked the sound of being punched in the stomach. "I do not, of course. But I do believe I have the better end of that deal," he murmured. His gaze went from her to something in the distance, and Stella turned in his hold to look. Her slight inhalation of breath had Darius tightening his hold on her.

"Who's palace is that?" she asked in awe. A large white villa, fronted with red columns and topped with a terra-cotta tiled roof, was sprawled over a flat of land near the northern shore. Another building stood nearby, and beyond it was a grove of olive trees.

For a moment, pride filled Darius, and all thoughts of his age disappeared. "Mine," he replied. "Although the olive orchard was planted for you."

Stella turned her attention back to him, her eyes wide. "Me?" she repeated.

He nodded. "The sennight after our betrothal," he murmured. "So, unfortunately, it will be a few years before you can harvest any olives."

Stella tightened her hold on him, her head pressed into his chest. "Gratitude," she murmured.

"I do not expect you to spend your days in the trees,

however," Darius replied, reveling in the sensations he felt in his head. "You can paint frescos or weave fabric. Ride Augustine, if you wish."

Stella smiled, no longer experiencing any qualms about having become Darius' wife. "So besides being in the king's favor, you are also a man of means?" she half-questioned.

He nodded. "I have had many years to build up my coffers, it is true."

"Then being older does have its benefits, does it not?"

Once again reminded of his age, Darius winced, but before he could say anything, Stella smiled and then reached up and kissed him.

For the rest of the trip to his villa, Darius felt young.

30

A NEW BRIDE

The following morning

"It's not so very bad, is it?"

Stella whirled around from where she stood at the north window of her bedchamber, surprised to find the *oikonómos*, Iris, regarding her from the doorway. Dressed in a simple blue *chiton* belted at her waist, the older servant held her gnarled hands together in front of her and then bowed her head in greeting.

"It is beautiful," Stella replied, thinking Iris referred to the rugged landscape and the sea beyond. On this day, clouds pregnant with rain appeared on the horizon, and the surf pounded onto the rocky shore below. Despite the threat of rain, the sun was still shining. "Everything here is beautiful," she added, waving a hand to indicate her bedchamber and the villa beyond.

Someone was missing, though.

Darius.

The slight tingle at the edge of her consciousness was gone, as well.

"I am gladdened. My master wanted everything to be perfect for your arrival."

Stella gave a start. "You knew he was bringing me here?" she asked. How was it everyone but her seemed to know Darius of Agremon intended to take her to wife?

"He told me of you a long time ago," Iris said as she entered the bedchamber. She glanced about the room with a critical eye, as if she were sure something was amiss. "I will see to your bath on this morning." Then she moved to the bathing chamber. The sound of running water prefaced her return to the bedchamber, where she hurried to a trunk and pulled out a robe and folded linens.

Curious as to why she was hearing falling water, Stella peeked into the bathing chamber and gasped as she watched a thick stream of water fill a bronze tub. "How is this possible?" she asked as she moved to poke a finger into the column of water. Warm but not steaming hot, the water was quickly filling the tub.

Iris brought the robe and linens into the bathing chamber and moved to turn two bronze wheels. The water abruptly stopped.

"What happened?" Stella asked, jumping back in alarm as her hands knotted into fists at her breast.

A grin further wrinkling the old woman's face, Iris pointed to the bronze wheels. "That one is connected to a pipe that leads to the cistern where the water is made hot by the earth. Too hot, lately. So the other is for water from the nearby cold spring."

"The earth?" Stella repeated in alarm. A memory of the geyser erupting from the ground the day before had her wondering if the earth was the reason for the steaming, stinky water. Perhaps it also made the ground tremble on occasion.

The housekeeper gave a shrug. "They say the mountain to the southwest is a volcano and once erupted in a cloud of ash and rocks," she replied. "And it may one day do so again. Until then, it allows this oikos to have hot water for the kitchens and for your bath." After she sprinkled crushed lavender in the water, she turned to help remove Stella's gown. She dropped her hands when Stella stepped back.

"I can bathe myself," Stella said, reminded of how humiliated she felt when Helena bathed her two mornings prior.

Then she remembered how Darius had bathed her yesterday morning, and a shiver shot up her spine. His touch had been so light, so sensuous, so slow and so reverent. And yet before she'd had a chance to fully appreciate what he was doing, he had her out of the water and onto the bed, pleasuring her and then thrusting his cock into her, as if any patience he might have possessed was long gone.

Had he done so only because he was aroused? Or had he done it as a means to take her mind off the pirates? To erase the sensation of being held captive in foreign arms?

Perhaps a bit of both, she thought, remembering his arousal.

Stella glanced over at the bronze tub, anxious to immerse herself in the warm, scented water.

Iris shook her head. "My master will not be pleased if he learns I did not help you," she said in a whisper.

"I will not tell him," Stella countered.

"He is concerned for your safety."

Stella gave a start, the paralyzing fear she had felt the day before coming back, when the pirate had threatened to slice her throat with a dagger. Despite willing her limbs to move—to do something—to free herself from the pirate's hold, she was left feeling powerless.

Before the images of what Darius and his men had done to the three pirates could replay themselves in her memory, she gave her head a shake and allowed the housekeeper to help her out of her gown and into the tub.

"Your *ypirétria* will arrive on the morrow," Iris said, referring to a lady's maid. "She is young, like you, but has been training to be a servant her entire life."

Stella lowered herself into the warm water and allowed a sigh of satisfaction. "The soreness will go away after a time," Iris whispered, as if she expected someone else might be listening.

"Soreness?" Stella whispered back. Then she realized the woman referred to her nether region, and a blush suffused her entire body. At least the lavender-topped water hid most of it.

"My master claimed your virtue, did he not?" Iris countered as she moved about the bathing chamber, arranging the linens and a skirt and jacket on a dressing table. Her eyes suddenly widened and she said, "Pardon, my mistress. I forget about the priests on this island."

Stella regarded the oikonómos for a moment, wondering at her comment. Her words implied she wasn't a native of Strongili. "Darius claimed me before I was expected to go to the priest," she said in a hoarse whisper, aware that the tingle she associated with Darius had returned to the edge of her consciousness. A sense of relief settled over her as she asked, "Should I be concerned that he paid coin to the priest so he could do so?"

Iris allowed a shrug. "Concerned? No. Honored, yes," she replied. "My master is well regarded on this island. On Creta, as well. But he brings with him some habits from his old country that do not always suit those here on this island."

Stella remembered a conversation she'd had with Darius when she was a youth. He had spoken of the large island to the south. The home of the kings of Minoa. Strongili might have produced the finest of what Minoa traded with other lands, but Creta is where they lived. "Is that where you are from? Creta?"

The old woman nodded. "Most of my life. King Cydon asked that I come here when he had this villa built. And then he decided to give it to the lochagos instead of living in it whenever he visited Strongili. I was once the oikonómos at one of his villas on Creta," she explained.

"Was that a palace, too?" Stella asked. She had heard tales of the magnificent palaces on Creta. Of grand chambers with frescos on every wall and colorful textiles covering the furnishings. Although Iris referred to this villa as a palace, and it was rather grand, the rooms were not how Stella had imagined those on Creta.

Giving her head a shake, Iris held a linen draped over one arm as she offered her hand to Stella. "Oh, no. The king lives in the Palace of Knossos, but he hosted his guests at the villa where I worked."

"What of Darius? Did he live in a palace on Creta, too?"

Iris allowed a shrug, not sure she was free to say what she knew of her master. For one thing, she had noticed he didn't appear to age. She had seen him many a time in the villa on Creta, and he still looked the same as he did the first time she had served him. "Darius used to live in modest accommodations near here, but the king insisted he have a better oikos. A waste, if you ask me."

Stella took the proffered hand and stood up. She accepted the linen from Iris, sighing when she realized how soft the fabric was. "Why a waste?" she asked as she wrapped it tightly around her suddenly chilled body and secured the ends above a breast.

Holding onto Stella's hand until she was safely out of the tub, Iris replied, "He is rarely in residence." At Stella's look of alarm, she added, "Perhaps he will spend more time here now that he has taken a wife."

"That is the plan," a deep voice said from the bedchamber.

Stella jerked her attention from the housekeeper to find Darius casually leaning against the archway, his arms crossed over his chest and his expression unreadable.

Iris bowed her head. "Pardon, my master," she murmured.

"You may return to your duties, Iris," he said as he pushed himself away from the doorway and stepped aside so the oikonómos could leave the bathing chamber. The old woman moved far faster than he thought possible, obviously embarrassed at having been caught speaking about him with his new wife.

He hadn't expected anything different, though. He had left that morning knowing Stella would have questions. Questions about him and about her new home.

Stella watched Iris take her leave and turned her gaze on her husband. For the second time in her life, she feared the man. Despite the size of the chambers, he looked larger than he had the day before in his tent. "You will not let her go because of what she said, will you?" she half-asked.

Darius furrowed his brows as he made his way to stand before her. "Of course not," he replied. "She has been my oikonómos for... for perhaps far too long."

Color once again suffusing her cheeks, Stella regarded Darius a moment before giving him a nod. "She seems very loyal," she said.

"She is," Darius agreed with a nod.

"I expected to wake up in your bed," Stella murmured, her eyes traveling over the dark leather armor that covered his chest.

Allowing a wan grin, Darius leaned down and kissed her forehead. "I had to meet with my men in Tholos at daybreak. I knew if I did not bring you to your bed, I would still be in mine. With you beneath me." A grin touched one edge of his lips and softened his features. "Or on top of me."

Stella dipped her head, a wash of color suffusing her body once again despite the thrill she felt at hearing his words. "I thought I might have done something... wrong." Indeed, the disorientation she had felt at finding herself in a bed she had never slept in and in a room she did not recognize—and Darius nowhere to be found—had her wondering if she was still in the same villa in which she had fallen asleep.

Darius lowered his lips to hers and kissed her. "Nothing wrong, and what you do, you cannot help."

Her eyes widening in alarm, Stella asked, "What do I do?"

His eyes darkening at her query, he murmured, "Fill me with desire. Make me want you. I barely think of you and my cock hardens," he whispered as he wrapped an arm around her back and pulled her against the front of his body.

Stella knew he spoke the truth when she felt the evidence of his erection just beneath his armor. Inflamed with desire for him, she said, "Then you best join me in my bed." Her fingers worked to undo the fastenings of the leather breastplate as she spoke, but his hands were quicker.

Within seconds, the armor was on the floor. Another moment, and his tunic and loincloth joined the armor. At the same moment thunder rumbled outside the window and the first drops of rain began to fall, he had her stripped of the linen and on the bed. The sizzle of lightning and the odor of ozone tinged the air when he plunged himself into her, and they were both lost to the storm.

31

A PREVIEW OF DISASTER

An hour later

Barely awake, Darius slid down the bed a bit and rested his head against the side of Stella's breast. He inhaled slowly, noting the scent of lavender mixed with his wife's natural scent. *Leave it to Iris to see to a new bride's comfort,* he thought as he dozed.

"What am I to do here?" Stella asked in a whisper.

Darius allowed a grunt, not sure what she was asking. "Besides lie with me?" he half-asked. There was a hint of humor in his voice despite his words.

Stella jerked, which had his head dislodged from where it had found the perfect place to rest. "Is that all that is expected of me?" she countered. "As your wife?"

Rolling onto his back, Darius slid an arm beneath her shoulders and pulled her so she was mostly on top of him. "I have servants to see to the household," he replied, his eyes closed.

"So... you took me to wife to have a bedmate?" Stella

whispered, not exactly sure how she felt about that particular motive.

"I took you to wife because I like spending time in your company. Because... because I value your opinions. Because I was lonely, and I wanted a companion," he murmured. "And a bedmate," he added before he placed a kiss on the top of her head.

"You could have had any woman in Akrotiri," Stella said, lifting her head so she could see his face. "Or the entire island."

"I didn't want any of them," he replied, a hand cupping the back of her head and pulling it down to his chest. "I wanted you."

Stella considered his words, a sense of wonder as well as worry settling over her. "Wanted?"

Darius was silent for a time before he suddenly turned over, sending Stella beneath him. He hovered over her, his eyes darkening with what appeared to be anger. But his words were quiet. Soft. And so welcome.

"*Want*. I want you. Always."

Blinking, Stella allowed a sigh and a slight smile. "Enough to make love to me again?" she asked in a teasing whisper. Although she was still a bit sore from the night before—Darius had insisted she believe his claim that he would always see to her pleasure as well as her safety—she felt the throb of desire deep in her body. Knew she was ready for his cock to impale her. For his fingers to help send her into a maelstrom of pleasure so intense, she thought her body was no longer in one piece.

Chuckling, Darius leaned down and kissed her nose. "Always," he replied, surprised when she easily opened her legs in invitation. His rigid cock found its new home with a minimum of effort. Barely moving, he buried himself in her wet haven, and he allowed a long sigh of satisfaction. "Always," he repeated as he moved his hands down to her hips to hold her steady.

His movements, deliberately slow and taking him to the verge of ecstasy, seemed at odds with the movement of the bed. For a moment, he thought Stella was out of sync with his thrusts, and then he heard shouts from somewhere downstairs.

His release, which he had desperately tried to hold off until he was sure Stella had experienced hers, came far too soon. Lost in the intensity of the in-between, he sighed and dropped his head to one of her shoulders. Even there, the bed seemed determined to shake him from it.

Her breathing labored, Stella was concentrating on how her quim clenched his manhood. She wanted to coax it back to moving when it was nearly jerked from inside her.

The sounds of shouting had her listening intently, and then her attention was captured by the waving fabric above them. The entire canopy over the bed seemed to shift, setting off another wave in the filmy fabric.

"Darius," she whispered in alarm.

He tightened his hold on her even as he raised his head. He grimaced, as if in pain, and slowly lowered his head to her shoulder. The sounds from the rest of the household died down to the point that he heard nothing, and he finally allowed a long, low moan.

"What was that?" she asked.

"The gods trying to help me, I think," Darius replied after a moment. "Or else our lovemaking has triggered an earthquake," he teased.

Stella's eyes widened in alarm. She remembered the last time the earth had shook beneath her. When she was in a tree, trimming away the small branches on the inside. Shaken to the point she had dropped her knife just to be sure she didn't hurt herself.

She had remained in that tree, gripping the trunk for support for a very long time before she felt safe enough to crawl down and retrieve her knife.

"Earthquake?" she repeated.

As if repeating the word had summoned it, another earthquake jerked the bed beneath them, its force nearly separating Darius from her. Instinctively, he gripped her tighter with one hand while the other grasped for something solid to hang onto. At the moment he had the edge of the mattress anchoring him, the shaking subsided once again.

"Earthquake," he confirmed. He lifted his body from hers a bit. "Did I hurt you?" he murmured, aware something had changed within the house.

"No," Stella managed to get out, once she let out the breath she'd been holding. "Are you well?"

Darius wanted nothing more than to stay atop her for just a few minutes more, but he slowly pulled his cock from her body and moved to get off the bed. "Apologies," he said to her murmur of disappointment. "I must see to the others."

He pulled on a chiton and hurried from the bedchamber, leaving Stella to pull the bed linens over her naked body and struggle to calm her breathing.

In only three days as Darius' wife, she had been manhandled by marauders, nearly scalded by a geyser, and now had been shaken by an earthquake. She dared not think of what else might go wrong, but she felt dismay when she realized the brightly colored fresco on the bedchamber's longest wall now displayed a crack that split the artwork nearly in two.

As mistress of the household, she realized she really should be by her husband's side, taking stock of the damage that might have been done in the rest of the villa. Ensure no one had been hurt.

She rose from the bed and pulled on the skirt and jacket that Iris had laid out for her, eschewing sandals and dressing her hair in favor of simply hurrying out of the bedchamber to join Darius.

She let out a gasp when she realized the fresco in the large hall had partially crumbled. Blue and green plaster chunks lay scattered over the tile floor. In the reception chamber, a vase had tipped over and shattered, while a crack had opened in the ceiling above.

"Do be careful of where you step, my lady," Iris' voice came from behind her. "Hades must have been angered on this day."

Stella turned to find the housekeeper holding the pieces of a pot she recognized as having come from Creta. "Is everything broken?" she asked in alarm, just then noticing the deafening silence surrounding them. The sounds of birdsong no longer made their way into the villa, nor did she hear anything from the kitchens. "Is anyone hurt?" She resisted the urge to run from the villa and check on the grove of olive trees. If any of them had become uprooted, she wanted to be sure they were lifted and replanted as soon as possible.

Darius appeared from the other end of the villa, his expression fierce. "I have not yet been to the kitchens," he replied, "But the servants all seem to be in one piece." He allowed a heavy sigh. "The villa may have suffered the worst."

"But it can be repaired," Stella said with hope.

"I will send for a carpenter," he replied, moving to join her. "You should have stayed in our bed," he whispered, his gaze taking in the pieces of broken pottery littering the floor. "At least until it is safe to walk on the floors."

"You have made me mistress of this villa," Stella reminded him, one brow arching up with her response.

"A position for which I did not think you would take on so soon," he countered. "You are but three days my wife."

Stella was about to argue, but thought better of it. "The fresco in my bedchamber cracked," she said instead.

Darius nodded. "I noticed," he whispered. "Perhaps you can use your pigments to repair it and the one in the hall," he suggested. "I will see to it one of the servants acquires some plaster and lime for you."

The thought of painting had Stella's eyes widening with excitement. "I will do so," she agreed, glad to know she would have something to occupy her time when Darius returned to his regular schedule. Then she sobered. "Do you think the entire island felt the shaking?" she asked, her worry now for her parents.

He winced, knowing exactly what she was thinking. "Probably," he replied. "I will have one of my men ride to Akrotiri. Have him check on your father's oikos."

"Gratitude," she answered, just before he bestowed a kiss atop her head.

"The vase from Creta is ruined," she murmured.

"It can be replaced," he replied. Six-hundred years of

living had taught him that the things made by a human's hands rarely lasted long. Even the artifacts rumored to be made by the gods were not permanent.

The thought of leaving her behind as he made the rounds of all the watchtowers on the island had him reconsidering. "Perhaps I will bring you with me this sennight," he suggested. "You can ride Augustine, and I can introduce you to my men."

Had anyone asked him if he would ever bring his wife along on his weekly tour of the watchtowers, he would have said no only a few days ago. Now he couldn't imagine leaving her for six or seven days.

Perhaps it was merely his cock that would miss her. He thought of the young, unmarried men on Creta who worried more about who they might next share a bed with than pirates, and he suddenly understood.

The past few weeks had been torture, as if part of him knew Stella was ready for his bed while another part argued that he had made a deal that could not be altered.

At least Andros had been accommodating—once he saw the size of Darius' purse. Or perhaps he had been frightened of the lochagos and thought to simply do his bidding.

Darius wondered how he must have looked as he arrived at the old man's oikos, his manner not the least bit friendly. He didn't know what he would have done if Andros hadn't agreed to let him have Stella an entire year early.

He might have struck him down. Killed the old man, and his wife, too, had Helena put voice to a protest. But neither had so much as questioned his appearance.

Perhaps they knew he had no patience for anything but compliance.

Desire for Stella had done something to him. Made him almost feral with his need of her. He knew it had been building for some time, but he couldn't decide what might have been the catalyst that had him behaving like a lovesick whelp.

Stella regarded him a moment, shocked by his suggestion that she join him as he did his work for the king. "I would be honored," she replied with a nod.

Darius blinked. "Then we shall leave in the morning," he said, reaching out a hand to pull her against him.

The pleasant tingle at the edge of his consciousness flared into a fully formed burst of pleasure, and he knew then why it was he craved her. Never before had the touch of a woman caused such a sensation. Never before had a woman sent him into such ecstasy with just her presence.

Something had been missing from his life all these centuries. He knew now she was what he needed. What he wanted. What he craved.

Darius held Stella a long moment, basking in the pleasure that seemed to engulf him. Then his stomach grumbled, and he was reminded they hadn't yet broken their fasts.

Stella giggled. "As much I like being held by you, I am reminded you require sustenance," she murmured, one of her fingers trailing down his chest and stomach. "I do hope the cook has been able to make a suitable breakfast despite the earthquake."

About to suggest he be allowed to simply feast on her, Darius let go his hold, and they made their way to the kitchens.

32

A NEW WIFE LEARNS HER HUSBAND'S WORK

The following day

Augustine knickered in greeting when Stella appeared at the stables the following morning, her satchel stuffed with some clothes gripped in one hand.

Her new ypirétria, Naia, was in her bedchamber preparing her clothes for the day when Stella emerged from Darius' bedchamber. Already briefed by Iris, Naia understood the haste with which Stella wanted to be made ready to leave and was quick with dressing Stella's hair and helping her to pack.

Stella had no idea what the girl would do for the next six days as she toured the watchtowers with Darius.

Arriving before Darius meant she had some time to speak to Augustine.

"I missed you, too," she whispered to her mount as she slid a hand along the side of his head. "So I shall spend a good deal of time in your company these next few days."

Augustine continued to knicker, his eyes nearly closed as Stella spoke to him.

Stella's attention then went to a horse she didn't recognize. "And who might this be?" She directed her query to Pietros, but it was Darius who answered.

"That would be Melanie," Darius said with a roll of his eyes, just as he entered the stables. He carried a bedroll over one shoulder and his shield on his other arm. "She was supposed to act as a brood mare, but she will not allow Augustine to get near her."

Pietros held the reins of Arion and dipped his head in greeting as Darius loaded his equipment onto the horse. Meanwhile, Stella moved to stand before the mare.

The two regarded one another for a time before Stella finally lifted a hand to touch Melanie. Although she didn't seem to welcome Stella's touch—the horse shoved out her lower lip and was on the verge of baring her teeth—she was soon nickering softly.

Arion suddenly knickered as well, tossing his head up and down.

Darius turned his attention to Pietros, who merely shrugged and then said, "He may be jealous."

But Darius watched as Stella's eyes widened and a grin brightened her face.

"What is it?" Darius asked, moving to where Stella stood.

"She carries Arion's colt," she whispered. "And although the fenced pasture is acceptable, she would prefer to spend her days among the olive trees where there is more shade. She will not run away, for she likes it here."

Darius frowned. "But..." Stella followed his gaze as he

dared a glance at Augustine. The older horse seemed oblivious to their discussion.

"Augustine prefers another mare," Stella whispered. "The one belonging to Glaukos. She has already thrown two of his colts. Whereas Melanie prefers Arion because he is younger."

Staring at Stella in disbelief, Darius said, "How is that possible? I only just took possession of Arion a few months ago."

"It only took the one time," Stella countered, one of her shoulders coming up in a shrug.

Darius blinked before giving his head a shake. He had no reason to doubt Stella's words—she had always had an innate ability to communicate with animals—but he wasn't sure he believed the claim that Melanie wouldn't run away if she was allowed to roam free.

There was only one way to find out.

He turned to Pietros and said, "See to it Melanie is allowed to spend her days in the olive orchard, but if you have to go looking for her at the end of this day, then she must remain inside the fences."

"Yes, Lochagos," Pietros replied, just before he turned to see to it Stella's satchel was packed in a saddlebag on Augustine.

A few minutes later, Darius and Stella rode out to the southeast under a cloudless sky.

THE NEED TO reach not one, but two watchtowers on the first day meant the horses were allowed to gallop when the terrain allowed it. Stella thrilled at the ride, quickly learning how to use the reins even though she knew

Augustine would do her bidding if she merely touched him and imagined what she wanted him to do.

Although Darius had made the trip to the watchtowers on the eastern side of the island many times, he was wary of what damage the earthquake might have done to the well-worn path they followed. The ground hadn't cracked, though, nor did it appear as if any geysers had made an appearance. Only one steam vent spewed a white cloud, but Darius remembered it from prior rides along the same path.

He saw the most obvious effect of the earthquake when they reached the first watchtower.

Stella sucked in a breath as Augustine pulled up next to Arion. "I hope no one was hurt," she said. Half of the watchtower had caved in. Some of the stone blocks had tumbled to the ground near the base, but it was apparent the rest had fallen to the inside.

Darius had Arion racing to the tower, his shouts louder even than the thundering hooves.

"Here!" one of his men called out as he appeared from behind the tower. Aries followed a moment later, holding out his hand in greeting.

Halting her mount well back from where Darius held Arion, Stella listened as the two men assured the lochagos they were uninjured. They had both scrambled out of the tower when the first quake hit, and then the tower had partially collapsed during the aftershock.

"I went in to see if I could get to the top, but there are stones blocking the stairs," the one called Thiones explained. "We need men with pry bars to help us remove them." His attention was diverted by a ship on the horizon, and he excused himself so that he could return to his makeshift outpost atop a boulder.

"We have been watching the coast from the rocks on the beach," Aries said, his gaze going to Stella. He arched a brow. "Stella of Akrotiri rides with you?" he half-asked.

Darius nodded, although he also frowned at the query. "She does. Why do you call her that?"

Aries allowed a shrug as his attention returned to his master. "I heard her say it that way a long time ago, back when I lived near the port," he explained. "She was but a child then. Clever and good with the animals. I hear she is the only girl on the island with red hair."

"What else do you hear of her?" Darius asked in a hoarse whisper.

Dipping his head, Aries was about to deny there was more, but said, "She is the only reason Andros the olive farmer has the best harvest on the island."

Although Darius had always suspected Andros relied entirely too much on his adoptive daughter, Aries' words seemed to indicate he wasn't the only one who thought so. He was also relieved to know she wasn't reviled, or worse, feared because she sported red hair. "His harvest may be in jeopardy, then." Darius turned and waved for Stella to join him.

Well aware the two men had been talking about her, Stella commanded Augustine to bend his front legs so she could dismount. The horse dutifully knelt and then returned to standing once Stella was completely off of him.

Darius watched and gave his head a shake, one brow arching in Aries' direction. "I have never seen him do *that*," he murmured.

Stella stepped up and gave a nod to Aries. "It is good to see you again," she said, a grin lighting her face. "I do not know what you are called."

"Aries, son of Klumenos," the coastguardsman said, just as Thiones joined them.

The second man gave his name as he held out his hand. Stella shook it, and was about to introduce herself, but Darius asked, "Is there trouble?"

Thiones shook his head. "The ship on the horizon sports the pennons of a fisherman, so there is no threat from him." He turned his attention back to Stella. "Apologies, but I do not recognize you."

"I am Stella." She dared a glance at Darius, wondering if he had already told Aries why she was with him. "It was my wish to meet those my husband commands," she added as she placed a hand on Darius' arm. The familiar tingle in her head intensified, and she felt a shudder pass beneath his skin.

The word 'husband' had Aries' eyes widening. "I did not know you had taken a wife," he murmured, hoping his earlier words about Stella hadn't offended the lochagos. "I would offer refreshment, but..." His words trailed off as he indicated the damaged watchtower.

"I intend to make it to your father's tower before the sun goes behind the mountain," Darius replied. "I will send men to help clear the stones and others to rebuild the tower. Give my regards to the men who relieve you at sunset."

"Gratitude," Aries replied.

With that, Darius led Stella back to Augustine and lifted her onto the saddle. "Stella of Akrotiri?" he teased, remembering she had once introduced herself to him using that name.

Stella stared at him a moment before she dared a glance at the retreating back of Aries. "I am," she replied, her head held high. "And wife to Darius of Agremon." She furrowed a brow. "Which has me wondering. Just where exactly might Agremon be located?"

Darius shook his head and allowed a wan grin. "I wish I could remember," he murmured, especially after the images he had called to mind only a few days ago.

Mother, he thought, wincing at the pang of hurt that seemed to grip his heart just then, knowing he had lost her in the awful fire that had left him homeless and alone, hungry and desperate.

One day he would spend time to simply wallow in his memories. To discover if he could sort exactly where he had come from, and when. Until then, he had a job to do, and a new wife he wanted to impress. "At least we know where Akrotiri is," he said with a wink. With that, he mounted Arion and they headed for Kamari.

CONDITIONS WERE BETTER AT KAMARI, but not by much. Although no stones had fallen, the watchtower featured a vertical crack along one side, and those on duty reported a few damaged oikoi in the small port city.

"Is my son proving himself at his new post?" Klumenos asked after Darius had introduced him to Stella. Although Klumenos had never before seen the young woman, he had heard tales of a red-headed girl who spoke to animals. The lieutenant afforded her all the courtesies, but he was quick to get to the business at hand.

"He has done nothing to embarrass you, I assure you," Darius replied. "However, the tower there is damaged and in need of repair. Far more than this one," he added as he motioned to the cracked exterior. "Any damage on the inside?"

Klumenos shook his head. "Nothing much. But..." He paused, allowing a long sigh. "These earthquakes—"

"Are getting more frequent," Darius interrupted.

"The ground grows hot in some spots," Klumenos said as he pointed to where a small tree had dropped all its leaves.

"It has died," Stella said in a hoarse whisper, her gaze having taken in a number of plants that seemed on the verge of dying. "If this continues, the saffron crop will be threatened."

Darius turned his attention on Stella, shocked by her words. "Saffron is our most important export," he said.

"Followed by olives," Klumenos offered. "Either the gods are offended, or this island has become cursed. At some point, people will be forced to leave." He paused a moment before adding, "After Death has taken me, I pray."

Dipping his head in agreement, Darius thought of how his next meeting with the king would go when he told him the news. With any luck, someone else might tell him of the most recent earthquake before he was next scheduled to sail to Creta. One of the king's advisors or a favored ship's captain who was in port when the earthquake occurred. Far better word came from them than from Darius.

Strongili might continue to provide a good living for its citizens for a few years or longer, but it was becoming more and more evident that the slumbering volcano was about to wake up. Once it did, the entire island would be at risk. No place would be safe once an eruption started.

"Where will they go?" Stella asked in alarm.

"Creta, at first," Darius replied. "From there, they could choose one of the other islands to call home. Naxos or Rhodes."

"I will never leave," Klumenos announced. At the look of shock Darius displayed, he added, "I am an old man. My wife is an old woman."

"You are but... forty summers?" Darius guessed.

"True, but too old to call a new place home."

Stella surreptitiously reached out and touched the ypolochago. "You will live to see a hundred years," she argued, and then shrunk back when both Darius and Klumenos regarded her with furrowed brows.

Darius was the first to recover. "She speaks the truth, Klumenos. Should it become necessary for all of us to move to Creta, I will see to it you command one of the watchtowers there."

Klumenos gave Stella a look of doubt before he allowed a sigh. "If I must, I suppose—"

"Meanwhile, your son is in need of manpower to help remove stones from the stairs of his watchtower. They block his way to the top, and he is forced to watch the waters from the boulders on the beach."

Nodding, Klumenos turned and motioned for one of his men to join them. He gave the order for him and three others to take horses and head to Gialos. "Pack to spend the night there," he ordered, his gaze going to the setting sun. He turned his attention back to Darius. "Will you stay here on this night? We have meat. We have ale."

His stomach growling in response, Darius agreed to share their meal, but he declined the offer of a place to sleep for the night. Despite having Stella at his side for the entire day, he desired her. Wanted to make love to her, and he knew he would wish to do so again in the morning.

What kind of power did she have over him that he would make decisions based on when he could next bed her?

Or perhaps she was merely a novelty. After not having a woman for so many years, he simply required more than a few nights with his wife. Another sennight or more, and he would be fine with leaving her at the villa while he made his rounds of the island.

He could only hope. For if Stella continued to have this kind of power over him, he would have a difficult time continuing in his position as lochagos.

33

DOMESTICITY

For the next thirteen years

Although it took several sennights and a bold suggestion by Glaukos that the lochagos leave his wife at their villa—*she is a distraction for my men, and some believe she brings bad luck*—Darius finally agreed to make his rounds of the watchtowers without her.

Stella welcomed the opportunity to spend some time alone, much as she did in the olive orchard during her youth. She spent the mornings in her own orchard, seeing to trimming the trees as Augustine and Melanie hid beneath the canopies of leaves.

A nearby cave provided a respite from heat, and soon she had it outfitted with the comforts of a bedchamber. The secret grotto gave her and Darius privacy from servants and a view of the sea to the north.

In the afternoons, she mixed paints and plaster and worked to restore the damaged frescoes in the villa. Once they were repaired, she began work on her own, covering entire walls with intricate works of art.

One day each sennight, she visited the agora in Tholos with Iris, choosing produce and praising artisans for their beautiful creations.

Occasionally she hosted an ypolochago's wife and children for a meal and conversation. Each time they took their leave, she felt jealous of the women. Despite an attentive husband who showered her with gifts upon his return and who bedded her morning and night when he was at the villa, she still hadn't conceived a child.

AT THE END of their sixth winter together, Darius woke up to find Stella weeping next to him, tears dampening their shared pillow.

"What is it?" he asked, alarm in his voice. He was halfway out of the bed before Stella could place a hand on his back.

The touch calmed him enough that he slowly settled back onto the bed. "What is wrong?"

"I am not yet with child," she whispered.

Darius allowed a long sigh and closed his eyes. He knew this day would one day come. Knew that he would have to tell her she was probably barren. That he had no seed. "Have your monthly courses begun?"

Her keening wail was the only response he needed to hear. Gathering her into his arms, he kissed the top of her head and rocked her for a time.

"I was never able to get a child on any of my three wives before you," he whispered, the words loud in his ears.

Stella sobbed for a time before she lifted her head to regard him. "But you had a son—"

"Conceived by another man," he whispered, using a thumb to wipe away the tears from one of her cheeks. "A deceit I regretted for many years."

Usually when she cried, which was rare unless she was especially touched by one of his gifts, the tingle at the edge of his consciousness turned to pain, giving him a headache. This time, he felt no pain from her.

Just despair.

"I have never expected you would bear me a child," he said then. At her look of surprise, he added, "We are both foundlings, Stella."

"But what has that to do with it?"

For years, he had practiced what he might say to her, knowing he wasn't about to admit he was an Immortal, nor tell her that she, too, would be immortal some day.

"We are of a kind not meant to create children of our own. I believe we are meant to take in foundlings. Bring them up as our own."

Stella hiccuped as he kissed the tears from her other cheek. "Foundlings?" she repeated.

He nodded, noting how her features had matured in the six years since he had taken her to wife. She almost looked as he imagined she would on the day he would see to her death. On the day her immortality would bring her back to life and keep her the same for the rest of their years. "Have you ever heard how it was you came to be on Strongili?"

Sniffling, Stella shook her head. "My mother said she found me in a basket beneath a tree."

"The priest in the temple said you were brought to the island by a large bird. Do you remember that?"

Stella blinked and shook her head. "I was but a babe,

but... a bird?" she whispered in disbelief. "I cannot fathom such a story." She paused then and furrowed a brow. "Is that how *you* were delivered to your mother?"

Darius inhaled slowly. Although he'd had that vision of his mother staring down at him, delight on her face, he could not remember anything before that moment. "I do not know. But I do know that I cannot live my life without you." He kissed her then, pouring every bit of love he could into the simple gesture.

When he finally ended the kiss, he pulled her tighter against his body and held her, enjoying the flare of pleasure that replaced her despair in his head. "Will you please remain my wife?"

Stella nodded. How could he think she wouldn't? No other man would abide a wife who could not give him strong sons and dutiful daughters.

"Be patient, my love," he said then. "Foundlings do not appear on our island very often. But when a babe has been left without parents, we shall see to taking it in," he promised.

Nodding again, Stella reached up and kissed Darius on the corner of his mouth. "Will you still make love to me?"

She felt more than heard his initial response. "As often as you will have me," he murmured. "Now, perhaps?"

He felt more than heard her response as she pushed him down onto the mattress and climbed atop him. "Yes, now," she replied.

He was more than willing to do her bidding, even as the earth shook beneath them.

34

DYING FOR THE VERY FIRST TIME

1613 BC, the thirteenth year of life with Darius

Chaos reigned around Stella. The sky had gone from a beautiful blue washed with wispy clouds of white to a dull ash gray in only moments. The ground beneath her, once a green punctuated with red from a million poppies, was now the same ash gray. It was nearly impossible to discern the ground from the sky.

Standing on the portico of the villa, Stella allowed the tears to flow. Everyone else in the household had left the morning before, Darius' orders not allowing even Iris to remain. Then he had taken off on Arion to patrol the edge of the island. *All the way around*, he had said, to be sure everyone had left the island.

Few had taken to boats on the north end of the island. Most had traveled south to the ports at Akrotiri and Exomitis, where the largest ships would take them to Creta. A few had left on merchant ships bound for islands to the northeast while others had departed on the last trading ship. Filled with a saffron harvest and olives, it had disembarked over a sennight ago.

A number of ships had been pressed into service for the evacuation, their cargo dumped on Creta so that they had room to take on passengers for the return to the largest island in the Aegean.

Stella's gaze went toward Tholos, sure she would see Darius riding in her direction. But there was nothing on the horizon except falling ash and tiny black stones. The earth once again shook beneath her feet, and she struggled to remain upright as she winced at the sound of broken pottery coming from inside the villa.

Although Iris had seen to packing what she could, Darius had ordered her to leave for Creta before she could finish, explaining that she and the other household servants would once again be in service to the king in one of the guest villas at Phaistos. *I will not be able to take all of this*, he had added when she wondered about the wealth of goods that decorated the villa. *Leave it.*

Stella felt the same disappointment Iris had expressed with her parting words. Over the years, Darius had gifted her with beautiful pottery and fine fabrics, jewelry and crafts. She had stuffed what she could into her trunk, but the larger items would be left behind.

A low rumble had Stella moving closer to one of the columns. Breathing would be easier inside, but she worried for Darius' fate and wanted to watch for his return.

What if he couldn't make it all the way around the island? What if the earthquakes or geysers had made the roads impassable?

She moved to the end of the portico and gazed at their

secret cave. At the olive orchard that was now turning a light gray. At the yacht Darius had seen to mooring near the cave. Barely visible through the rain of ash, their means of escape was still bobbing on the water.

She had already moved the bedding from the cave onto it, and had one of the servants help with adding jars of water and bins of bread. Their trunks, packed full with clothes and as many possessions as Stella wished to keep, were also on board. Purses of gold lined the bottom of one, but Stella had seen to it there were coins in other parts of the yacht as well. Purses that could be strung around their necks should the voyage to Creta prove perilous.

Stella made it back to the main villa just as one of the front columns swayed too much and finally broke free of its moorings. The cypress trunk fell outward, as if in slow motion, the column top rolling away once it hit the ground. The column ended up as a harsh red slash in the gray ash that covered the ground.

Sure she heard a shout, Stella hurried back outside, her gaze once again going west. She wiped a hand over her face, sure the tracks of her tears were smeared with ash. A quick glance down at her tunic had her grimacing and glad she had packed her best clothes in her trunk.

Dirty with ash and barely able to breathe, her knees turned to rubber when she spotted the silhouette of a man on a horse. He was shouting something, but she couldn't hear. Making her way to the front of the portico, she stood and watched as the horse raced in her direction. The tingle at the edge of her consciousness returned. Relief unlike any she had ever felt in her life engulfed her, just as the earth once again shifted beneath her feet.

Struggling to remain upright, her last image was of another column swaying. Swaying and finally breaking away in a thunderous roar, the wooden column tumbled down. Despite the crack and roar that warned of its detachment from its moorings, Stella was too slow in her retreat away from the villa. Engulfed in a cloud of ash, she was aware of falling to the ground and of a pain so great she could no longer breathe. Darkness descended, and she had no choice but to succumb to it.

Her last thoughts were of Darius and how she wouldn't be able to welcome him home with a kiss.

35

ESCAPE

The roar that came from Darius was as loud as the thunder that rose behind him. Another eruption had begun in the bowels of the volcano. In a moment, a new shower of ash and pumice would begin to rain down on the island, further hampering his efforts to get to Paradisos. To get to Stella.

Arion snorted ash from his nostrils, his whinnies of protest becoming more frequent, his head rearing back as Darius struggled to maintain control of the beast.

"We're almost there," Darius said in as calm a voice as he could manage. Never in his six-hundred years had he felt such terror, such fear as he did at the moment. Not for himself, of course—he would live no matter what happened—but he had left Stella alone the morning before, believing he had time to ride around the island and ensure every last person had made it onto a ship. Since then, the world had turned an ashen gray, and the earth beneath rumbled in protest. If anything happened to Stella before he reached her...

He shook the thought from his head. He knew better than to allow his fears to get the best of him.

Surprisingly, Arion seemed to settle down, and Darius urged him into a run. The gray ash covering the ground made it impossible to determine the terrain. Impossible to be sure he wasn't sending the horse in a hole or onto an uneven rock. But up ahead, he could see the outline of his villa against the gray sky. The columns were dark red against the gloomy landscape, a welcome sight after all the destruction he had already witnessed.

The west side of the island had nearly been impassable. Columns had collapsed, blocking the paths that connected the villages. Limestone boulders, dislodged from the sides of the mountains, tumbled down to the sea. Every obstacle he encountered required a detour, further delaying his return to Stella.

Now he could see her. Feel her in his head. Knew she was alive.

That is, until he felt the earth shift beneath his mount and watched with horror as a column broke away from the villa's portico and began its descent to the ground. Despite Stella's attempt to move out of its way, the column drove her to the ash-gray ground and pinned her to it.

At Darius' shout of disbelief, Arion reared and whinnied.

All at once, the tingle in his head vanished.

ARION SEEMED to recover before he did, the beast rushing ahead until a column had him stopping in protest. Darius was dismounting even before then, his feet sending up clouds of gray ash with every step he took until he was next to Stella and the column that had crushed her.

Too heavy to move—Darius attempted to roll it off her body even before he knelt next to her—the cypress trunk was already coated with gray ash. He would have to remove it, though. At any moment, she would come back to life—at least he hoped she would—and probably die again just as quickly.

Arion's arrival had Darius glancing up in surprise, the horse's nose nudging Stella's body. "We have to get this off of her," he said, nearly cursing when he realized he was speaking to his horse. The sight of the length of rope wound around his saddlebags had him coming to his feet, though. He quickly wrapped one end around the column, his fingers digging ash from beneath where it touched the ground so that he could shove the rope under it. Knotting it tight, Darius tied the other end around Arion, just in front of the saddle.

The horse seemed to know what to do even before Darius gave him the command to pull. Hooves slipped on slick ash before they took hold in the ground. After a few jerks with the help of Darius' brute force in pushing from the other side, the column dislodged from where it rested and finally rolled off of Stella.

The beast reared in protest at being tethered to the column. Knowing Arion was in danger of hurting himself, Darius used a dagger to cut the rope from around the tree trunk. Then he lifted Stella's limp body into his arms and began the longest run of his life, his destination the yacht near the grotto.

Arion whinnied and reared, and was soon following,

the rope still tied around his middle. At the water's edge, he reared up, his front legs kicking the ash-filled air.

Despite the coating of ash on everything in the yacht, Darius could make out the pile of bedding from the grotto. He gingerly stepped on board the broad-bottomed vessel, making sure his footing was sound before he made his way to the makeshift bed Stella had created.

He pushed aside the top layers of bedding with a sandaled-foot before he lowered Stella onto it. He formed a tent with one of the blankets to shield her face from the falling ash before lowering his lips to hers. It was then he noticed how gray outlined the trail of tears on her cheeks, a smear on one side a sign she had used the back of her hand to wipe them away.

Despite the amount of time that had passed, she was still lifeless.

Perhaps he had misjudged. Perhaps she wasn't an Immortal. Despair gripped him before Arion once again whinnied.

The horse seemed determined to join them on the yacht, a front hoof poised to step on board before pulling away as the boat bobbed on the water.

There was room for the horse, if the beast stood in the center and didn't move about too much. Arion had been on ships before—he had been transported to Strongili from Iberia aboard a cargo ship, after all. Darius decided then he couldn't leave him on the island. He would die from lack of water given how the rain of ash was coating everything. If something should happen en route to Creta, he knew the horse could swim.

He just didn't know how far or for how long.

Taking a chance, Darius led Arion to the center of the

deck and used the rope still tied around his middle to secure him to the mast. A moment later, and he had the yacht untied from its moorings and floating away from the island.

As for navigation, he would have to skirt the north edge of the island and follow its curved eastern shore before heading south to Creta. Given how ash from the volcano continued to fall almost straight down from the sky, sails would do no good until he could catch a northerly breeze farther out to sea.

That meant he would have to paddle. There were oars, of course, but there was also the wheel at the front that could be turned by pushing pedals with his feet.

The thought of having to move his legs up and down for hours had exhaustion and thirst descending all at once. Hunger would soon follow, but food could wait.

He glanced at the provisions, heartened to see jars secured against the sides of the deck. Finding the one with water, he uncovered it and drank deeply. He was about to put the jar back when he felt the flicker of something at the edge of his consciousness. A soft nicker from Arion had him turning to where Stella lay. He put the jar down and made his way around the horse.

"Stella?" he shouted.

A low moan was the only response. He quickly pulled her into his arms, relieved when the tingle in his head flared into a brilliant light. He kissed her eyelids and cheeks. "Stella?"

Her eyes opened, and she blinked several times, the tips of her lashes dusted in gray. Stella stared at him a moment, her brows furrowed. "Arion is thirsty," she whispered before she coughed a few times.

Darius squeezed his eyes shut, reveling in the sensation of her in his mind, of how she felt in his arms. And then he laughed. And laughed some more. Not from feeling humor so much as feeling immense relief. He would never dare laugh at her unless she intended to evoke humor with her words.

"It is not funny," she said in a whisper, her expression conveying her confusion. "He is thirsty." She reached out and touched his cheek. "As are you. There is water. I made sure there were several jars brought on board. Just as you ordered."

Nodding, Darius reluctantly lowered her to the bedding. "I will see to it Arion drinks," he said, and then made his way back to the jug of water. He removed the lid and allowed a curse. "The opening isn't large enough for him to drink from," he added before he surveyed the rest of the containers that lined the interior of the yacht.

"He can use the bread bin," Stella suggested as she attempted to sit up. A hand went to her head and then to her side, sliding over the grimy folds of her chiton. She wondered at the ash that fell around her and the sound of a distant rumble that seemed to grow louder by the moment. The rumble crescendoed and then lessened, much like thunder during a rainstorm.

But no rain fell from the sky. Only flakes of gray ash.

She wondered why there was no birdsong. Why her head felt different, why her body tingled all over. "What has happened?" she asked in a hoarse whisper.

Darius had located the square container and was considering how to respond as he removed the loaves. He knew from the low rumble to the west that the volcano had spewed forth another cloud of ash. Soon, it would rain down upon them, further darkening the sky.

The sun was already barely visible, the golden ball having taken on a reddish cast. He almost wished the northern winds would blow, except he needed to get the craft clear of the island or it would end up back on the beach. With luck, he could get them around the eastern shore before dark. Before the night winds started. Then he would hoist the small sail. Barring an unusual day of little wind, they would make Creta the following evening.

He would be unable to use the stars for navigation if the ash cloud remained above them. On one hand, he wanted the northwesterly winds to blow—he wouldn't have to do more than steer the yacht—but on the other, the wind would make the sea too rough for the small vessel.

These thoughts and more crowded his mind as he went about seeing to his horse.

After he had the container placed below Arion's head and filled with water, he brought the jar to Stella and offered her the rest. "Do you remember anything?" he asked as he held the jar for her, watching her drink. When she indicated she'd had enough, he set aside the pottery and added, "From before?"

Her attention wasn't on him, though, but on the shoreline. On the rocks they would hit if the yacht continued on its current course. Darius followed her line of sight and cursed. Wanting nothing more than to hold her for a time, to ensure she had not only survived but that she had completely recovered from her injuries, Darius realized he would have to see to piloting the yacht or it might end up broken on the rocks.

He reached over Stella and pulled an oar from its mooring. Poking the end against the first boulder in their path, he pushed as hard as he could. Slowly, the vessel moved away, but with another slight wave from the north, it would again move too close to shore. He moved to the front of the vessel and settled into the seat, his feet pushing hard on the wooden pedals in an attempt to get the paddlewheel moving.

His first few tries were met with failure—they weren't yet in deep enough water for the wheel to move freely. He used the oar to paddle, alternately pushing away from the rocky shore and steering the vessel east.

Once Darius had them clear of the shore and in deep enough water, he had the paddlewheel moving and the yacht heading east.

Keeping the shoreline in sight was more difficult than he thought it would be. Ash continued to fall in curtains, threatening to blot out the sun completely. The island was already covered in a layer of gray. Even the normally turquoise water reflected the soot gray sky. At least there seemed to be a dark band where the sea met the shoreline, the water apparently rinsing away the ash as each wave washed ashore.

Movement from behind had him pausing in his task so he could turn to look. Stella had moved to the other side of the yacht and pulled out a jar of grain. She scooped some out and offered it to Arion, her quiet murmurs of encouragement a balm even for him at that moment.

"I suppose he told you he was hungry," Darius said, trying to keep his voice light. In reality, he could feel nothing but contempt for the beast at that moment.

"Something like that," Stella agreed, just as she carefully settled next to him. She had one of the flat loaves of bread in her hand. "Your hunger is louder, though." She broke off a piece and fed it to him.

"Gratitude," he murmured, studying her face. At nine-and-twenty, she looked elegant—regal—compared to the sixteen-year-old he had taken to wife. Taken with the intent of watching her age until she better matched his apparent age. Then he would have seen to her quick and painless death, one that would activate her immortality and keep her looking the same age for all eternity.

Five-and-thirty, he had decided.

Well, she hadn't made it that long.

He had secretly hoped he would never have to kill her, of course, but for her to have suffered as she did—being crushed by a wooden column—was more painful than anything he might have done to her.

From the way the tingle at the edge of his consciousness had strengthened since her awakening, Darius knew she was now impervious to the Darkness. She couldn't die. At least not for longer than a few minutes.

Wiping the ash from his face with the back of his hand, he leaned over and kissed her, heartened when she returned the favor. When he pulled away, he continued to gaze at her face as if to memorize everything about it.

The oval shape of it was nearly perfect, broken only by the slight triangle of hair at the top of her forehead. Despite the dusting of ash, her red hair was evident, and caught up in the style favored by Minoan women. The shape of her nose, the contours of her lips, the arch of her eyebrows—all of it would remain the same for the rest of eternity.

Green eyes, dark in the overcast light, stared at him as

if she was waiting for him to say more. So he repeated what he had asked her earlier. "Do you remember anything?"

Stella broke off another piece of bread and offered it to him. "I was afraid," she murmured. "I thought I might never see you again."

"I will *always* come for you," he said, his brows furrowing. He could feel her fear. "Never doubt that, Stella. For the rest of our days..." He broke off, realizing that he felt *relief* at her having died on this day. She hadn't died by his hand, or by the hand of another he would be forced to kill to avenge her. "And there will be many of them," he finished.

One of her hands moved to the side of her head. "I do not believe I have ever felt you more panicked than you were when you carried me here to the yacht," she said.

Darius considered her words. He had thought her still dead when he lifted her into his arms. "You were... awake?" he asked, sure she was lifeless when he brought her on board.

Stella dipped her head. "Not awake, but I was... I was *aware*. Of you. Of Arion. I could feel you in my head." Tears sprung to her eyes then. "You have never felt like that before," she said with a shake of her head.

Frowning, Darius wondered if she referred to the tingle she felt at the edge of her consciousness, or something else. "Describe it," he urged, giving a quick glance to his right to ensure the shoreline was still in evidence. The sun was starting to sink in the sky, and soon it would be behind the island's mountains.

He hadn't given a thought as to what they would use for light once the sun was completely set, although the gray skies would probably keep everything around them from going completely black.

"You were *afraid*," she accused.

Darius nodded. "I was," he admitted. He still was to some degree. Whatever happened on this night, he knew they would live through it, but he doubted they would have an easy time getting to Creta.

He didn't want to be forced to swim to the large island. He didn't want Stella to have to swim. Her small body wouldn't last long in the frigid water. And he certainly didn't want Arion to have to swim.

"Do you remember what happened to you?" he asked, hoping she wasn't reading his thoughts. "Do you know how I found you?"

Stella tore off more bread and fed it to him, letting the back of one finger brush his cheek. She knew it set off something inside him, for his brows lifted and his eyes darkened. "I remember an earthquake and all this ash falling from the sky," she replied. "I remember a fire. I remember a column falling onto the front lawn. And another..." She stopped and seemed to hold her breath. "I remember pain so great, I could not breathe." She ignored his hiss and added, "I was sure I died." Tears streamed down her cheeks, leaving dark trails in the gray smudges on her face. "There was darkness and the thought that I would have to wait a very long time for you to join me there."

Darius stopped pushing on the wheel's pedals and pulled her into his arms. He held her tight to his chest until he could feel her heartbeat slow, until her shaking body stopped trembling. "Perhaps you did die," he murmured, his lips pressed against the side of her face.

"But you are very much alive now, and that is all that matters."

When he saw how wisps of her hair blew from her face, how the flakes of volcanic ash danced through the air sideways, he turned his head to the north and knew their moment of intimacy was over.

The wind was about to blow.

36

A SEA CHANGE

Stella watched as his attention left her. She couldn't help the disappointment she felt at how his gaze tore from hers and turned to the north. To the west. But a slight breeze had changed the air around them. Broken the eery quiet and interrupted the falling ash. "What can I do to help?" Stella asked as she carefully stood. Although she had been on the yacht before, it had been on days when the waters were calm and the sky was clear.

Her attention went to Arion. The horse had been quiet since she had fed him some grain, apparently content to simply stand tethered to the yacht's small mast and take a much needed nap.

Darius moved to undo the ropes that secured the ship's single sail to the mainmast. He motioned for her to move to the other side of the mainmast, where the mound of blankets and hides were stacked. "When I start to lower this beam, grab onto it from your end and lower it at the same rate I do," he instructed. Although he could have easily unfurled the thick fabric sail by himself, he sensed her need to have something to do. Something to keep her occupied. Keep her mind off what had happened back at the villa.

"Won't Arion block the wind?" she asked, noting how the horse stood facing the direction they intended to travel once they were around the eastern-most beach. The wind would hit his backside before reaching the sail. With a bit of encouragement, she thought he might be inclined to lie down on the deck. His massive body would take up most of the available space, though.

"We might need him to," Darius replied. Although he wanted the wind power, he feared it would be too much for the small craft once they cleared Strongili and were out on the open sea. He had sailed the craft on many a fine day, but he had never done so on the route they would need to travel.

Nor had he sailed at night.

"We will keep the sail low, so it does not overburden the mast," he explained.

"Where are we going?" Stella asked, carefully mimicking Darius' moves with the sail. He had done something with a rope that had the top mast lowering on the mainmast until it was the height of her shoulder.

"Creta," he replied, as he tied the bottom of the sails to a wooden beam he had lifted from the deck—the boom, Stella remembered. He unfolded the two legs at each end of the boom and then steadied the structure by sliding the legs into perfectly aligned hollow braces secured to the deck. "Keeps the boom perpendicular to the boat," he said, when he noted how she watched every step he performed. The top wasn't nearly as well braced, but it would have to do. He had no tools to make any changes.

Arion appeared interested in his work, although the horse made a sound of protest when his vision was suddenly obscured by the sail in front of him.

"If you wish to see, then you will need to hold your head up higher," Darius said, his comment eliciting a nicker from the beast.

"I used to be able to see Creta," Stella said, her eyes widening. "On a clear day," she added, her gaze sweeping to the south. It was nearly impossible to tell where the sky met the sea on this afternoon. "When I stood on the edge of my father's property."

"Creta is nearly seventy milion away," Darius replied as he secured the last rope. The sail filled and billowed a bit before holding its shape. Beneath them, they could feel the craft pick up speed over the water.

Stella's eyes squinted in an attempt to see the shoreline. "We are moving," she breathed. When the yacht hit and then jumped over an inbound wave, she reached out and steadied herself by grabbing onto Arion's mane.

"We best get you back into your bed," Darius said, knowing there would be rougher seas ahead. A low rumble sounded from the island, and he turned his attention due west. The island's eastern mountains prevented him from seeing the volcano, but he was sure it had just spit out another round of ash. "Cover your head as best you can. We're about to..." He wasn't able to finish the sentence when Arion let out a whinny of complaint. What looked like a rock had bounced off of Arion's back and onto the deck. Another landed near the front of the vessel.

Darius cursed, realizing this latest eruption included more than just ash. He scooped up the one near Arion. Although it was warm, it wasn't burning hot as he feared.

"It's full of holes," Stella murmured. She had picked up the other stone and was holding it in the palm of her hand.

"Pumice," Darius murmured. His eyes widened. "Get under the blankets, Stella. Now!" he ordered.

Stella recognized his command voice. Even if she hadn't been married to him for the past thirteen winters— hadn't known him for nearly twenty years—she knew better than to question him. She dropped to the deck and slid into the bedding, drawing the top hide over her head just as another stone hit the deck and another landed on the bedding.

When Arion seemed on the verge of panic, Darius said, "Can you... calm him?" he asked.

Stella poked her head out of her makeshift tent. "Calm him?" she repeated. Her heart was racing, and she could barely breathe. But she understood his query. Sometimes, Arion was as attuned to her as she was to him.

She reached out one arm and touched the horse with the tips of her fingers. Arion immediately responded, his head dropping so his nose was nearly in his water. Stella closed her eyes and thought of blue skies and large mead- ows. Of fields of poppies and of her and Darius making love beneath a nearby tree. Of Melanie, because she secretly knew Arion had been the one to get a colt on the spirited mare. Twice.

In the meantime, Darius pulled the top hide from the pile and quickly spread it over Arion's back. "Prepare to be pelted," he said to his horse, hoping the rain of stones wouldn't last long. He could hear them hitting the water around them, the plops sending up wavelets on the surface of the water that passed by too quickly for him to see if they sizzled when they hit.

If they maintained this speed for an hour or more, they would clear the effects of the volcano.

At least, he hoped that would be the case.

When one of the stones hit his arm, he cursed. Sure it was hot, he lifted it from the deck and cursed again as he quickly tossed it overboard before his fingers suffered a burn.

He glanced at Arion, noting how the horse was nickering softly, his head lowered as if he were in a trance. A wave of jealousy had him pulling another hide from the stack covering Stella. He wrapped it about his shoulders and moved to the back of the yacht to reset the rudder. Having just passed the easternmost shore of Strongili, he knew they could simply head due south and the wind would eventually take them to Creta.

He glanced over at the mound of bedding that held his wife. Grinned when he saw how her fingers touched his horse just above his hoof.

Perhaps Stella could do for him what she was doing for Arion, for exhaustion had set in, and he knew he would not be able to stay upright much longer.

Lifting the hides, he glanced down at his wife and gave a start. She was completely naked, her skin flushed and her breasts swollen, her nipples tightened into rosy buds. One of them poked through a lock of her red hair that cascaded over the front of her torso.

Never in their years together had she appeared so erotic. So wanton.

And never before had he needed her like he did at this moment.

"I am in want of you," Stella said, her lips forming a pout.

Giving her a weary nod, Darius took his time removing his chiton and his perizoma, stunned at the wave of desire he felt coming from his wife. He used the chiton to wipe the ash from his face and hair, from his arms and legs, and then tossed it to the deck.

With one last look at the receding shore of Strongili—perhaps the last time he would lay eyes upon it for a very long time—Darius lowered his body into the bedding with Stella, pulled her atop his body, and was soon buried in her.

37

A TIDAL WAVE OF EMOTION

For the entire time they had been on the yacht, and especially from the time Stella had opened her eyes, she knew something had happened. Something had happened that had somehow changed her.

At first, she thought the disorientation had to do with the chaos that surrounded her—the erupting volcano and the rain of ash, and the temblors that shook the earth beneath her feet—but there was more to it. Her awareness of Arion and his distress seemed to have increased tenfold. She could sense his fear, his hunger and thirst, without even touching the beast.

Her sense of her own body—her skin and how it stretched over her muscles and bones, how her limbs moved, her hearing and her sight—every sense and sensation was magnified.

Perhaps the most startling change was her increased awareness of Darius. Despite her state of unconsciousness earlier that day, she had sensed his near-panic even before he lifted her into his arms. His fear had filled her as if it were her own. And then, when she was in his arms, the tingle that always foretold his presence flared into an intense and pleasurable sensation. One filled with concern and reassurance, longing and belonging.

Love.

He had said the word a time or two. Murmured it in the middle of the night. Whispered it when she seemed worried she had done something wrong. Coupled with the way he would hold her body against his own, as if protecting her from the rest of the world, his show of emotion would leave her happy.

She had always known he seemed attuned to her every emotion. Seemed to know what she was thinking even if she didn't say a word.

Did she now have that same knowledge of him?

Stella might have been overwhelmed by the thought, but with her new ability came the certainty that they would survive simply because Darius believed it. Knew it with all his being. And when she touched him, the sensation was so intense, she had to allow it to wash over her and through her, or she would have been forced to give up her hold on him.

And she didn't want to be so close to him and not touch him.

The pleasures she experienced when he held her were addictive. Calming. Exciting. Reassuring.

Loving.

She craved him.

Had he been experiencing the same sensations from her all the time they had been betrothed? Did he sense her fear, her joy, her disappointments, and her contentment in this magnified manner?

If so, perhaps it explained why he had spirited her from her home when she was barely sixteen. To take her to wife as he did, before he was entitled to do so.

For when sensing his emotions as she had done on this day, she knew he was jealous of his horse—all because of the attentions she showed the beast when she had first awakened from the odd slumber.

She was aware of Darius' needs, of course. They had been far more noticeable. Although he saw to quenching his thirst, he ignored his hunger. He would still be famished if she hadn't fed him an entire loaf of bread whilst he pedaled them around the north end of the island. His exhaustion would also go ignored until he finally collapsed.

But what surprised her the most was his desire for her. Despite the falling ash and rocks, despite the chaos they had left behind on the island—chaos that might certainly be replaced with an entirely new disaster at sea —he wanted her. The intensity of it was almost animalistic.

And the thought of his cock inside her had her body reacting in a manner far different from their usual nightly couplings. She wanted him with an urgency she couldn't explain. This wasn't just desire she felt for him.

She felt lust. Uncontrollable, desperate lust.

So when Darius used his waning strength to pull her body atop his, to position her so he could simply impale her with his cock, she had taken the opportunity to drive their coupling. To set the rhythm of the ancient dance of mating. To coax him to a near release, and then slow her movements. To tease him until his hands grasped her hips. He pulled her hard against him, his own hips lifting so he could drive himself into her as deeply as he could go.

Stella inhaled sharply, her eyes widening in delight. Desperate for her own release, she had finally lowered her body until the tips of her nipples touched his heaving chest and her tongue could flick over one of his nipples. He was still driving his cock into her, deeper with each thrust. But at the touch of her tongue on his tender flesh, he let out a growl and seemed to burst inside her. One more thrust, and his body went limp beneath her.

Warmth washed through her lower body. Warmth and waves of pleasure that seemed to amplify for several seconds until she didn't dare breathe. Didn't dare speak. Didn't dare move.

Thick arms pulled her down to his chest and enveloped her in warmth. With her cheek pressed into the small of his shoulder, sleep took her to a pleasant place.

All would be right with the world.

DARIUS THOUGHT for a moment that the world had ended. That he had ceased to live, his mind transcending to some other level of consciousness while his body experienced pleasures so intense he could no longer breathe.

What else could explain what had just happened?

He didn't wish for explanations, though. Didn't need them. What he had at one time imagined could be a life with a truly immortal Stella—back when he had first met the young girl as she worked in an olive tree—their life together had just begun. A few minutes of bliss was just the beginning of a lifetime of untold pleasures.

If he could die on this night, he wouldn't mind one bit.

Not if Stella died with him. For whatever came next in their lives—whether it be a life in a new land or a return to one of his old countries—they would forever be together.

The sensation of being lifted and lowered niggled at the edge of his consciousness. Another wave seemed to pass beneath him, lifting him higher and then taking him lower. On the third such lift, he seemed to hover for a long time before the sensation of sliding down finally had him opening his eyes.

He stared at Stella's breasts, the sight bringing a grin to his lips. "You do know how to please me, beautiful wife," he whispered.

Stella dropped her attention to him, her eyes wide when the downward slide suddenly ended and a wave of seawater washed over the front of the yacht. The bow lifted again, but this time more sharply. Arion let out a whinny of complaint as he struggled to keep his balance.

Desperately wishing it were just a bad dream, Darius lifted Stella from his body and managed a quick kiss before saying, "Get him to lie down." His voice was no longer tinged with sleep but with the urgency of command.

Stella nodded and struggled to pull on her chiton. She noted how Darius didn't bother with his, but moved to lower the sail.

Stella stood up next to Arion, her hands going to the side of his head. Despite the shifting waves beneath the yacht that threatened to toss her to the deck, she spoke in low tones. Her voice, void of panic, instructed Arion to step sideways. Then she encouraged him to drop to his knees. A moment later, he was lying on his side, a series of nickers indicating a combination of complaint and contentment. After that, he closed his eyes.

"What did you do to him?" Darius asked in wonder.

Stella regarded her husband a moment before angling her head. He stood with one arm outstretched, a hand gripping the mast for the support. In his glorious naked-ness, she couldn't help the shiver of excitement that coursed through her. Couldn't help the memory of their lovemaking that had her wishing they could return to their makeshift bed.

She had seen to it Arion's hooves were directed to the other side of the yacht from the bedding.

"I did to him what you did to me earlier," she replied.

Darius frowned, and she felt a wave of jealousy pour from him.

"Not that," she scolded as she hurried to join him, lifting onto tiptoes to kiss him on his cheek. "I just provided some reassurance, is all." Her gaze had gone beyond him, though.

Although the dark sky above wasn't clear—remnants of gray ash borne by the winds were evident—low clouds pregnant with rain moved at the same rate as they did. A quarter moon provided enough light so she could see the surface of what appeared to be an undulating sea.

"Hang on," Darius ordered, as the yacht suddenly lifted and then dropped down the wavefront. The bow didn't break the surface, though, instead simply riding the lift of another wave and hanging almost atop it for what seemed like an eternity.

Stella clung to Darius as he tightened his hold on the mast. To the north, the golden-red glow of the volcano lit the sky. A low rumble reached her ears, and Stella knew she had been hearing a quieter version of it for some time. "Another earthquake?" she asked, attempting to keep her tone light. She held out a leather lanyard from which hung a purse filled with gold.

Darius noted how there was a similar purse draped around her neck, the bulge of coins nestled between her breasts. He understood her fear immediately. Should something happen to the yacht, they might lose everything they had brought with them. By each keeping a purse on their bodies, they would at least have gold when they reached Creta.

His gaze went to the old trunks. Secured to the sides of the yacht with rope—much like the jars of food and water, and amphorae of olive oil and wine—the trunks held whatever of the household items and clothing Stella had managed to cram into them.

Hoisting the purse in a fist, Darius turned his attention back to Stella and said, "You were wise to bring these." Jerking his head back to the island, he said, "And that was another earthquake, I am sure of it." He hung the purse around his neck and then pulled on his loincloth. "I expect our ride is about to get rougher," he murmured, his lips brushing her hair. "Which means you will be safer if you are down on the deck."

She looked up at him. "And you?"

He turned around and faced their direction of travel. Creta wasn't yet on the horizon. He didn't expect it would be until sometime the following day. By mid-morning, he hoped.

Unless they were traveling far faster than he had originally thought.

"Darius, my love," Stella said, her attention aimed due

north. The golden glow on the horizon was no longer visible. In fact, nothing was.

"Get down!" Darius ordered. He moved to the front of the yacht, taking a seat at the paddlewheel's pedals. No matter how fast he got the wheel to rotate, he knew it wouldn't be enough, but he had to at least try to stay on the back side of any wave that might break over the sea.

Stella dived onto the bedding and managed to get beneath a few layers when the sensation of weightlessness occurred.

Arion nickered, his head lifting a bit to regard her. She was sure there was a moment when the horse was completely lifted from the deck. Her stomach recoiled, and she thought for a moment she might be sick. And then gravity once again took hold, although not in the direction she expected. Wind whipped her hair as their speed over the water increased and everything seemed to cant sideways before they were angled down toward the front of the yacht.

Stella reached out and placed a hand on Arion's back. All at once, the creature relaxed, settling his head onto the deck so the top of it almost touched the mast. She hoped he would sleep, but given the incessant lifting and lowering of the yacht on the waves that passed beneath them, she didn't expect he could. Had their situation been different, she might have found the rhythm of the undulating waves soothing. A means to fall asleep faster.

But what would she find when she awakened?

Concentrating on the thought of sleep as a means to keep Arion calm, she closed her eyes and imagined she was back in her bed at the villa. Darius was by her side, one arm wrapped about her middle and holding her against his solid body.

The feel of him over the years remained the same. Until earlier that day, everything about Darius seemed the same as the first day she had met him. His mannerisms, his voice, his stance, and especially his appearance. He didn't look any older these days than he had the first day she had met him in the olive orchard.

In the meantime, her father's face had wrinkled, his hair had gone gray, his spine had shrunk and curved, and then he had died. Her mother's hair had lightened from jet black to nearly white, and crow's feet had formed on either side of the corners of her eyes. Although she still appeared elegant, age had slowed Helena's steps.

Stella thought of how her own features had changed since that day Darius had taken her to wife. How the cheekbones of her face had overcome the roundness of youth. How her breasts had swelled, her hips had widened, her legs had lengthened.

So why hadn't age affected Darius?

The pleasant tingle at the edge of her consciousness brightened as she angled her head to look at him, and she noted how his head turned so his chin nearly rested on his shoulder.

Did he know she was thinking of him?

A need to be closer to him—to touch him—had her emerging from the pile of blankets. She struggled to maintain her balance as she wrapped the top blanket around her body and then covered the short distance to the front of the yacht. She would have been satisfied to sit on the deck next to Darius, but he reached out an arm and pulled her onto his lap. He was no longer pedaling, but she knew they were moving at a fast clip. Wisps of the hair around her face were blowing in their direction of travel.

She nestled her head into the small of his shoulder and reveled in the musky scent of him. At the same moment she lifted her head to look over his shoulder, the yacht rose once again, and continued to do so.

Ignoring the odd sensation in her middle, she studied the scene behind them. The golden glow of the volcano was barely visible. Despite the quarter moon that winked in and out of existence with the passing of clouds, it was nearly impossible to determine where water met sky.

Then she realized why.

They were well above it. The wave on which they rode continued to rise, and somehow, their small craft stayed atop it. Ash once again surrounded them, although the flakes swirled and danced in the air.

Stella felt Darius' hold tighten on her. She tried to anticipate when they might start the descent, thinking the wave would pass beneath them as all the others had and leave them momentarily weightless. But instead, they were simply carried along.

"What's happening?" she whispered in awe. If she hadn't been in his arms, she might have felt fear. But there was no fear coming from him. Just a sense of weariness and wonder.

"This is a wave the earthquake created," he murmured. He hoped it might diminish, but it seemed to grow larger the farther from the island they traveled.

A *boom* followed by a slow rumble rolled past them, and Stella's eyes widened as the golden glow brightened on the northern horizon. Brightened and then slowly faded as debris from the eruption began falling to the sea.

Stella was sure Darius cursed, although she couldn't make out the word over the roar. She did hear Arion let out a whinny of complaint, but the horse remained on his side.

"Should I go...?" she started to ask, but Darius tightened his hold on her.

"Stay right here, my love," he said, his voice hoarse as his head leaned back. He gazed at the sky, a grin forming after a moment. "We will be on Creta when the sun rises."

The sensation of his presence in her head flowed with reassurance and adoration, tiredness and desire. Stella wondered how it was he felt no fear. No terror. How could he not be afraid? Their entire world was disappearing beneath a layer of ash and pumice, and what wasn't buried was probably now shaken to the ground by the earthquakes.

Had she been alone, she was sure the sound of her pulse in her ears would drown out anything else. She would have died of fright.

"Do you trust me?"

Stella pulled her gaze from the mesmerizing scene behind them to regard him with surprise. He had asked that very question a long time ago. Never had she not trusted him. "You know that I do," she murmured.

"I expect our arrival on Creta will be... a bit rough," he said, his voice still sounding hoarse in her ears. "These waves will probably be too much for the docks."

"What are you saying?" Stella asked in alarm.

Darius rearranged how she was sitting on his lap, one of his arms moving beneath her knees. Stella held on by wrapping her arms around his neck, ignoring how the blanket dropped away from most of her body. "If we stay atop this wave, we will end up well inland," he reasoned. "Beyond the shore. But I promise you, whatever happens to us, we will survive. We will live."

Stella allowed a nod, for what else could she do? A quick glance back at Arion had her almost asking about him. Could the horse survive a rough landing?

"He will do what he must," Darius said, as if he could read her mind. "He is a clever horse."

He hoped those who lived close to the northern shore of Creta knew what was about to happen. If the wave on which they traveled didn't diminish in size—and soon— those closest to the shore would have a wave wash over them. Given the blast that had happened a moment ago, another might already be on its way.

Bracing for the inevitable, Darius held onto Stella and realized there was absolutely nothing else he could do.

Meanwhile, Arion let out a loud whinny and jumped into the dark waters, disappearing beneath the wave on which they rode.

38

AN END IS A BEGINNING

Darius held tight to Stella, knowing that if he didn't, she would join Arion in the water. But he understood immediately why the horse had taken refuge in the black water—land lay immediately in front of them, mountains just beyond.

Suddenly, the small yacht rose and then seemed to stay suspended above the wave for a long time before it dropped back onto the water's surface with a hard landing. Darius nearly lost his hold on Stella as they coasted down the wave front.

Without looking behind him, Darius knew the wave was rising, that once it crested, its edge would crash down onto them. But even before that could happen, the front of the giant wave washed onto Creta's northeastern shore.

For a moment, he thought he spotted a figure, maybe two, scrambling up the hillside. Had the inhabitants of the village directly ahead of them had some warning then? Perhaps they had heard the rumble of the earthquake. Surely they could see the sickly glow in the sky to the north—that is, if they were awake. Dawn wasn't yet evident in the eastern sky.

Had they felt the earthquake this far away?

IN THE DIM LIGHT, Stella knew something was different. The wave behind them shrunk down, while they surfed on a sheet of water that seemed to grow more shallow the farther inland they traveled. The yacht shifted to the left and then to the right before it came to a grinding halt on large, flat rocks. Stella was ripped from Darius' arms and rolled to the front of the yacht, and Darius was nearly upended from his seat.

Water continued to flow past them, cresting the rocky hillside straight ahead before finally giving up its climb and subsiding back down. The yacht shifted back a bit, and Darius feared they might slide down the hillside. But the yacht came to an uneasy stop, its bottom resting on a slanted boulder.

The deafening roar of rushing water quieted as it slid back down the hill and out to the sea.

"Are you hurt?" Darius asked as he knelt next to Stella. She was already lifting herself onto one arm, the other pushing her drenched hair from her face.

"I do not think so," she murmured, ignoring the pain from her hard hit against the yacht's inner wall.

Darius turned his attention to the north. The sky, glowing yellow and orange in the direction of Strongili, was nearly black above them, but he could make out the shape of the water as it fell back to the sea.

"I cannot believe it," Stella said as she surveyed their surroundings. They were several stories above the shore, which the receding water was just then exposing. If they hadn't ridden atop the wave, they would have been covered by the gigantic mass of water and tossed about. Who knew if they would have even ended up on shore.

She frowned when she noticed the damage done to the yacht, though. Despite being tied to the sides of the yacht, their trunks appeared to have tumbled over, while the mast listed to one side. There was a gaping hole in the bottom, where the wooden planks that made up the hull had been torn away. Then she realized the entire yacht was angled to one side. She gingerly stepped out of Darius' hold and struggled to stand upright.

A plaintive whinny made its way to them as thin sheets of water continued to slide back down the rocks. "Arion?" Darius murmured, stunned the horse would have survived the ordeal. Perhaps he had stayed close to them, riding the wave, and was merely washed ashore onto high ground as they had been.

"He's limping," Stella said as she made her way over the low edge of the yacht. Her wet chiton clung to her body and made movement difficult

"Stella, be careful," Darius called out as he stood up and made to follow her. He couldn't even see the horse, let alone determine exactly where they were. About to step out of the yacht, he couldn't when it once again shifted on the rocks. When it seemed to find a more solid footing, Darius scrambled out and surveyed the area.

The pale gray of dawn colored the landscape in gray and black, making it difficult to discern shapes. Below them and off to the north, he could make out the remnants of buildings. At first glance, they seemed intact. Perhaps their inhabitants had survived their drenching. But then it became apparent that the power of the wave had washed the buildings off their foundations.

Darius cursed as his gaze swept the horizon to the east. He recognized Itanos, or what remained of it. The port city at the eastern tip of the island appeared as if it had washed away. Given its location meant that the village below them was probably Kamaizi. If they followed the coast, they might reach the palace at Gournia by day's end.

He thought of the palace at Malia, and the port city Amnissos—the port of Knossos—and knew in an instant they both would have suffered a similar fate as these coastal villages. Probably every watchtower along the northern shore had been upended by the force of the massive wave.

Tsunami.

Before the word had finished forming in his head, Darius stared at the horizon and cursed. Loudly.

The sea was rising once again.

In less than an hour—half that, given the speed at which this second tsunami was making it's way south— another wave would crash onto the island.

He turned around and gave a start, stunned to find Stella naked but for the purse of gold that still hung around her neck. It was a wonder she hadn't been strangled by it. Her chiton, now shredded, was acting as a bandage on one of Arion's legs.

"He is limping because he suffered a cut on his foreleg," she said, exhaustion evident in her eyes. Although she struggled to hold back tears, she was seeing what Darius had just noticed, and she began to shake her head back and forth. "We have to get to higher ground," she said.

His gaze going to the west, Darius realized they would have to move in that direction and farther inland to escape the next wave. "Agreed," he said, before making his way back to the yacht.

If they headed southwest, they could make it to the top of the mountain that would lead to Vasiliki. Although it was nearly at sea level, he thought it might have been spared the worst of the wave given how the island's shoreline curved up just north of the village.

Seeing the damaged boat in the growing light, Darius thought it a wonder they had managed to stay inside its shell. Had Arion been with them, he surely would have lost his footing and become more injured than he was.

"We have little time. Gather what you can, and be sure to drink some water," Darius said as he lifted a saddlebag of food onto Arion's back. Despite his injury, the horse didn't complain but merely stood still as the bags were stuffed with another purse of gold and some small weapons.

Stella opened her trunk, amazed that her clothes were mostly dry. She pulled on a skirt and jacket, struggling with the closures. As to what they could take with them, she knew Arion couldn't handle the weight and size of the trunks. She pulled out another purse of gold from the bottom before she closed hers tightly and then moved to Darius'.

"Eat something," he ordered, holding out some damp bread and then taking the gold from her. "I will see to my things." He stuffed the gold into one of the saddlebags and opened his trunk, relieved to see it hadn't been damaged. Removing his leather armor, he hurriedly pulled on what he could, deciding it would be simpler to wear it than to carry it.

Stella did his bidding, choking down the first food she had eaten since the day before. She located a jar of grain among those still tied to the inside of the yacht. Although it had tipped over, there was still some in the bottom. She offered it to Arion, who seemed to understand he needed to eat right then or lose the chance. Then she tied the rope around his neck so that she would have something to hold onto.

Darius took Stella's bedding, now soaked with seawater, and did his best to wring it dry. Then, with Stella's help, he arranged it over Arion's back. She stuffed her satchel with some clothes and her jewels, and soon they were making their way up and west over the rough terrain.

"Do you think anyone could have survived down there?" Stella asked when the village on the coast came into view. Well below and to the north of their location, the small town at first appeared undamaged. But buildings had collapsed. Entire structures were far from where they had been built. She was sure she could hear a distant wailing, and she knew someone had discovered a loved one had perished.

Somewhere nearby, a baby's cry sounded.

Shaking his head, Darius said, "Well, it sounds as if someone has survived," he murmured. "Keep moving up," he ordered as he turned in the direction of the crying.

"No," Stella said as she handed him the rope. "I will go."

Darius started to argue, but realized he would be a frightening sight for any child, dressed as he was.

He urged Arion to climb until they were on the ridge of a mountain range that continued west. From this vantage, he could see the sea to the south as well as to the north, and the wall of water was nearly upon them.

At least it appeared as if they were above its crest. He knew they could be washed away if they were any lower on the island.

About to continue west on the ridge, he paused when he heard Stella call out. Turning, he watched as she made her way around a rocky outcropping.

In her arms, she carried a basket.

Inside was a baby.

EPILOGUE

Heraklion, three days later

"How was your meeting with the king?" Stella asked once Darius had joined her on the palace steps. The huge palace complex had suffered the same wall of water as the rest of the northern shore of the island, but the main palace building was mostly intact. "Does he still hold you in high regard?" She carried the baby boy in the crook of one arm. Still wrapped in the blanket in which she had found him swaddled, the babe had survived their early morning trek on the mountain top until the last of the three successive tsunamis had finished their destruction of the north and eastern shores of Creta.

Earlier that morning, the third since that fateful day, she had joined Darius in the palace's reception chamber and met the man who was to decide their fate and that of the infant she carried. "Can we keep him?"

Darius nodded, giving a glance at the boy. He remembered the figure he had seen climbing the hillside just before the wave hit, and thought perhaps it had been the boy's mother. She had probably been awake and feeding him, then saw the impending wave and did what she could to climb to safety. Given the violence of the wave, it was doubtful she had survived, but the rushing water had carried the basket farther up the hill until it was caught in a rocky cradle.

"The king has given his permission and his gratitude," Darius replied. "For a moment, though, I feared he might order your presence in his bedchamber."

Stella's eyes widened. "He would not," she countered, although not with much conviction. She had been uncomfortable in his presence, cowed by his majesty and the riches that surrounded him. Despite being older even than Darius looked, and already having a beautiful queen, Tektamanos had gazed at her with open appreciation.

Darius shook his head. "Your red hair magnifies your beauty. But I think he fears my blade," he replied with a quirked lip.

Stella couldn't help the grin that lightened her face. "He seemed ever so relieved when you appeared before him."

"He thought me lost when I did not report to him after the last ship arrived from Strongili," Darius explained. "We stayed at least a day too long, although I cannot help but think we, too, would have been lost in that first tsunami when it hit the coast." He tried not to think of how difficult it might be for him to find Stella if they had been washed out to sea, drowning and coming back to life until they were washed up on some island's shore.

As for what might have happened to all the others who had escaped Strongili, he didn't yet know. Adamaos and his family had left for Naxos a month ago. Argurios and his men had been reassigned to the southern shore of Creta the year prior. Any former residents of Strongili who settled in villages on the northern shores of Creta were probably dead.

At least early reports from the coastal villages on the southern and western coasts indicated they were almost intact, as were the interior settlements.

"What of Iris, and the other servants? Our horses?" she asked.

"Safe at a guest villa near Phaistos," he replied. "We will go there next."

They had spent the past three days making their way north and west until they had reached one of the inland palaces, their speed hampered by Arion's wound and the rough terrain.

Exhaustion had them stopping at dusk the first day. They had removed the now-dry bedding from the back of Arion and made love on a flat of land just down from the mountain ridge. Once Darius had Stella tucked against the front of his body, she did the same with the babe, and they slept beneath a clear sky.

"What will happen here?" she asked.

"Some rebuilding," Darius replied. "Although..." He stopped, knowing most everyone who had lived in the destroyed villages was lost, as was an entire fleet of ships, plantations and crops. "It will not be like it was," he finished. "Creta has suffered too much."

Stella winced at hearing the words that only confirmed what she suspected. "Has the king asked you to stay?" she queried, lifting the babe to her breast when he began to fuss a bit. After only a day carrying the month-old infant, her breasts had begun producing milk. The sensation had been so foreign, she didn't know what was happening until the hungry boy had latched onto one of her nipples and begun to suckle.

"He has. I am to oversee the remaining coast-guardsmen here." Heartened to learn Glaukos and Aries were still alive—they were now in charge of watchtowers on the west end of the island—Darius had decided he would go there after seeing to Stella and the babe. "We must still defend the northern shores, even if there is nothing to protect."

"Who would invade from the north, knowing there is nothing there?" she argued.

Darius sighed. "It will be some time before word of what has happened here reaches the countries to the north and east," he explained. "Once it does, Creta—indeed all of Minoa—will be vulnerable. The king is sure the Mycenaeans will take advantage." He agreed with the king's assessment, if only because the savage invaders had targeted Creta so many times in the past, but never with enough men to defeat the Cretan navy, or the coastguardsmen, if they made it to shore. "In the meantime, I will transport you and the babe to our new oikos, and then see to retrieving our trunks."

"You believe they are still there?"

Darius allowed a shrug. "It is not as if there is anyone near to find them," he replied. "But I made a promise your trunk would go with us wherever we went, and I intend to keep that promise."

Stella gave a shake of her head, surprised by his sense of priority just then. "Our world has turned upside down, and you are concerned about my trunk," she chided.

He angled his head to one side. "Well, I confess to wanting the gold that remains in the bottom of it. Our lives are about to become more expensive. Short supplies mean higher prices," he explained.

Nodding her understanding, Stella regarded him for a moment. "I confess I am uncertain as to your desires," she whispered, realizing the babe at her breast had fallen asleep.

"Since I only desire you, I cannot think of what you might mean," Darius said as he led her down the palace steps and beneath the shade of some olive trees.

Stella allowed a wan grin. "I feared you might have decided to leave Creta. To leave your position as lochagos."

Darius shook his head, and then leaned down and kissed her before resting his forehead on hers. "I will not leave until the king tells me I must go. By then, I will know where we should next live."

Stella gave another nod and then kissed him, aware of how the babe she still held was cradled between them. She noticed how Darius' attention had dropped to the infant. "What will you name him?"

Arching a brow, Darius placed a hand atop the babe's fuzzy head. "The king said he must have a bold name. A name suitable for a warrior," he replied.

After waiting a moment, Stella matched his expression. "Well?" she prompted.

Darius allowed a chuckle. "Damon of Creta," he suggested.

Sounding out the name in a whisper, she gazed down at the sleeping babe and sighed. "Perhaps he will grow into it," she murmured, having a hard time imagining such a tiny thing could one day be a warrior for Creta.

"I will see to it that he does," Darius replied.

With that, he led her to the cart that would take them to their new villa and their new life on the largest island in the Aegean.

AFTERWORD

Thank you for taking the time to read Stella of Akrotiri: Origins. *If you enjoyed it, please consider telling your friends or posting a short review. Word of mouth is an author's best friend.*

Thank you,

Linda Rae Sande

ABOUT THE AUTHOR

A self-described nerd and lover of science, Linda Rae spent many years as a published technical writer specializing in 3D graphics workstations, software and 3D animation (her movie credits include SHREK and SHREK 2). Mythology, immortality, and ancient Greece have been lifelong interests.

A fan of action-adventure movies, she can frequently be found at the local cinema. Although she no longer has any tropical fish, she does follow the San Jose Sharks. She makes her home in Cody, Wyoming.

For more information:
www.lindaraesande.com
Sign up for Linda Rae's newsletter:
Regency Romance with a Twist